HEATHER BOYD

USAT BESTSELLING AUTHOR

AN AFFAIR OF HONOR

REBEL HEARTS 2

PROLOGUE

London, 1814

MATILDA WINSLOW BLEW A FALLEN lock of her hair from her eyes and then crawled under Captain Ford's bed to retrieve an item that had rattled to the floor while she'd been changing his sheets. She stretched to reach a strap that appeared to be wedged behind the headboard.

When tugging from beneath failed to free it, Matilda scrambled out again, frustrated. The captain was leaving very early the next day, returning to his ship and command, and she needed to finish this job. Mrs. Young insisted the bedding be changed before he returned to the house.

She wasn't supposed to be in his rooms at this hour. No one was. The captain, when he was ashore, ran his home under a firm set of rules that no one dared cross.

Matilda considered her options. She couldn't leave it there in case it was important to the captain. The bed was too heavy for her to move on her own, and although she could call for help, she hated to do so. The other servants didn't like her very much, having decided from the beginning to make fun of her at every turn. Calling out to them was decidedly unappealing, so she had no choice but to climb onto the enormous bed, hoping she could reach the mysterious item without having to remake her morning's work entirely.

It was dark behind the headboard, and she thrust her hand into the narrow space.

She touched cold metal and jerked her hand back in surprise. Matilda peered into the gap and discovered the straps attached to a buckle. Puzzled by their presence, Matilda grabbed the item and tugged it into the light. It was not what she'd expected to find.

It was a horse's harness, but a strange design indeed if it was intended for a normal-sized horse. The straps were made of red silk, the buckles bright silver and definitely too delicate for any beast of burden. On further exploration, she retrieved a leather mask, not unlike a satin one she'd seen the captain wear to a masquerade ball recently. It was engraved with swirls and markings to define the eyes and was sized to fit the full way around the head, almost like a cap that laced at the back with more red silk ribbons.

Intrigued, she searched again and brought out a riding crop and cat-o'-nine-tails that appeared new. The latter gave her gooseflesh just to look at it, but the strands were so soft that she wasn't sure it could be used for punishment of any member of the captain's crew.

She sat back on her heels, flexing the crop between her hands, puzzled. Why would the captain keep such items hidden behind his bed? Surely, they belonged in his dressing closet with all his clothes, although some items deserved to be in the stables. She picked up the mask again and studied the item, running her fingertips over the smooth sections where his cheeks would rest. Beautifully made, and the leather was supple as if it was worn often.

Matilda scurried off the bed and moved to the mirror to find out, but when she saw her appearance, she nearly died of mortification. Her hair looked dreadful. She appeared a waif who had run backward through a briar patch.

Matilda quickly released her hair from the few pins she owned, smoothed the strands until they were tidy, and swept it up again into a neat and modest arrangement. Feeling better about herself at last, she lifted the captain's mask into place.

The leather was soft against her skin, and wearing it made it seem as if a stranger was in the room with her. It hid her identity so well she was curious to know more about the purpose. She'd never seen Captain Ford carrying it out the door on his way to a society entertainment. She probably should not pay so much attention to the handsome captain; as a servant, his comings and goings were none of her business. Nevertheless, she had long ago admitted the man was more than a little intriguing. He was quiet, he never yelled, but somehow his brief stays in the town house managed to terrify each and every servant so much that they fell over themselves trying to please him.

He was dangerous in a way Matilda could never quite pin down. He made her wonder if falling into her employer's arms might not be the scandal her upbringing told her it should be.

Through the eyes of the mask, she saw the door open behind her, and she gasped as she realized her employer had returned.

Matilda dropped the mask from her face and swept it behind her back, hoping to hide what she'd been doing from Captain William Ford.

His dark eyes bored into hers, flickered to the bed where her discoveries were still on display, and then back to her. His brow furrowed, which she'd learned was not a good sign. He was displeased, as he often was around her no matter how hard she tried to be unobtrusive. She couldn't have picked a worse day to linger in his room.

The click of the door lock was very loud in the room. "Miss Winslow," he said in his soft way, causing gooseflesh to rise all over her skin.

"Captain."

He came close. "What are you doing here at this hour?"

Matilda clenched the mask behind her back. "Making the bed," she explained weakly and then prayed he would not notice she'd failed to straighten the comforter from when she'd been standing on it.

"The bed is made, although somewhat imperfectly." He stopped a foot from her, and then his attention flickered to the mirror behind her back. His brow rose. "Show me what is behind your back."

"I. Oh. This mask?" She offered it to him, seeing no point of hiding it any longer. He must have seen she'd been holding his possession through the mirror's reflection, a major transgression for any servant. She'd been warned before not to touch his personal items. "It fell."

His expression grew cold. "And the other articles. Did they fall too?"

"No." She swallowed the lump in her throat when he would not take the mask from her shaking hand. "Only one item truly fell. I still have not retrieved it from behind the headboard. It is out of my reach, only I did not know you stored these other items there and recovered them by mistake. I promise to put everything back the way I found them."

His hot fingers wrapped around her wrist and held her in place. The mask dropped from her hand. "Too late for that."

His grip tightened, and her heart pounded. "Captain?"

One brow lifted. "Have I not issued clear instructions that I do not want servants lingering in my bedchamber?"

"Yes, captain." She shivered, too aware of his proximity and unyielding stance. "But I was ordered to change your sheets today."

"If that is true, then what were you doing standing before the looking glass?" His gaze narrowed. "Admiring yourself?"

Matilda licked her lips. Oh, she was in so much trouble. Mrs. Young would waste no time in turning her out for displeasing the captain on his last day ashore. She could not afford to lose this position. Surely, he had some compassion in him for a woman who'd only stolen a moment to neaten her appearance.

"I wanted to fix my hair," she admitted, glancing down in shame. "I was given no time to use in the mirrors in the servants' hall this morning and I did not know how frightful I looked until now. Mrs. Young believes servants have no business fussing with their appearance. I apologize."

"You always look beautiful, even when your ebony tresses are half falling down. Especially then." His lips pursed, and he released her. "Turn and look your fill in the mirror."

Startled by his suggestion, Matilda hesitated to obey. Staring at her reflection wasn't actually what she'd been doing. Her hair was tidy now, and she had just been curious about how she would look in a mask, having never attended a masquerade ball before.

She turned a little as Captain Ford placed a chair some feet before the mirror and sat facing her, hands on his thighs as if he was waiting for her compliance.

Waiting for her performance—as if she were a character in his very own private play.

He scowled. "The mirror, Miss Winslow. Look at yourself in it now."

To follow his orders meant she would have to stand directly in front of him. What harm could come of that since he insisted it was all right? She took a step, placed herself before the mirror, and stared at her reflection. She had always resented that her skin wasn't fair. She was too much like her mother in appearance, her father had often claimed with a hint of regret. Her saving grace was her eyes, her prettiest feature by far. She widened her attention to the rest of her appearance. A poor maid wearing a drab brown gown that did not flatter her complexion or figure stared back. She lowered her eyes, properly shamed before the captain. Overall, she was nothing special to look at. "You were making fun of me."

He frowned. "I'd never do that."

"Why not? Everyone else does." She complained and then bit her lip. Her employer wouldn't want to know about her problems, and especially not on his last day ashore.

"Everyone else is either a fool or jealous, Miss Winslow." He pulled a face. "You could wear sack cloth and still be the most remarkable and distracting woman in the room."

His words made her skin heat with a blush, but she smiled too. She liked the idea that he had noticed her, even if he was so far above her. But was unwise to think a captain in his majesty's navy could want to pay too much attention to a lowly maid when he was as handsome as William Ford. However, the way he scowled at her sometimes had made her feel so very insignificant. Did he not want to like her? He probably didn't. "Thank you."

"Now come here and sit on my knee," he said quietly.

She spun about. "Why?"

"Your punishment," he said calmly. "You cannot play with my possessions without consequences."

She blinked as he reached forward slowly to capture her wrist, his gaze fastened to her face until she blushed.

"I issue orders and expect to be obeyed in all things. Especially in the bedchamber." His brow rose. "Or do you imagine yourself above my rules? I do not like snoops, Miss Winslow."

"I'm sorry, Captain." He tugged, and Matilda stumbled forward. He eased her down on his knees. "It won't happen again," she promised as she clutched at his shoulders to steady herself.

Eye to eye, her pulse raced. He was so very handsome and sure of himself. The very thing Matilda never was around him. All of Matilda's senses seemed ready to fly apart just by being so close to him.

His gaze drifted to her lips. "Don't be sorry. But accept my punishment now and do as I ask in the future."

She nodded, breathless at the way he was regarding her mouth. "Yes, Captain."

His eyes widened and his tongue slipped out to wet his lips. "Yes, to what?"

Matilda wriggled on her scandalous perch; sure he would steal a kiss and more. "They say a maid who is foolish enough to fall into her employer's arms, deserves her ruin and the loss of her employment. I do need to be punished."

"Never consider that I could turn you out for any reason," he whispered, his breath hot against her throat. "What happens between us is strictly our business and will remain a secret. I will punish you, bring you pleasure, and that will be an end to the matter."

She squirmed even more as she considered what sort of punishment he might deliver that brought pleasure. She was not afraid of him. At the very least she might be expected to polish his bedchamber from one end to the other as punishment for her misadventure today, at the worst he might kiss her witless. Make love to her. Her sex throbbed with unexpected anticipation. "Very well. Punish me however you like."

No sooner were the words spoken than he flipped her over, so she dangled over his limbs. Matilda gasped in surprise as he held her there by placing one arm over and around her waist firmly.

His other hand connected with her backside the next moment, and she cried out, kicking at the shock of his idea of punishment. She expected ruin, not a spanking. "What are you doing, sir?"

"Captain," he reminded her. "You agreed to be punished in any way I deemed fit." He struck again, so hard that her eyes filled with tears and her face grew hot. "I do not want you touching that mask ever again. Never wear it. It is not for the likes of you."

"I won't wear it again."

He held his hand still on her bottom and kneaded her flesh through the gown. "Do you understand that a line was crossed today?"

"I understand," she whispered. "Captain."

"You continue to place yourself in my path, so there's nothing else to be done but continue as we are."

She frowned and clutched at his leg to steady herself. "I don't understand."

"You, and only you, have my permission to linger in my bedchamber for as long as you want. I'll make the arrangements before I go. You may touch any possession of mine except that mask and do your hair before the mirror. Mrs. Young is an old woman, threatened by your youth and beauty." His hand smoothed over her bottom, and she held her breath. "Look at yourself in the mirror now, Miss Winslow."

She turned her head as he pulled her skirts up and exposed the bottom he'd spanked. Matilda's heart began to hammer. A smile lingered on the captain's lips as he lightly touched her exposed skin with just the tips of his fingers. As the gentle caress continued, her face grew hotter and hotter.

"Look at me admiring you," he said as his fingers trailed along her thigh, sliding down over the gaping hole in the stocking tied below her knee. Matilda was transfixed by his gentle touch, by the devilish light in his eyes. He teased his fingers into her best stockings, widening the tear. "You must replace these after I'm gone."

His hand lifted slowly, and he brought it down sharply on bare bottom again and then continued.

Matilda gasped through it all, overcome by sensation, pain, and anticipation for the next strike. She clung to his leg, stunned, and fascinated by how his punishment affected her senses. An ache began between her legs, a sensation she'd never experienced before. She was breathless and restless. Captain Ford's face was a mask of severity now. He did not smile or look at her again. His attention was reserved for her rear and the red flush growing on her skin.

Suddenly he glanced up and met her gaze. His eyes were wild, dark, and focused solely on her. Matilda panted. He gripped her tingling bottom tightly, then turned his hand a fraction and used his fingers to part her thighs. His brow rose. "More?"

She nodded, but was unsure of what he'd do next. As his fingers dipped between, touching a place only Matilda had tentatively explored before in the privacy her narrow cot afforded, she closed her eyes. She was assailed by strange sensations that made her feel warm all over. As his gentle caress grew bolder, she could not help the need to push her body into his touch.

He brushed against her sex while she shuddered and moaned to his bewitching touch. He continued to rub through her damp curls, more insistent with each stroke, and the sensations were so different that she couldn't account for them. She squirmed a little as an ache began where he played with her; a burning need to widen her legs further so he might press his fingers into her body.

"Look at us," the captain whispered. "Look at what I'm doing to you. How perfect is the moment just before your surrender?"

Matilda struggled to catch her breath. She did look, focusing on his hand moving between her thighs, on the pink of her bottom beside his pale wrist, on the flush of color on his cheeks. She ached so badly an unladylike moan tumbled from her lips.

"Please," she begged of him, knowing there must be more to come. She was alive in his embrace in a way she'd never felt before. She could barely hold still.

"Trust me," he whispered, leaning over her body so he could speak into her ear. "You're as eager as I am but will learn not to rush such moments. I will make the wait worth your while."

He teased her again, but so skillfully that Matilda began to shake. She stiffened and cried out as her body convulsed, taken over by sensations beyond her experience.

She hung her head as her senses spun out of control again and again until his touch gentled on her sex.

The captain's fingers slipped away, and he eventually loosened his tight grip on her waist. He relaxed against the back of the chair and uttered a shockingly masculine groan. "An exquisite end to this affair." He chuckled softly. "I had hoped you might hold out longer before falling. Next time you will."

He reached into his coat pocket and pressed a cold coin into her hand.

She stared at the new-minted sovereign as pleasurable satisfaction gave way to unease over what she'd allowed.

"Oh, God." She was a fool. Matilda twisted to look at Captain Ford's smiling face.

Matilda dropped the coin. She flew off his lap, shoving her gown down as she went, and fled the room as fast as she could unlock the door. She did not pause to tug up her mangled stocking; she did not heed his calls to wait. She could not bear to hear him offer more money as if she had expected to be compensated for her favors.

CHAPTER ONE

London, 1815

MATILDA WINSLOW CAME to a screeching halt behind the tottering housekeeper and tried to contain her impatience before she ran the gasping woman down. She shuddered at the wail echoing through Captain William Ford's cozy London town house.

It was not a pretty sound.

It was a sound no man should make.

"Dear God, have mercy," Mrs. Young whispered as the sound trailed off. She struggled toward the steep mahogany staircase as if she were walking through knee-high mud. "He lives. He lives."

But at what price? Matilda shivered and followed with mincing steps, trying to remember that the older woman would not take kindly to a servant brushing past her on the stairs. Mrs. Young must always be first. Matilda struggled with showing deference to a woman with limited sense, and she had no doubt been both lucky and foolish to still have this employment.

Now that she could clearly hear Captain Ford crying out in pain, she understood she'd hardly any idea of how desperate the situation was when she'd first heard the startling news that he'd been returned to shore and to his London town house. The entire household had been belowstairs and most had erupted into frantic activity to cover up how little they'd been doing in his absence.

Matilda tripped along in a daze, her heart in her throat as the sounds continued to rise and fall unabated. She had hoped to find another position before his return, but without any sort of reference, she'd been unsuccessful. She cringed as Captain Ford cried out again. He uttered agonized, incomprehensible gabble that, in her three-year acquaintance with her employer, she would never have suspected he'd be capable of making.

The housekeeper turned to her, her cheeks an unhealthy shade of gray. "We will need to be strong. Go on without me, do what is needed."

She stared at the woman; struck by the notion she had not heard correctly. "Me?"

"Yes, you. It is time you earned your wages for a change," the woman hissed.

That was not fair. Matilda worked harder than any of the other maids. All they did was flirt with the footmen and lift their skirts for anyone who had enough coin.

Mrs. Young caught the banister, her fingers white on the rail, and swayed into it for support instead of moving upward. The usually self-sufficient old woman could barely stand. Matilda didn't want her to fall on the stairs for the fuss she would make later on so she caught the eye of the nearest footman. "Assist Mrs. Young upstairs at once."

She skirted the protesting housekeeper, and although she

would most likely be reprimanded later, Matilda hiked up her skirts and ran up the entire flight of steps toward Captain Ford's bedchamber and that horrible noise.

She sped along the halls and paused outside his dressing room, risking a peek first before entering. The Roberts brothers, twin footmen who should have returned downstairs to their posts by now, lingered at the bedchamber doorway, maids Jenny and Jane stood nearby, whispering to each other as was their habit. One had tears in her eyes, but most probably they were tears meant for themselves. With Captain Ford returned, their easy employment would certainly end.

Matilda shooed them away. "Back to your duties before Mrs. Young sees you."

She ignored their protests and pushed her way between the towering footmen. The captain's valet, Dawson, had returned with his master, and at the sound of her voice, he turned toward her. A sensible man she knew fairly well, Gregory Dawson had dark circles under his eyes, and his expression was bleak.

His appearance was unkempt too, his jaw covered with several days of stubble, his usually impeccable clothes wrinkled and stained in some places with what appeared to be dried blood. He looked about ready to fall down from exhaustion. She grasped his forearm, offering compassion and her strength. He was particularly attached to his employer for some reason, even going so far as to follow him to sea by his own choice.

"Miss Winslow," he whispered with relief at seeing her.

"Mr. Dawson." She shivered as another moan filled her ears. "What has happened?"

The man paled further. "He's dying."

Matilda swallowed hard at the idea of a world without Captain Ford and then noticed strangers in his room. "Who is in there?"

"Mr. Simmons and Mr. Fellows, physicians both. They came with us direct from the docks." Dawson shuddered as Captain Ford moaned brokenly again. "They don't mince words."

Dawson shifted to lean against the wall, revealing the whole of the room to Matilda.

She shuddered at the sight of four men holding William Ford down. "Why was he not taken to the Naval Hospital for treatment?"

"He's not expected to live very long," Dawson whispered. "The hospital was said to be overflowing, so I brought him home to die because I knew he'd prefer to be here where it is quiet."

Tears filled her eyes, but she dashed them away. She had wished injury on William Ford many times over the past year for his treatment of her, but this was beyond anything she'd ever imagined he'd deserve.

She bit her lip, unable to comprehend that nothing could be done to save the captain. "Surgeons perform miracles every day. My late father treated many men and never gave up until the last moment of a patient's life. He saved many when I had felt their recovery hopeless. Has word been sent to the duke, to any of the captain's family?"

"Yes, Lieutenant Ford made landfall ahead of us and went ahead with the message."

"Good. Mrs. Young should be on her way up." As an afterthought, she added, "Make sure she has a chair as soon as possible. Keep an eye on her in case she faints."

"How like you to care about everyone." He smiled tightly and then scraped his fingers through his hair. It didn't help him look more composed. "It is good to see you again, despite the circumstances."

"It's good to have you home." She touched his arm again. "Get some rest, and I will see what I can do to help."

Matilda entered the room and at once was assaulted with the odor of turpentine. The unpleasant scent brought reminders of all the times some poor broken soul had been carried into her father's simple home to be mended over their kitchen table. She breathed through her mouth until her nausea passed and tried to recall what her father might have done in a similar situation.

"Hold him still," Mr. Simmons barked out while the captain twisted and moaned brokenly beneath clutching hands.

The captain should be calmer.

She eased closer, assessing the men in the room and the mood. Every face was grim. No one would meet her gaze. "What are you doing to him?"

The doctor grimaced as he peeled back a blood-soaked scrap of linen from the captain's head. "What must be done?"

The captain bucked again, and the men struggled to keep him on the bed.

"Well, don't stand about gawking, girl. Out!"

Girl! She'd argue that description, but she was the only maid in the household with experience that might lend assistance to the physicians. "My father was a surgeon. I helped him save lives. What can I do?"

The physician assessed her with a scathing flicker of interest and then scoffed. "You either help hold him down or wait outside with everyone else."

He didn't believe she could help. How typical that men of science refused to believe a prettier face than theirs might have skills to offer too. She wasn't surprised by his skepticism, merely annoyed.

Matilda moved toward the bed. She had experience with the treatment of minor wounds, though she had rarely been called upon to use her knowledge since coming to work for Captain Ford. The housekeeper did not like any reminder that she possessed more of an education than the old goat did herself and always consulted with an apothecary.

The captain's arms and legs were already pinned; another fellow held his head still, but his body writhed between all of them. She could barely make out his face beyond his uncovered eyes. His lashes were dark and appeared moist. The rest of his head had been swathed in linen some time ago judging by the grubby state of it.

Matilda leaned across the bed and pressed her hands down on the captain's heaving chest.

Simmons glanced her way. "There's not enough room for everyone to stand. Get on the bed beside him."

Although surprised by the request, Matilda carefully climbed up. She knelt beside William Ford, and the odor of him—sweat, turpentine and other strong scents—almost made her gag. She pushed on his ribs firmly and breathed shallowly. "Like this?"

Captain Ford chose that moment to buck, and Matilda was almost tossed off entirely.

"You'll need to apply more weight, Miss Winslow," Dawson suggested as he drew close. "Let me do it."

Matilda shook her head as she took in Dawson's sagging shoulders. He stared at his employer with tears in his eyes. "You're already exhausted, Dawson. Go and sit down before you fall down."

"You don't have to do this," Dawson said. "Not after..."

She stared at the valet in horror. How could he know her shame at the captain's hands?

Matilda turned away from Dawson quickly. She had hoped no one had known she'd been caught red-handed and punished for her curiosity. It was her own fault. When Captain Ford had closed the door behind him, effectively trapping her in his room, she had known he'd ruin her. She'd given him permission to do whatever he liked. She had enjoyed it too until he'd handed her a coin for services rendered as if she was a prostitute.

"I'll be fine," she whispered and concentrated on the patient rather than the man and how low he'd made her feel since that day.

Although entirely improper, sitting on the captain to hold him down might be her only option what with the way he was thrashing about. She was light and didn't want to be thrown off and hurt in the process of helping. Matilda carefully lifted her skirts and straddled William Ford, settling him between her thighs and pinning his sides with her knees. Thank heavens she'd taken to wearing drawers or she might truly be thought a wicked woman. A hot blush filled her cheeks as the doctors stared at her improper position. The surprise in their eyes caused Matilda to make sure the drawers covering her legs were hidden from view too. She carefully settled all her weight on the patient's belly and then pressed her hands to his upper chest.

"What are you doing, girl?" Mrs. Young gasped, having finally arrived. "Have you no shame?"

"She is doing what only she could," Dawson insisted.

The next time Captain Ford moved after the doctor's treatment; he did not move very much at all. "I think this has helped," she whispered.

"Agreed." Dawson turned away, dragging Mrs. Young toward a comfortable chair near an open window, then stood back to observe. Mrs. Young began to pray loudly.

As Matilda sat on Captain Ford's chest, she became aware that his breathing was strained and sounded very wet. He gurgled.

The bandages around his mouth were stained pale red and damp, as if they'd been constantly soaked. Her eyes widened with understanding. "Quickly, lift him up."

"What?"

"He cannot breathe." She pushed away the men holding Captain Ford's arms to no effect. "He must be allowed to sit up."

The doctors stared at the captain and then each other. "We can't see the wound if he is upright."

"For goodness' sake, let go of his arms and lift up the whole headboard then. He's been trying to get up, to breathe, and you won't let him. His mouth is full of liquid. He's drowning in it."

"Do it," Dawson ordered as the men holding Captain Ford hesitated to follow her instructions.

As soon as he was released, Captain Ford struggled upright, latching on to Matilda even as he cried out in pain. He clung to her tightly, gasping and sputtering around his moans.

Matilda cradled his well-padded head to her shoulder as the men quickly moved to the headboard, planted their feet, and raised them both up at an angle. Matilda eased the captain back against his pillows as soon as she could and immediately noticed his bandages had bloomed reddish brown around his mouth.

"Good God," Fellows murmured and then turned aside to gag into a handkerchief.

Matilda controlled her revulsion at the sight and concentrated on helping the captain breathe easier. "Get those bandages away from his face now. Cut them off if necessary. Bring fresh linen and warm water to clean him with."

It shocked her that these medical men were so slow to act. Had they no idea how to treat the captain properly?

"You'll need to bring in bricks from the yard," Dawson advised the idle footmen who'd reappeared at the door at the commotion. "Bring a dozen or so to support the weight."

The doctor leaned over the captain holding a pair of scissors and carefully cut through the remaining layers of bandages, freeing a corner of his mouth and nose. Captain Ford drew in a huge breath and closed his eyes as the doctor recommenced peeling the bandages away from the wound one layer at a time.

The bed rocked a little when the bricks were brought in and set in place. The fellows who had been holding the bed up flexed their shoulders but did not move to hold the captain down again. They stepped back and then silently filed out of the room.

The captain caught her eye and stared at her. He was breathing easier, and he did not fight his treatment anymore.

"You'll be all right now," she whispered.

His left hand slipped over hers, and his fingers tightened around her wrist in viselike grip. The captain's eyes darted left and right, examining those around him. When he did it again before meeting her gaze, she understood.

"Your family are all in the country." She swallowed the hard lump in her throat. He hated strangers in his home, but she could imagine he'd want those he loved at his bedside at a time like this. "I'm sure they will be here soon."

She shifted a little as her knees cramped.

When Mr. Simmons removed the final strip of bandage covering the wound, the captain spluttered out a garbled curse. He squeezed her thigh painfully and then fainted dead away.

Matilda stared at the angry wound that stretched over what had once been the captain's perfect left cheek. "Oh, no."

He had once been very handsome, and her eyes stung at the horror she faced now.

The injury gaped, a jagged and deep cut.

Mr. Fellows rushed outside. The sound of his retching in the hall soon followed.

Mr. Simmons turned his face away for a long moment. "It's a miracle he's survived this long. We'll make him comfortable, but we must prepare for the worst."

"No!" The defeat in the surgeon's tone angered Matilda on the captain's behalf. "If William Ford has lived this long, he undoubtedly intends to recover. Fords never quit nor do they ever give up, sir. It isn't in his nature, nor should it be in yours. Fix him."

Matilda looked to Dawson for support, expecting the valet to agree with her and remind the doctor of whom he was dealing with. Captain Ford was the most stubborn, taciturn man she had ever met. He would fight for life surely.

Dawson met her gaze sadly though. He bowed his head and covered his eyes as if overset by a grief he wanted no one to see.

"No," she whispered in shock. She turned on Simmons, who as the elder surgeon should be the most skilled and the one to convince. "He can survive this if you're the surgeon I think you are. You know what needs to be done to aid his recovery."

The housekeeper gained her feet and approached the bed. Matilda flinched as the older woman placed a hand to her shoulder. "This may be more than he can bear. We must pray together."

"He wants to live," Matilda insisted before grabbing a wad of fresh clothes with which to catch the ooze from his mouth and dabbed at his unmarked cheek. "He will."

Mr. Simmons sighed. "To have any chance, the wound will need to be cleaned and stitched again. It will be painful for him. He is already weak. He may not survive the attempt, and there is no guarantee it will heal properly. He may be horribly disfigured."

"Better disfigured than dead." The room fell deathly silent at her remark. There likely hadn't been an ugly Ford in history, and if the captain survived to see that day come, he might not thank her, but he would have his life to live.

She'd been around those next to die thanks to her father's profession, and she couldn't imagine Captain Ford succumbing. He might be in pain, but he was too lucid to have given up yet. His recovery truly only depended on whether Mr. Simmons was as clever as he was purported to be.

"Come away, Miss Winslow," Mr. Dawson murmured. "I can't let you watch him suffer under the butcher's hand."

"No, I will stay right where I am." The captain stirred beneath her, and she rose up on her knees until her face hovered over his. "You will get better."

He tried to speak, but no words came out that made any sense.

Matilda smiled tightly and then leaned toward his ear. "If you die, your sisters will look through your things, touch your precious belongings. Do you want them to know what you really keep in this room?"

Matilda knew too well what he hid from everyone. The mask and other things had disappeared, she suspected to a locked chest kept beneath this very bed. He had a darkness and a taste for inflicting pain on women despite his seemingly proper appearance.

She peeked at his face as she drew back. His eyes had widened a little, and then they darkened to a dense black. She shook her head as her body tightened in response to his obvious irritation. What the captain wanted to do with her would be her ruin if she gave in to her feelings again.

"Of course you will recover." She studied him as coldly as she could. "Besides, you don't really want a mere servant to have the last word, do you?"

He changed the grip he had on her hand. He made a sound of protest and squeezed.

"Shh, you must remain calm and allow Mr. Simmons to do his work." She loosened his grip; the right hand that had spanked her until she'd cried had a deep cut down his thumb and would need salve applied to it and new bandaging. She would attend to that herself. Later. The most pressing concern was his face.

She set his palm over her knee and pressed down carefully so she didn't cause further injury. "I won't leave your side no matter what the doctor does to you."

His eyes closed, his fingers flexed on her knee.

"I think he's ready. Fetch the laudanum and a narrow spoon. I recall seeing one for infants in the nursery cupboard."

The captain's fingertips dug painfully into her knee.

She glanced down at him, startled by his response. "I am not suggesting you are a babe in arms. The smaller spoon will make it easier for you to take the medication."

His stare promised retribution and equal humiliation if word of him eating from an infant's spoon spread beyond this room. That was exactly what she'd hoped for. He still had fire in him if he could be so easily offended, and that fire would help him fight for life.

"Hold that anger close to your heart and let it lend you strength for what is to come, Billy Boy."

He stared at her, breath churning as tension between them grew.

She smiled with satisfaction that her jibe, use of his childhood nickname, got under his skin. "This will hurt."

His fingers squeezed her knee painfully again.

"Be still now. You'll need your strength for what is to come."

Mrs. Young sobbed. "This is madness. We'll be blamed if he dies."

Matilda spared her a fleeting glance. "Better to do something than nothing at all. Do it. Do it quickly and all at once," she urged, resettling herself over the captain's body. It was a strange perch, but at least from here she could observe Mr. Simmons at work and distract the patient while he endured the pain.

Mr. Fellows returned and carefully spooned laudanum into the side of Captain Ford's mouth. It was a higher dose than she'd expected him to be given, and she prayed the man knew what he was about. The doctors turned away to discuss the procedure in private.

Matilda watched Captain Ford sink slowly under the influence and breathed a sigh of relief when he struggled to keep his eyes open, and the pressure of his gripping fingers softened and slipped away. "He's almost out," she called to them.

She moved to brush a lock of hair back from the captain's brow and then snatched her hand back. He deserved her compassion but wanted none of her affection. If he had, he'd never have tried to pay for her favors.

She settled her hands on his chest and felt the strong beat of his heart. He would live. Later she would decide if she could remain in his employ now that he'd returned to shore. It was almost certain that his recovery would take many months.

While he convalesced, she would have time to think of what to do while she awaited her beau's return.

CHAPTER TWO

About three months later

THE DREAM always started the same way. Fabric rustled and William Ford became aware of Matilda Winslow creeping into his room through a connecting door. Candlelight played over her features and prim nightgown, and he was spellbound in a way he had no right to be.

When the woman set her candle aside and climbed onto his bed to reach him where he lay in the center, he remained still lest he shatter the illusion that such moments could last.

Tonight he was properly awake and aware he was not dreaming this visitation. Matilda Winslow, a provocative maid in his employ, was in his bedchamber and crawling close. He had no idea when the woman's nightly visits had begun, but they couldn't continue without consequences for her.

He had been convalescing for several long months, and tonight was the first time he truly cared what had happened to him or around him.

He'd almost died, many times in fact.

He could still feel the slice of the blade through his cheek; he could still remember parts of battle and the harrowing journey to make landfall in England. He dreamed of that often. Vivid recollections that soaked his skin in sweat. The surgery performed on his face in this very bed he'd prefer to forget except for one small detail.

He'd rarely been alone since he'd returned to this house.

He'd had Matilda Winslow to watch over him every day and night it seemed.

An unbearable torture for him.

Matilda inched toward him, always so gentle in her movements to avoid jostling him and causing further pain. She had taken on her duties as nurse to an invalid with complete dedication. He sometimes forgot they were virtually strangers. She was a maid. A young woman in his employ. A pretty maid whose frequent touches caused his palms to itch.

Her fingers ghosted over his brow, no doubt checking him for fever as she so often did, and then she peeked at his face.

Her eyes widened. "I didn't mean to wake you, Captain."

Matilda had spent every night since the surgery at his side or leaning over his bed, tending to him as if he were her only concern. He'd grown used to her being around, but it had to stop. Especially now he was feeling more himself. This one last night was all he could permit himself of her gentle company.

He licked his lips as the scent of her body curled around them, waking him to the fact that he was only human and weak. If she remained close, he'd become aroused, and that wasn't something she wanted from him.

He eased a little to the side, turning his hips so the bedding did not lay too tightly over his growing arousal. "You didn't," he whispered. His voice was rusty from disuse, and he felt that he slurred thanks to the hideous scar dissecting his cheek. "I was not sleeping."

Matilda beamed at him warmly, a smile so welcoming he feared it. "You spoke."

"Obviously. Did you really think me silent because I couldn't find the words?" He'd kept silent so he wouldn't reveal how often the woman was on his mind. He considered her, and what she should be doing for his care, far too often for his own peace of mind. "I'd never let you get the last word," he said stiffly.

Matilda cried out and impulsively flung herself against his chest in an unwarranted display of affection. Maids did not embrace their employers unless they had an intimate and forbidden relationship. Matilda Winslow had rejected his passions by running from him once before. He feared revealing his needs to her yet again.

It wasn't right to torture himself like this, but he did not immediately push her away. Matilda was a soft, impulsive woman though who didn't have the faintest inkling of how great a test she was to his honor. He'd already failed once quite spectacularly.

He kept his hands down, pressing them into the sheets.

"I knew you'd recover," she whispered.

"So you did." He'd not been so overwhelmed with pain that he could forget how Matilda had fought with the surgeons on his behalf. She had insisted the doctor not give up. She had not been turned from her conviction he wanted to live, even if she'd been so very wrong.

Before her arrival in his bedchamber, William had fought off the hands that clutched at him so he might be left alone to die in peace. Matilda hadn't allowed him any peace since the moment he'd first laid eyes on her, and today was no different from any other.

His wish to die had changed the moment Matilda Winslow had sat on him. She'd been impassioned that day. Enough so he'd allowed her will to hold sway over his life. She'd issued orders for his care with authority, understanding what needed to be done to save him with surprising interest for his welfare.

He would be grateful until his last breath that her faith in his recovery had been greater than his own, but expressing softer feelings was not easy for him. As it was, they'd already passed too close to the bounds of propriety and his own limits.

He hesitantly touched her loosely tied hair as she clung to him, and desire pecked holes in his defenses and restraint, urging him to act and take what he wanted from this infuriating creature and damn the consequences. He'd done that once and frightened her. That day he'd found her at his mirror, admiring herself in the mask he insisted his lovers wear during discipline, had proved his wickedness knew no bounds.

He would not make that same mistake again.

Matilda was very warm against his body and fragile. She was nothing like his usual lovers who knew what to expect from him and enjoyed being disciplined by his hand or by a riding crop. She wasn't the sort of woman who could want him.

Her hair was tied back with a white ribbon, and as he pushed her back, he kept hold of it. Her hair spilled forward over her shoulder in a lush dark wave, and his breath caught. If only she weren't so shy, or a maid, he would pursue her. He'd catch her and bend her over his knee.

Again.

He cursed under his breath, denying himself what he wanted even though he yearned for her. Their relationship needed to go back to the way things had been before he'd spanked her if he was to have any peace, but this was not the way to do it. He had to do a better job of keeping a proper distance, and toying with her hair wasn't it. He had to be strong and strict with her. "I'd have a chance if you'd stop crushing me," he grumbled meanly.

She sat up, supporting herself on one arm but still smiling down into his face, failing to be put off by his harder tone. "I also suspected that you could talk all along. How could you stay so quiet for so long?"

"Habit, and I happen to like the sound of your voice," he whispered, then cleared his throat, uncomfortable when her eyes widened in surprise and pleasure. He hadn't meant that how it must have sounded to her, but to him he might have asked her to dance on his cock until the sun rose.

He struggled to purge that thought from his head. Matilda Winslow deserved his utmost respect and courtesy—and that meant keeping his desire to discipline her to himself. "The wound pained me a little on first try, so I thought I had better wait a good long while before further attempts. I'd rather not be stitched again."

She rubbed his arm, a soothing gesture she'd done many times over the past weeks and months. At first, he'd been uncertain of the gesture and what it signified, but Matilda had appeared to sense his melancholy.

She settled more comfortably. Closer. "Well, that was sensible. How do you feel?"

Dear God, the woman didn't make anything easy.

"Like I've been to hell and back." He glanced at the ceiling. He should send her away, but after all she'd done for him, the woman deserved a little conversation. "I don't think I can adequately describe how surprised I am to be alive. When I was wounded, I feared for my life."

"We all did, but in usual Ford fashion, death must wait till you are ready to go and not a moment sooner," Matilda remarked humorously. "What do you remember?"

"Too much," he whispered, drowning in memories for a brief and unpleasant moment, instantly annoyed when she brushed her hand over his shoulder once more. He owed this woman his life, and he should say something about her actions. The dimness of the chamber only added to his wicked train of thought.

Despite the impropriety, he found her wrist and held it tightly. Restraining her made him feel more settled and confident for what he needed to say next. "I cannot properly express my gratitude for the care you've given me. I don't know what would have become of me had you not wished to save me."

"You saved yourself." Her posture softened, and he could just make out a gentle smile curving her lips. "Whatever influence I managed to have over your recovery was purely so that your sisters had no reason to cry."

He frowned. "Why are you here?"

She sighed softly. "Dawson insisted that I sleep in the dressing room in case you needed anything during the night. I always peek in on you before bed."

"Why you particularly and not another?"

"My father was a penny surgeon during his life, and I had the necessary experience of tending wounds and a stronger disposition than anyone else. Mrs. Young and the other servants have done nothing but weep and wail for months." She paused a moment, then shook her head. "And Dawson remembered your instructions that only I was allowed to be in your rooms. He said you would prefer me over anyone else."

"Ah," he said, remembering that long-forgotten discussion with some discomfort. At the time, he'd wanted to ensure that no one else accidentally found his sex play implements. It might have also had something to do with making sure Matilda's hair never mimicked a bird's nest again as it had done earlier that morning. "I had forgotten your father's career, but I did not think you had much interest in it. Have you studied much?"

"Some." She shifted a little, as if embarrassed by having an education. Matilda had not always been a servant, that much he knew. She'd come into his employ not long after her father's death. He'd been moved by her bleak face on the day they'd met and had impulsively employed her, even though Mrs. Young had not been in favor of employing a pretty girl when she had no letters of recommendation.

"I am grateful for your experience." He shrugged. "The other maids would indeed have been too foolish for the sickroom."

She cleared her throat. "My father believed a familiar face could aid in the recovery of a grievously ill patient."

"He was correct. I would rather have your pretty face hovering over me than a stranger's." He frowned. He had not meant to reveal a partiality, but Matilda's presence had been an excellent distraction from the pain and frustration. Had she any idea of the effect her innocence had on him? The danger she placed herself in was foolish. He released her wrist and sat up a little, keeping the sheets high over his hips still. "There were a few occasions I feared the doctor would resign because you made them wash their hands so often."

"Sickness can linger on the hands, but the doctors think little of women's intelligence in such matters and of my experience in particular." She shuddered. "I saw you at your worst that first day. After that, the physician's disapproval of my continued presence influenced me very little, Billy Boy."

The taunt, a nickname not used since his youth, made his palm itch. He would not tolerate the name on her lips again. He scowled. "Do you have any idea how much I hate hearing that name? Do not repeat it."

"That is why I said it that first day—to distract you from what was happening. I can explain if you will listen." She glanced down at the bedding guiltily and ran her finger along the heavy linen.

He was somewhat appeased by her submissive behavior. "You can try."

"Mrs. Young likes nothing better than to recount the past, and I recalled her mentioning the taunt and your reaction to it when you were a little boy. You had quite the temper as a child. The surgeons were giving up. I feared you were, too. So I said it, hoping there was everything to gain by throwing propriety aside and goading you. I saw the anger in your eyes that day and was glad I could provoke you. It gave me hope you would not give up without a fight."

"Remarkably observant." He caught her wrist again and stroked the soft skin on the inside. "But don't dare test me again without expecting consequences."

She shivered, and he hardened further at that sign of her unease around him. The thrill of having a woman even temporarily in his power only ever increased his desire.

"Your sisters have been writing every day and offering all sorts of treatments for you," she said in a rush, attempting to draw away.

"Dear God, that is grim news." He released her, bent one knee so the sheet hid his state better, and leaned on it. He hoped the gesture would set her at ease. He was master of his desires tonight. "What did you do with the advice?"

"I considered some of their suggestions, but then Mrs. Young took the letters from me before I could memorize them all." She frowned. "I do hope they were answered to their satisfaction. They seemed very concerned about you."

"I see." Anger rose in him that the housekeeper had interfered. He let out another curse under his breath at his train of thought. Far better for Matilda that she be kept at a distance than become more involved in his life and with his sisters, but still...

"I would have liked to have written back to Miss Evelyn. She suggested I kiss a crown and place it directly over your heart to ward off infection, which of course could not have any effect on an injury like yours." Her brow creased. "Does she really think that could have worked?"

"Evelyn has been infatuated with the occult in the past, but I had hoped she'd grown out of that foolishness," he mused, shaking his head in disgust. Clearly, he'd been away from them for too long, and his father's romantic nature had corrupted them into bird-witted ninnies. Now he was better, he would oversee their reading much more strictly and see what sense they had left. "I will speak to her about such nonsense when I see them again."

"That would be a good idea." Matilda appeared a practical, no-nonsense kind of woman, and he was pleased. "Her suggestion speaks more of a romantic dream than of any science. I am aware that sometimes it is only faith that keeps despair at bay, but it was very surprising to read such a thing from someone with her education."

He studied the woman who had bullied him back to life. Their conversation tonight was the most Matilda had ever spoken to him directly, aside from reading the daily newssheets and his correspondence. He was intrigued by her clarity of thought. She had been hiding a fine mind. "You've nerves of steel to have stayed at my side for so long. More courage than ten officers to witness what you must have done."

"My father tried to shield me from the horrors of his work, but it seems what I did see merely prepared me for what was to come." Her head dipped. "It is a necessity for a servant to avoid squeamishness. I don't have the luxury of fainting, as so many of the delicate ladies of your class are prone to do."

"Matilda," he said, his voice carrying a warning. There had always been an odd remark or expression when she read that hinted at bitterness at the antics of the *ton* mentioned in the papers. For all of her headstrong ways with the doctors, she possessed a finely tuned moral compass. He'd had to remind himself more than once that she was not of his world. They were quite different in every respect.

She'd probably kept her father's home until his death and overseen servants herself. He imagined she'd done very well at it, too. Since coming here, she would have only dusted and waited on his sisters, who treated her as their own plaything while he had watched her with growing hunger.

And then what had he done but punish her when his own vices had spun out of control?

He tightened his grip on the sheet as lust crept up on him once more. He did not deserve her kindness and compassion. He was not a man anyone could love and had no delusions his nature was normal.

He had in truth not expected her to be still employed in his home. He'd thought she would have fled while he'd been away at sea. It was astonishing she hadn't found other employment while he was away, though without a reference she might not have had a choice but to stay.

Before his injury, he'd briefly entertained the idea of offering her a new role in his life, but time had been short, and he'd not been able to locate her before leaving last year. He couldn't very well place such an offer in a letter and leave it behind. He'd changed his mind about the wisdom of making her his lover while they'd been apart, and especially so after his injury had thrown them together again.

Even though Matilda had the perfect temperament—quiet, trustworthy—she deserved better.

He'd do well to reestablish some boundaries. "Watch your tone when you speak to me."

"Yes, Captain." She swung off the bed and then patted her hair as she discovered he'd let it down. "When did you...?"

She quickly scrambled for the ribbon, but since he'd hidden it in the palm of his hand, her search was in vain. However, in her zeal to find her property, her enticing curves were revealed by the candle's flickering light, and he had a fine view down the front of her nightgown. He swallowed, itching to run his hands along her sides. Then scold her for flaunting herself before him, too.

It was well beyond time he took himself back to a brothel and purged his unreasonable urges for punishing lush women.

She stood up and huffed, drawing her hands down the long strands of her hair to neaten her appearance. "I trust you are able to call for Mr. Dawson's help now if you need it during the night?"

Mention of his valet soured his night. The man's fussing was driving him to distraction. "I won't need Dawson."

"Of course." She ducked down and collected her slippers, then fussed with her hair again. She seemed extremely uncomfortable with it loose. "If there is nothing else."

"Wait," he begged, but he sat up too quickly and clutched at his face as his newly healed skin stretched uncomfortably. "I have a great many questions that require answers."

Matilda hurried for his nightstand, scooped out a little of the cream kept there, and pushed his hand aside impatiently. She carefully patted the rosemary-scented ointment along his tingling scar. William held her shoulders to steady himself as she rubbed gentle circles over the rough edges. Months without relief had made him aware of every touch upon his skin as if it were a flame. He flexed his mouth as she recapped the jar, then slid his fingers down to her narrow waist.

"That should help," she whispered as he caressed her.

"Thank you." He studied her as he inched his fingers around her lithe body. He almost couldn't breathe for the anticipation and tension thrumming beneath her skin. "Don't go," he whispered.

The words were out of his mouth before he knew what he'd asked for.

Her gaze fell. "Tomorrow you must write to your family and inform them you are well again. They will want to visit. Tomorrow morning, after you've taken your breakfast, is the appropriate time to ask your questions. Mrs. Young will want to speak to you too, and she can fill you in on all you have missed."

The housekeeper set his teeth on edge. Mrs. Young would have done nothing but pray and allowed him to die neglected. "I will retrieve my sisters' letters and give them back to you. I will speak to you alone tomorrow."

She shivered and took a pace back, slipping out of his grasp. "As you wish."

"Why do you fuss over me and then run away?"

"It is not right. I need this position."

"I'm not about to dismiss you. Quite the reverse in fact."

Her eyes widened. "Are you going to offer for me?"

William froze, startled by the suggestion. She had run away from his passions before. He could not have a lover who disliked the tone of his desires. "I had not considered it."

"You held my hand a great many times in the beginning," she whispered.

"I remembered something of that," he acknowledged guiltily. He had a hazy recollection of comfort whenever she was close. A nightmare made smaller and insignificant after her whispered words of kindness. "I don't recall you making any attempt to stop me from touching you. Not even once. You were kinder to me than I deserve."

"You were ill." She brought her hand up to her chest. "It was sometimes easier to let you have your way. You were not yourself."

No doubt he'd been exactly himself, full of want to control her, but he would not reveal that truth to her now. Not if he could never have more than she was comfortable giving up. A marriage of unequal passions was utterly out of the question.

He threw himself out of the bed and followed her. "My actions reflect only on me."

She stared up at him, her bottom lip quivering. "Yes, Captain."

She should flee now. Her wary gaze drew him like a magnet, and he took a pace forward, unraveling the ribbon in his hand. "Come here and I will repair your hair."

She held out her hand for the ribbon, but William shook his head stubbornly. It was his mistake to fix. "Turn around and face the mirror."

She jumped, and he realized he'd said much the same thing to her that sunny afternoon he'd spanked her bottom red. He waited to see if she would comply, and when she slowly turned like she had the last time, he was pleased. Good servants were hard to find. Obedient ones like Matilda were extremely distracting.

William wasted no time in gathering her hair and running his fingers through the dark locks. He plaited the mass into a thick rope and tied it off with the ribbon and a bow the way he'd prefer it worn at night. He held her shoulders, admiring his handiwork, and then drew the light lemony fragrance that clung to her skin deep into his lungs. His cock ached as she held still, almost in his arms but not quite close enough to reveal his desires should she brush against him. "That should suffice," he said in a voice thickened by growing lust.

"Thank you." A hesitant smile teased her lips as she turned.

He kept his hands on her upper arms and his breath caught.

Dear God. If he didn't release her soon, he might go mad. She seemed the type to...

His bedchamber door creaked open. "Captain?"

Dawson's voice cut through his desire in a horrifying second.

He released Matilda and shoved her rudely toward the dressing room door before she was seen standing in his arms by his valet.

Tomorrow night, no matter what else occurred, he would take himself to the brothel and deal with his desires in the only way he could. There were women there who liked what he could make them feel far more than Matilda Winslow ever would.

CHAPTER THREE

MATILDA DUMPED the soiled linen in the laundry for washing, then turned to follow the sound of rushed steps toward the servants' hall. She passed the butler as he clutched a bottle of red wine in his hands, rattling his keys as he locked up the wine cellar behind him.

"You are tardy, Miss Winslow."

She was early. There wasn't much point in protesting that she was ahead of her own schedule. Mr. Carter commanded the servants by his own rules, most of which had nothing to do with kindness or forward thinking. "Yes, Mr. Carter."

She hurried to her place at the long table of the servants' dining hall for her first meal of the day. It had been a week since the captain had emerged from the relative privacy of his bedchamber, and she'd been up for several hours already, preparing the house for the new day, lighting fires, dusting tables in every room and hallway on the ground floor.

Now that she no longer needed to perform the lighter work of hovering near Captain Ford's bedchamber, she was already tired.

The months she'd spent at his bedside were the easiest days since she'd entered his service.

The cruel whispers swirling around her daily made her hours of drudgery worse, and she had no one to comfort her here.

She did her best to ignore the other servants as she sat down to eat, but it always stung that everyone thought so little of her efforts. Because the captain had singled her out, they assumed her his lover. They believed she'd shared his bed during his recovery because she desired him, or desired his money. Jenny and Jane, the other two upstairs maids, were the most dim-witted imbeciles with but one thing on their mind—attracting any man no matter what they offered—a pretty trinket in return for their favors pleased them very well. They teased her constantly, assumed her after the captain's attention.

The captain gave her nothing but trouble.

She glanced down the table, missing the steady presence of her beau Harry Lloyd but grateful he might never hear these terrible whispers about her character. They had met when he was a footman here, but he had gone away to make his fortune so they might marry one day soon. It was disappointing that she'd not had word of him recently, but the promise of his love kept her warm at night. It could not be too long till he came back to collect her, and they could start a life together somewhere nicer.

She took her place well down the table from the highest-ranking servants in the house and forced a smile as the house-keeper strolled in with Mr. Dawson following close on her heels.

"His Lordship passed another quiet night," Mr. Dawson informed everyone, smiling broadly at the news.

"That is very good." The butler nodded approvingly as he poured wine for Mrs. Young and himself. "He's had a trying time of it, but it seems he is out of danger at last."

"Indeed he has." The housekeeper glanced over everyone as she snatched up her brimming glass.

No one but the upper servants took wine so early in the day, and Matilda fumed. Such gluttony turned her stomach.

Mrs. Young's eyes lingered on Matilda, and her glass twitched in her hand. "We will still endeavor to keep as quiet as possible, so he is not disturbed and stay out of his way."

The household was walking on eggshells around William Ford as they went about their duties. He'd been irritated for most of the week and usually scowled when he saw her working nearby.

"He has no plans to go out today," Dawson remarked, casting a quick glance in Matilda's direction. "He's settled in the library and seems in exceptionally good spirits. He has asked to speak to you at eleven, Mrs. Young."

There were a few among the servants who sighed with relief. The others glanced her way, no doubt wondering what she knew of the captain's evening activities that might have attributed to his good mood.

The captain confused her. One moment speaking to her as an equal, touching her hair, and the next shoving her away and refusing to even acknowledge her existence. He'd been cold and abrupt all week, and he made her consider that running away might have been a better option than continuing to live another day under his roof.

Matilda held her breath, but Dawson never mentioned a similar summons for herself to see the captain. She was disappointed. Captain Ford had not recovered her letters from Mrs. Young yet nor had he passed them along. He had apparently forgotten his promise to retrieve them from the indolent housekeeper—if he ever intended to get them back for her at all.

Matilda lowered her eyes as the butler said grace, adding

thanks for the captain's continued good health while she gave thanks the man had finally ventured downstairs.

Amen.

She had to dust the first floor today, which contained the drawing room, his dressing room, and bedchamber. Those rooms needed a good airing too. She didn't particularly want him anywhere close at hand to observe and comment on her efforts.

Heaped platters were passed around, starting at those servants of highest rank down to those far lower. When the first plate of meat landed next to Matilda, there was decidedly less to choose from than she'd hoped to find. She filled her plate sparingly, leaving enough to the young scullery maid and boot boy so they'd keep up their strength. A servant's life was hard, and they were very young and still growing like weeds. The footmen always left everyone else too little to fill their bellies, and that made her angry. However, there was nothing she could do about it. She had absolutely no influence belowstairs.

"Want to wager we find her in the library later," someone whispered.

Matilda made the mistake of looking up and discovered Jenny and Jane were smirking at her. The pair of maids laughed outright at her scowl. Matilda resumed her meal, annoyed by their continued speculation about her supposed affair with the captain.

They were convinced she'd bewitched him—if such a thing was even possible.

She sipped the cup of tea that had been set before her plate, pushing Captain Ford and his critical gaze from her mind. Her easier duties were in the past. She must face the realities of life in service once more. Every brief moment of idleness at his side had been a precious respite, gone and soon to be forgotten.

She swallowed another mouthful, noticing absently her tea left a strange taste in her mouth. She took another sip and then spluttered as she realized the tea had been laced with salt rather than the usual single spoon of sugar she'd been granted.

Across the table, the other maids were struggling not to laugh. Matilda pushed to her feet, begged to be excused, and without waiting for a response fled for the kitchen to find fresh water to rinse her mouth out with.

She spat the disgusting taste out into the nearby washroom basin several times until the vile flavor was gone. She hated this place. No one was kind here.

Heavy treads approached. "Miss Winslow? Are you all right?"

Matilda hurried to pat her mouth with her only handkerchief before Mr. Dawson saw what she'd been doing. She could never be sure if Mr. Dawson should be considered her friend or not. He was the captain's man and almost as critical as their employer. "The tea was too hot."

He lifted his hand. He had her cup judging by the familiar chip next to the handle. He poked in one finger. "Lukewarm at best. Are you sure that's all it was?"

"Yes, Mr. Dawson." Matilda didn't want trouble.

The way he'd been looking at her this past week made her suspect he'd seen her in the captain's arms last week too. He'd been different toward her lately. Concerned for her welfare in a way he never had before, asking her opinion about everything she ought not to care about as a lowly maid. Almost to the point of embarrassing her even more in front of the other servants with his deference.

Dawson slowly lifted the cup to his nose and sniffed, and then, as if he intended to take a sip, he brought the cup to his mouth.

She stopped him before he was able to taste the evil brew. "You don't want to drink that."

Regardless of her warning, he took a sip and promptly spat it out into the basin. After he rinsed his mouth with fresh water, he asked, "Who did this?"

Matilda shrugged.

"I'll speak to the housekeeper and make it stop."

That was amusing. Was Dawson really so naïve? "Who says she doesn't already know?"

His mouth gaped.

"Mrs. Young has been indifferent to my happiness for a long time," she remarked in a soft voice. Matilda suspected it was not just because of the time she'd spent alone with the captain. They did not rub together well—never had from the very beginning of her employment. Since those early days of gratitude, Matilda had come to see the housekeeper as a lazy old woman who lived well off the captain's largesse. The woman did as little as possible and never noticed Matilda did the work of two maids. Now the captain was recovered, it was only a matter of time before Mrs. Young found a way to be rid of her for good. Or was the woman hoping to overwork Matilda to the point she would leave without a reference or die of exhaustion? More than likely.

Dawson glanced over his shoulder. "I'll speak to the captain."

"And make things worse." Matilda shook her head firmly. "You'd better not."

"What will you do then?" He stared at the contents of the cup before upending it in the sink. "This must stop. You cannot wait until someone makes you ill."

She shuddered, knowing he was right. "It won't come to that. I have a plan."

Dawson paled. "You're not thinking of leaving, are you?"

She didn't answer him at first. Who knew who could be listening around the corner? A servant had no privacy and certainly wasn't allowed too many secrets. As it was, she always ran the risk of being caught scanning the newssheets for an alternative position. The only reason she stayed was because Harry Lloyd knew he'd find her here.

However, her lingering over the papers might be grounds for instant dismissal if she was found in one part of the house when she was meant to be elsewhere. If she allied herself with another servant, she might do a better job of finding other employment. And she would know, one way or the other, if Dawson could be considered a friend or foe. "I would never leave until Harry returns."

"Harry? Harry Lloyd?" Dawson said slowly. "What is he to you?"

"He's a very good friend."

"Surely not?"

"I'd best get on with my work." Matilda tossed her head defiantly, fetched her bucket of rags, and then inched past him. "Excuse me."

Too bad if Mr. Dawson did not care for the connection. Matilda did. She would be a bride and have a home of her own.

Since she had no appetite left for the fare of the dining room, she left the servants' hall and climbed the stairs to the first floor. With only Captain Ford in residence, the upper floor was as still as the grave. A peaceful place where time dragged, sometimes pleasantly.

She liked these rooms best of all, having spent so much time here while the captain recovered. The drawing room boasted a set of four tall windows that drowned the room in lovely soft light, and she took a moment to enjoy the view.

She barely went outside anymore. She missed long walks in the park, the comfort of greater society, and the occasional butterfly to follow through a field of wildflowers. Their delicate beauty fascinated her, but they were never seen in the great city.

She absently brushed dust from the back of a deep, upholstered armchair and looked about her.

Matilda was almost certain the captain's younger sisters would arrive any day. She imagined the house filled with feminine laughter. A rare commodity here. She could not afford to dawdle when there was so much to prepare for. It was a surprise they'd stayed away so long, though they had mentioned in their early letters that the duke had forbidden them to pester the captain until he sent for them.

Since the captain was on the ground floor in the library, Matilda chose to attend to his bedchamber first. Just in case he had returned unexpectedly, she tapped lightly on his door and then slowly eased it open. The large room was empty. The fire had burned down to embers, so she attended to that quickly, resetting it in readiness for the captain's return later that day. She had spent a great deal of her days in this room until recently and was very familiar with the way the captain preferred it kept—neat to the point of severity.

Absolutely no flowers or feminine touches allowed.

She shook his heavy linen sheets, smoothed them back into place, and plumped his single pillow. He always slept in the exact center of the bed, so she returned the pillow to its expected place. As she turned to gather an empty glass from a side table, her gaze landed on the headboard and then dropped to the locked boxed beneath.

She had nothing to fear from this room, but she still thought of that afternoon last year with mixed feelings. Anger certainly. Embarrassment often. Why did he keep those things and hidden away? Why had touching them made him so angry that he'd spanked her like a misbehaving child?

There was no way to find out without humiliation. The captain was no longer kind to her.

She glanced around the room, checking that everything was in order, and then backed out to the dressing room. She dusted the mantel and side tables, flicked dust off the windowsills, then lifted the window sash high.

She breathed in the thick scents of London, then quickly slammed the windows shut. Today wasn't the day to air the captain's rooms. Perhaps tomorrow the smoke of thousands of fires would have blown away.

The work of a servant never ended, and it had been a savage week spent on catching up on forgotten chores, so she moved to the drawing room.

Dawson was waiting, holding a tray. "Fresh tea."

Matilda stared at him in shock. "Please tell me you didn't speak to the captain."

"I didn't, but you should. I had no idea things had become so bad for you. He will not like it." He gestured to a nearby table and carried the tea tray there. "Drink and eat what you like."

Matilda swallowed, just a little nervous of his sudden kindness, but eyed the tray. She was thirsty. "I don't need it."

The valet moved closer, eyes fixed on hers but reflecting only concern and kindness. "Drink the tea, Miss Winslow, or it goes to waste out the window. I know what you give up each day to the younger pair. My eyes are opening to what is happening below-stairs, and I believe you and I are of the same mind about the subject of how the servants' hall is run. Shoddily, indeed. You have barely eaten this past week, and I cannot stand to do nothing about it."

She had not thought anyone had noticed, but perhaps she wasn't as circumspect as she hoped. "Very well," she whispered, hoping the captain would not return and catch her making use of his drawing room like a proper lady. He would truly have a reason to punish her then.

She poured tea into one of the finest cups kept in the house with a tiny worry for the impropriety, added just a single spoon of sugar, and sipped the hot liquid slowly. The tea was a stronger-flavored cup than she was used to receiving in the servants' hall, and it was wonderful. She was reminded of the comforts of her old home and how much she missed her old life.

"Cake too," Dawson murmured as he picked up her dusting cloths and attended to the room in her place.

She gobbled the cake quickly, blushing at the hunger that had awakened in her. She set the cup aside carefully when she was done and hurried to him. "Thank you, but that is my duty."

Dawson smiled broadly. "I'm starting to think it shouldn't be for much longer."

"Whatever do you mean?"

His smile was enigmatic as he turned away. "Just wait. I have a feeling things are going to change for the better for everyone very soon."

With that, he collected the tray and sauntered away, headed for the servants' staircase.

CHAPTER FOUR

WILLIAM APPROACHED MATILDA QUIETLY, ready to admit defeat and give up trying to avoid her. Everywhere he turned, he always seemed to find her watching him with those soft, unguarded eyes.

She was currently dusting the furniture and had paused to look down the staircase at a commotion in the hall. He peered over her shoulder too, eyes widening in surprise. His half-sisters—Victoria, Audrey, and Evelyn—had returned to London and brought their grandfather with them. That his own father had tagged along boded ill for his day being a quiet one.

William had been dreading seeing the old man. "Do you think if I run, they can be avoided?"

Matilda started, as she'd done every time he'd spoken to her since he'd left his bed a week ago. Even the presence of other servants hadn't eased her anxiety around him, and he was sorry for that. Did she think that every time he spoke, he intended to seduce her or worse? He might yet if she kept up her ridiculous behavior.

She bit her lip and looked away. "Your chances of a clean escape are slim, Captain."

"I fear you may be right." William grimaced and then let his eyes linger on Matilda Winslow's face. There was an air of dejection about her William had never noticed before. Not even when he'd been at death's door had she appeared so bleak and cast down.

He'd been avoiding her on purpose and wanted the distance to increase this past week. However, the bold woman who'd climbed atop his sickbed and made certain his life was saved had withdrawn too far from him, and he didn't particularly care for her current demeanor. "Why can't they be more like you?"

"I beg your pardon?"

"You know what I mean." He pointed down the stairs. "You are calming. They are not. They fuss about house, moving things."

His sisters were exhausting, and they chatted incessantly. There was probably no rest for anyone when they were in the house, especially not for the servants.

"They are your sisters, and you should love them no matter what they do." For a moment he thought she was about to say more on the subject, but then she dipped a wobbly curtsy. "I must get back to my work."

She moved in the opposite direction, toward another room and escape from him.

Downstairs, other voices drowned out his family, and William peered back over the railing quickly as the butler greeted other callers. When he spotted the balding pate of Mr. Chudleigh's head and the golden ringlets of his daughter, Miss Maria Chudleigh, his mouth grew dry. Chudleigh was a crony of his father's and had the most ridiculous plan to see him wed to his only daughter. The pair hadn't wasted any time in hounding him. Just a week out of his sickbed and they were at his door.

He jerked around as they were led into his ground floor parlor to wait. "Damn this nonsense," he muttered, wondering how fast he could make an escape from the house.

Maria had come for him, aided by his father's misguided notion that they would suit, determined to make a scene before his family, profess her love yet again, and there wasn't a damn thing he could do to prevent the embarrassment. He'd tried to outrun her once before, but she was particularly devious and swift of foot.

"Is there something you need, Captain?" Mr. Dawson asked as he appeared from the direction of the servants' stairs, brushing specks of lint from his naval uniform.

William lifted his gaze. Matilda Winslow was poised just inside the drawing room, watching them both with wary eyes.

He wanted Matilda, and he shouldn't. Not this much.

Dawson glanced at Matilda too, and a slow smile spread over his face. William's temper rose. Dawson was an excellent valet in every respect save one. He was entirely too interested in Matilda Winslow, and of late he'd had a lot to say on the subject of her continued employment as a maid.

"Put that coat away. The admiralty has no use for me yet."

Dawson spun around to face him. "Very good, Captain."

He nodded. He should be furious that he was languishing onshore, but truth be told, he wanted nothing more than to live out the rest of his life in relative peace. As he'd lain in recovery of his wounds, he had pondered if he had possibly given enough blood in the service of his country. If the admiralty never wanted him again, he would lose no sleep at being overlooked for a command.

Dawson cleared his throat. "Perhaps I could have a few moments of your time later, Captain."

The butler arrived, ready to announce William's waiting visitors. "Captain, you have guests."

"I saw them, Carter." William waved him off with an impatient jerk of his hand. He dismissed Dawson too. "After dinner tonight."

Whatever problem Dawson had could wait. William had to

decide, and quickly, how best to extract himself from the impending family ambush waiting downstairs.

"Thank you." Dawson hurried away with a decided spring in his step. He frowned after Dawson but was unsurprised by his transparent delight. The man had been hinting all week the servants' hall was badly managed. He'd suggested changes needed to be made to the household staff sooner rather than later. It was probably time to do something about it. The housekeeper and butler were set in their ways, and according to Dawson the matter couldn't wait until William married someone to take care of the trouble for him. The house was inefficiently run, with the bulk of the work falling to only a few. The place needed a woman's touch.

However, marrying Maria Chudleigh was not part of his plan to fix what ailed his home. He did not find her the least bit appealing. She was too headstrong for what he needed in his life. When the time came, he'd marry someone he liked, a woman willing to be disciplined and capable of running his home with or without his involvement.

He was willing to wait his whole life for her.

A crash farther along the hall caught his attention. Matilda had toppled a vase of flowers. The vase was saved, but water splashed over the mahogany hall table and made quite a mess. He took a pace forward as Matilda simply stared at the slow-dripping water as if she was dazed.

"Miss Winslow," he murmured in concern. "Are you well?"

"Yes, Captain. Forgive me." She pinched the bridge of her nose and then threw her cloth over the puddle. "I'll clean this up immediately."

She was never usually so clumsy, but she had seemed out of sorts today. Tired too. Was it true that most of the work of the house fell to those most dedicated in his service?

He moved toward her as she knelt and dabbed ineffectually at the puddle, exhaling heavily as she worked.

After all she'd done for him, didn't she deserve something more from life than menial work? He smiled. Perhaps there was a way to solve both his problem and help her escape a life of servitude.

His solution was unorthodox, and if she'd been born a lady, he would never suggest it, but if he convinced Maria that he'd taken his maid as a lover and could never be persuaded to give Matilda up, the plague of womanhood might be shocked enough at him—disgusted too, he hoped—to give up her quest to become his wife.

It would be easily confirmed that Matilda had spent a great deal of time with him should enquiries be made. All he needed was Matilda Winslow's agreement and participation to pull it off.

He strode toward Matilda purposely. "You will do something for me," he demanded. Matilda stumbled to her feet, but he caught her before she tripped. "Not so fast. I need your help."

Matilda struggled. "Let me go."

"No." He tugged her into his empty dressing room for a private word and shut the door. "You're going to be my lover from today."

Her eyes widened. "Are you out of your mind?"

William cursed under his breath. He had wondered that very thing many times—mostly when Matilda was near. She had the most distracting effect on his speech, causing him to blurt out orders rather than gild them with necessary politeness. He had to do better than this if he wanted her help. He took a calming breath. "Quite possibly, but it is either convince others that I am hopelessly infatuated with a servant in my employ, or I will be blackmailed into marriage with that woman downstairs."

Her brow creased and her fear disappeared entirely. "What woman?"

It went against the grain to confide in anyone, but she had to help him. "Miss Maria Chudleigh claims to have acquired a declaration of love from me in writing of all things. She is here now, most likely to advance her claim that we are to marry during the season."

Her expression soured. "Congratulations."

"You don't understand. I don't recall even meeting Miss Maria on my last visit home, and I sure as hell don't profess my love for women willy-nilly. No man with any self-respect wears his heart on his sleeve and should not expect to suffer such foolish declarations in return. Miss Chudleigh wrote to discuss our marriage as if it were a fact, but I won't be blackmailed into a parson's trap. I would not have chosen her for a bride under any circumstances."

Matilda's jaw firmed. "I see."

"Good. Now, we are not speaking of a lasting union, or anything based in fact." He set his hands on his hips. "I want you to pretend to be in love with me long enough to drive her away, preferably into the arms of another man."

"Wait just a moment. I did not agree to help you." Her eyes widened. "I couldn't possibly lie about being involved with you. What will everyone say?"

"Did you not hint last week that the staff are whispering that I like you too much?"

She blushed. "They will learn the error of their ways soon enough, as I did."

"If I sent you away to another house, that would suggest I had already tired of you and confirm their suspicions." He saw her shock at his blunt appraisal. "I'll pay you very handsomely if you can act the part of lover."

Her expression shifted to surprise.

"If I have my way, you'll never need to work as a servant again. Someone else can clean up after you from now on."

Her gaze narrowed. "How handsomely?"

Matilda had overcome her aversion to taking his money at last. Thank heaven for the adoption of good sense. He approved of her reversal, and since time was of the essence, he made several calculations quickly. The right amount of honey could attract the sweetest bee. "An allowance. A town house. Servants of your choosing. Whatever you require for your comfort."

Her eyes gleamed. "Anything?"

He nodded curtly. "As long as I don't have to bleed or go bankrupt."

She folded her arms across her chest. "You will apologize first."

He moved close to her. "For what?"

Her jaw lifted and her eyes blazed. "For hurting me."

At last, an opening to discuss his mistake. The Fords lived by a code he thoroughly approved of—never admit fault—but when it came to Matilda Winslow, he'd make an exception. He should have exercised better control and protected her from his nature.

He leaned closer, brought his face down beside hers so his voice wouldn't carry. As much as he'd enjoyed spanking her bottom until it had glowed red after catching her in his room, he'd had no true right to ever discipline her, even if she'd given her permission. She had not known enough of his nature to accept what it was he offered.

That day he'd lost his head and had not fully considered how his desires must have seemed to an innocent young maid. And he was sure she'd been an innocent that day, judging by her frantic escape from his rooms. Afterward he'd made a vow never to run such a risk again, but he'd never stopped thinking about her bare skin, hot against his palm, or her reaction to his intimate touch.

"I apologize for spanking your pretty backside," he whispered.

Her eyes widened as if she'd not expected him to admit fault at all. She swallowed. "Apology accepted. A house in London to live in, five hundred pounds, and you'll pay my expenses from any Bond Street merchants for two years."

A great deal less than most mistresses demanded, or wives, from what he'd gathered. He breathed in her scent, a familiar mixture of rosemary and lemon, and his senses stirred. Dear God, he wanted to devour this woman, spend hours bringing her exquisite sensations of pleasure and pain if she would let him. He licked his lips as the urge to kiss her grew. "I can live with that."

Matilda spun on her heel and marched to the door that connected to the drawing room.

"Wait." He hurried to stop her. "No one will believe the pretense if you look too buttoned up or shabby."

She paused at the doorway, glanced over her shoulder and then down at her dress. "What does what I look like have to do with pretending to be in love?"

"Everything. Trust me. I am known to have particular standards when it comes to my lovers." And a preference for dark-haired women not unlike Matilda Winslow.

He reached forward and lightly touched her face for the first time. She had a strong jaw, slightly pointed chin, and her eyes flashed with alarm. His hand trembled, but he steadied himself. "You must look softer, irresistible."

He tugged a few strands of hair from beside her ears. The dark strands bounced into curls instantly, just as they had when he'd let her hair down. Next, he plucked the ugly tucker from the top of her bodice, prepared to draw it over her head.

Matilda reared back when his fingertips caressed the upper swell of her breast accidentally. "I will do it."

She moved to his mirror and pulled the scrap of lace over her head, then rushed to remove her damp apron. Without it, the plain gown seemed a good deal more fetching, and Matilda looked less like a servant who had made his bed every morning.

William moved behind her to tighten the ribbon beneath her bust to accent her figure. He caught his reflection in the mirror and quickly averted his eyes. Next to Matilda's feminine grace, he appeared an ogre, hideously scarred. He shifted his attention to Matilda and kept it there, liking what the mirror revealed with those few alterations. He grabbed the tightly bound mass of dark hair at the back of her head and wiggled it a little, softening her coiffure.

She pinched her cheeks and licked her lips. "Good enough?"

Too good. The changes made a world of difference and played havoc with his control. The gown, although serviceable and plain, was a good color for her. He dug a sea-green silk shawl and gloves, impulsive purchases with no purpose save that they'd appealed to him, from his sea chest and dressed her in them. He was gripped with a sudden idea that would guarantee him success. A fine silver chain and cross pendant he'd hoarded for years completed her transformation from distracting servant to delectable temptation. The revelation was utterly breathtaking. "You'll do," he managed to say, feeling uncomfortably hot.

He caught her newly gloved wrist so she couldn't flee and towed her toward the staircase, still dreading the coming meeting but determined. He would marry when he liked, whom he liked, and not a moment sooner than when he had had enough of being a bachelor.

At the top stair, he took a breath, threaded her arm through his, and led Matilda down the staircase as if she were indeed his lady.

CHAPTER FIVE

HIS BUTLER WAS WAITING on the landing, eyes wide at the sight of Matilda on his arm.

"I knocked over a vase upstairs," William said. "Have it cleaned up immediately, Carter."

"Yes, Captain." He hurried past them but glanced back a time or two before he disappeared. Yes, it was time for Matilda to leave his employ. The first course of action would be to find her somewhere safe to stay tonight once his guests had gone on their disappointed way.

"I do love my sisters," he informed her, returning to their earlier discussion about his family. "But I have never been comfortable showing how I feel."

"They deserve to have their season," she whispered, hand rising to the pendant at her neck and twiddling with it nervously. "Don't spoil it for them with your usual bad grace."

That deserved at least one strike on her pretty bottom. He gritted his teeth until the desire passed. "You are correct. They do deserve a chance to find a husband. I simply dread going back into society again and being stared at."

She paused on the last stair, turned, her gaze full of under-standing. "You cannot lurk indoors forever."

He would like to try. The few times he'd gone out this week had not soothed his temper. His first trip to the brothel had been a disaster. He'd looked, meant to indulge, but the women's shocked reaction to his altered features had ruined his intentions. He'd been gawked at, whispered about, until he'd rushed back to his carriage and drawn the curtains on the world.

The mirror didn't lie.

Matilda was the only person he knew who looked at him without pity in her eyes.

However, for this ruse to work today, she had to look at him with warmth and desire. And after today, it might be necessary to venture into society a few times just to be sure their ruse of lovers was believed. He pictured Matilda hanging on his arm at the theater, dancing together in a crowded ballroom and pretending she enjoyed every moment in his company while everyone whispered about them and his altered looks. It would take courage he hoped she still possessed in abundance. For if she was anything like him, she might hate every moment of scrutiny.

"I'll lurk if you'll lurk with me."

"I don't think that's a good idea. I'll convince them today, and you will pay me well enough for the trouble," she insisted.

She gathered up her skirts in one hand, and William caught a glimpse of her slender ankles encased in dowdy stockings. She still needed the new ones he could have paid for last year if she'd accepted his gift of coin for the purchase, and once he considered her stocking covered legs his mind traveled upward to her well-rounded bottom. He gritted his teeth. Damn, but dressing her up for this little play might not have been his best idea for continued peace of mind.

"Where is dear William?" Maria asked in a shrill voice that carried into the hall with perfect clarity.

Matilda's eyes rose with a question, and he nodded. "That's her," he whispered.

William held on to Matilda's elbow just a little tighter as his father replied, "Nothing could keep him away."

Father had wanted this alliance since he'd been a boy, never understanding why William fought the connection.

"He'll be here when he's ready," his grandfather proclaimed in a raised voice, surely meant to reassure William that at least someone in the room might be on his side.

William drew in a deep breath, squared his shoulders, and braced himself to face his family with his new and scarred face. He did not look the same as they would remember, and he was sure they would be taken aback when they saw him for the first time.

He kept his gaze down and only when he passed the arch and the thick rug appeared in his line of sight did he dare lift his face and show them the changes. "Here I am, for better or worse."

Audrey, Evelyn, and Victoria screamed and ran to him like wild creatures of the woods.

Feminine arms wrapped around him tightly, and through the overwhelming babble he discovered they didn't care one whit about the alteration of his features. They proved they missed him, as they always did when he'd been away, but this time their enthusiasm toppled them to the carpeted floor in a tangle of arms and legs. William came to rest on his back among the trio.

"Dear God, you're all heathens," he cried out as Eve prodded his scar with no fear or evident revulsion and Victoria scrubbed his head, disturbing his hair.

"Does it hurt?" Eve asked boldly, rubbing her fingertips over the rough and bumpy scar just as Matilda sometimes did when applying a cream to ease an itch.

He'd much rather Matilda's gentle fingers than Evelyn's prodding, so he moved out of danger. "Not now."

"You talk funny," Audrey said after adjusting her gown. At least she held back from attacking him with affection. "Your words slur just a little too."

"So they do." Despite his best efforts to cure himself, he still had trouble making his mouth do what he wanted all the time. When he smiled, he was left with the suspicion that he was utterly terrifying to others.

"It doesn't matter," Victoria insisted with a grin. "You still sound enough like our surly brother that you could never be mistaken for an impostor."

He sat up, shaking his head. "I cannot believe we're having this conversation on the floor."

"We don't care where we are," Victoria claimed. "We are so very glad to see our big brother."

He took in the faces of three women most dear to him, noting how much they'd grown, changed, in the past year while he'd been at sea. They were stunning, and his hope for a quiet and uneventful season died a sudden death. They would undoubtedly be popular with the gentlemen in society, and that meant he'd have to be right by their sides for each event they attended. He needed to keep a watchful eye over them and make sure they were not pestered or imposed upon and that his family didn't marry them off to unworthy men.

"Girls, girls," Maria said as she broke into their conversation.

William looked up into the pinched face of the woman who had schemed to become his wife for the past five years. She paled when she saw his face properly at close range and then collapsed back into the softness of a well-padded chair in a very fair impression of a faint.

William scowled at her behavior. He was not about to be lured over there to reassure Maria he wasn't a monster now.

He stood and helped his sisters to their feet while Chudleigh and his father fussed over Maria and helped her sit up. They offered her sherry and pillows and any number of foolish things.

William turned to his grandfather, the Duke of Rutherford, and bowed deeply. "Your Grace."

The old man, never one to stand on ceremony with family, hugged him tightly until he squirmed. Rutherford pounded his back a few times. "About time you sent for us."

William drew back, concerned by the catch in his grandfather's voice. The duke's expression was steely; there was no hint of the tears William had feared he might see. "The worst is over. I am as good as I will ever be."

"Could have been worse," the duke whispered, studying his face keenly. William's face was caught in a tight grip and turned so the shorter man could see the scar properly. "Thank heavens for that."

"No. Thank Matilda," he murmured when released. "She is the one who deserves the credit for keeping me alive."

When he glanced around for her, Matilda had backed away to wait in the shadows of the dining room. Dutiful. Silent. A perfect servant doing her best to be overlooked by her employer's guests. That would not do if she were to play the part he wanted her to.

He looked her over boldly and then tipped his head, hoping she'd remember to keep up her side of their bargain and pretend to enjoy his attentions. "What are you doing over there, *darling?*"

A hesitant smile fluttered over her lips as everyone gasped. "Waiting for the right moment to be introduced, *sweetie,*" she said with a small smile of triumph.

Sweetie?

Oh, that was good. He'd happily discipline her for uttering such a cloying remark if he could. She drew close, and when she reached his side, she slipped one hand over his shoulder. The gesture was perfect. Affectionate and just a touch too assured for her to be mistaken for anything but an intimate female acquaintance of his. William did not allow women to handle him in public.

He grinned at her boldness. He'd missed that about her. He'd missed her touch and never realized how much until now. "I should introduce you all to my Matilda."

"Your what?" his father burst out, eyes widening.

"Oh, how romantic," Evelyn shrieked. She clutched her hands to her chest with all the dramatic flair of a stage actress. "You married your maid!"

He faltered at her assumption. Claiming a marriage had taken place hadn't been his intent, but it absolutely solved his problem of how to thwart his father's matchmaking efforts. He wanted his father and Mr. Chudleigh to understand that enough was enough. He would not marry Miss Chudleigh. Being excluded from the marriage mart was exactly what he needed to send her packing. Claiming he'd already wed guaranteed they would never darken his door again.

Matilda's hand slid down his shoulder when he did not immediately speak up to deny they'd wed. He caught her wrist before she could run, then threaded their fingers together and squeezed tightly, holding her close to his side. Keen to appear affectionate, he raised her gloved hand to his lips and kissed it too.

"Indeed we are. We wanted to surprise everyone with the news." He stared at his father, unsurprised that the old man appeared ready to explode.

Matilda squeezed his hand in return, and her face transformed into an utterly besotted expression. He was astonished. He'd never seen the like before—not directed toward him.

"How could I say no when he was so adamant that he could not live without me?"

"But she's a nobody," Miss Chudleigh exclaimed, clearly recovered from her supposed faint.

He placed himself before Matilda, angry at Miss Chudleigh's utter rudeness. "Don't you dare speak of my wife like that," he growled.

Miss Chudleigh lifted a trembling hand to her lips. "You cannot be serious."

"He's always serious," Matilda murmured, rubbing his arm to soothe his temper. "If you truly knew him, you'd have already learned never to question his decisions."

William glanced at Matilda quickly and nodded. She was doing and saying exactly the right things to make his plan succeed. He couldn't be prouder of her performance under such trying circumstances.

"Now see here. This nonsense can be sorted out," his father promised the Chudleighs. "William has not been well. An annulment can be arranged soon enough, I'm sure."

"I'd like a whiskey," Rutherford announced loudly enough that everyone quieted to stare at him. He moved close to William, winked, and then addressed Matilda. "Mrs. Ford, would you care to join me in the drawing room? I believe William has long kept a decanter or two hidden there."

"He does indeed." Matilda appeared startled though and glanced at him for permission to go. He nodded decisively. There was no reason for Matilda to remain and listen to rude people. "Do join him. I'll be along shortly, darling."

"As you wish." She dropped his arm only to be claimed by his grandfather. "Your Grace."

"Matilda Ford? What a pretty ring that has," Rutherford began as they moved away. "We've never had a Matilda in the family before. How lovely. Come along, girls," he called out to Victoria, Audrey, and Evelyn, who rushed after him and very quickly formed a wall of protection around William's wife.

Once the group was beyond the door, his father rounded on him. "What are you thinking, marrying a woman like that? Did she trick you into it?"

"Of course not. I chose her."

His father started to shake his head. It was always a bad sign when that started up.

William turned to Mr. Chudleigh. "Sir, I hope you and your daughter will excuse us. You have intruded on something of a family celebration that I have long been looking forward to. This is the first chance my wife and I have had to be with my grandfather and sisters since my recovery. I am a very happily married man. Whatever my father has promised you will never come to pass."

Miss Chudleigh sobbed, clutching her father's arm, but Mr. Chudleigh thankfully ushered her out without uttering a word about his choice of bride.

William was not so lucky with his own father. "You will live to regret such a hasty marriage."

"Did you?" William bit out. "You barely waited a month after my mother's death before proposing marriage to my cousin's governess."

"The situation was entirely different," George Ford blustered. "You needed a new mother to curb your tears."

The usual resentment stirred at the suggestion that the second Lady Ford had mothered him at all. "How could she have comforted me when you sent me away almost immediately after Mama's death? From where I stand, my marriage is decidedly different than yours and truly none of your business."

"A marriage without love is no marriage at all."

"Is that why you and your second wife live apart now?

Because you are so deeply in love with each other? You squabble constantly over the littlest things." He folded his arms across his chest. "Why do you think Matilda and I are not in love?"

He didn't love Matilda of course, nor would he admit it if he did, but his father's comments made him curious.

"Passion!" he cried out. "I know you disapprove of it. It's obvious she flattered you when your defenses were down, made herself indispensable to ensure you felt you had no choice but to propose marriage just to have her. You will see her true colors once you are out in society. She will cost you a fortune and you'll have no one to blame but yourself."

William wanted to roll his eyes. He'd actually be happy to spend a little money on Matilda, but George Ford was so obsessed with being in love that he could not see the good he could do. He was quite sickening around his second wife, his half-sisters' mother, and he made sure to spend as little time with them as possible. If he were ever in love, he would not behave like his father.

"The only regret I have is not offering for her sooner," he added, embellishing a little more on their love affair than might be needed. He was dealing with a hopeless romantic. His father would never be satisfied with a curt statement of her suitability. "She is perfect for me and very beautiful."

He stared his father down until his shoulders sagged in defeat. Finally.

His father spared him a withering glance. "When you are ready to talk sense, you will find me at home."

George Ford stalked out, leaving his daughters and father behind. William rubbed over the scar on his face. He shared very little in common with his father, who lived too impulsively for his taste. He had always been more reserved than the rest of his family, finding their public displays of emotion uncomfortable to bear. He was not about to change. Not for anyone.

William poured himself a drink and silently toasted his success at overcoming yet another obstacle. He had freedom from marriage-minded misses. He had his life to live. Now all he wanted was a willing woman of his own and he'd be very happy indeed.

CHAPTER SIX

MATILDA SETTLED into a drawing room chair, the same one she'd beaten the dust from this morning, and waited for the other shoe to drop. It was just a matter of time.

The Chudleighs had quickly taken their leave she'd heard, the woman utterly devastated by William's announcement of his surprise marriage. A very great lie indeed. Miss Chudleigh's tears had seemed very real, but Captain Ford had not been moved by the woman's outpouring of heartbreak.

Not that Matilda had expected him to be kind after the way the woman had reacted to his scar.

She was a little worried about the scorn in Lord George Ford's eyes when he'd looked her over and how he might treat his son. She knew the captain had a temper, but she didn't know if he'd inherited the trait from his father.

She was also a little overwhelmed by the reactions to this false marriage. The captain's sisters seemed to think William must be in love with her, which of course they said had to be the reason he would marry her.

Matilda heard the unsaid "stoop" in that statement and gritted her teeth at the near slight.

Although the marriage was false, their presumption annoyed her as much as William Ford's obvious expectation that she'd fall in with the change to his scheme without voicing one single complaint about being so badly used.

She was glad she'd made a bargain with the captain for a house and sum of money after this disastrous affair was over. She'd never keep a maid's position in any household now. William Ford had made her unemployable unless she assumed another name.

How could he imagine she had any ability to pretend to be his wife?

She did not know him that well!

Or want to.

The duke settled in a nearby chair with a groan and his refilled glass. He studied her, his expression inscrutable. "I swear the journey from Newberry grows longer each time I make it."

Having no idea of Newberry Park's exact location, Matilda clenched her hands together in her lap and nodded politely. The duke had always been kind when he'd visited, but she believed William's actions today would not please him in the end. "You wanted to see me?"

She glanced around quickly, wondering why the captain's sisters had disappeared. "Yes," he said slowly. "Both of you actually, but William appears to have become delayed, no doubt because of his father. They do bump heads over every little thing."

Matilda nodded but decided it best to keep the rest of her opinions to herself. This marriage was not such a little thing. There was the threat of very real scandal. Lord George Ford could have more than a few words to say to his son in private, and none of them would be kind about his marriage to a maid.

"We owe you a debt of gratitude for the care you have devoted to my grandson, but I had been uncertain of how to repay you. I had thought a stipend appropriate, or something to that effect."

She blushed. Caring for Captain Ford after the first tension-filled weeks had been relatively easy. She had helped him eat what food he could manage to swallow to keep his strength up, cleaned the wound, and made sure he never scratched when his face itched. She had even bound his hands together late one night at his silent insistence when the itch of the healing wound had been driving him to distraction.

"I did what seemed best at the time," she murmured.

He sat forward. "You believed William would survive when men of science had grave doubts."

"I believed in the captain's stubborn nature above all else, Your Grace," she replied immediately and without thought for such a remark's likely reception.

The duke choked on his whiskey, and the heat of a blush warmed Matilda's cheeks. Perhaps it wasn't wise to be so candid. She should not have admitted her employer was too stubborn to die when most would have succumbed to a lesser wound.

"The housekeeper has been expansive in her description of my grandson's recovery in her letters, but I must confess I had not believed her suspicion that a romantic relationship existed between you both could be true."

Matilda glanced toward the door, hoping for Captain Ford's return, but could not hear his approach. She would not lie to the duke for him. Not for any number of riches he might bestow upon her. "We have no relationship beyond that of servant and master. It was a mistake."

Matilda was awkwardly aware that her dedication to the captain's recovery had set her apart from the other servants, and she was not surprised Mrs. Young had stirred the pot by relaying the particulars and her unfounded suspicions. Captain Ford's lie today would make her an utter outsider in the servants' hall tonight if she hadn't already been packed to leave this establishment forthwith.

She gripped her hands together as coldness filled her at the thought of having nowhere to go. What could she do to prevent her dismissal? How low would she have to abase herself to avoid being thrown out? "If there is nothing else, I must report to Mrs. Young and continue my work for the day."

"You must see that returning to your former position is impossible now," the duke said slowly. "If I have instilled anything in my grandchildren, it is the belief that servants are not to be toyed with. I would not like to have others believe William acted without honor where you are concerned."

Matilda swallowed. "The captain has always been a good employer."

Almost always, she silently added.

"When the message reached me of William's desperate situation, I knew he'd need the best care. My first thought on reading Mrs. Young's report of that first night was that she had made the right choice, especially since she mentioned your late father was a medical man."

Credit was due to the right person. "It was actually Mr. Dawson, Captain Ford's valet, who requested I remain with him, Your Grace. Mrs. Young tried to send me away when the surgeons first hesitated to treat him properly. I insisted they must at least try."

"I see." He shook his head, lips pursing a moment as he studied her. "You went above and beyond anything asked of you, but if scandal is how he means to repay you, then you are very badly treated."

She shrugged. "Further delay would have cost him his life, and this will pass."

"Perhaps not." The duke's expression grew tense. "Dawson is to be commended on his intelligence then in choosing you for William. I understand you didn't sleep, hardly ate, and cared for William's needs before your own. I did not anticipate a servant's sense of duty could reach so far; however, I am happy for it. You should be appropriately compensated for the trouble he's caused you."

"I am glad he has recovered." Matilda blushed again. She'd never been comfortable with praise and certainly not from a duke. "I expect no compensation for my part in the captain's recovery, I assure you. "

Not when William was already going to provide for her. He'd promised everything she needed, to ensure she and Harry Lloyd could start their marriage in a prosperous fashion far from the scandal of this affair.

The duke's eyes narrowed. "I assume that farce downstairs was William's doing."

Matilda nodded quickly. There was no point lying about it when he would be able to find out no marriage had taken place. "Yes, he was concerned about the arrival of Miss Chudleigh. He said his father meant to pressure him into a marriage he didn't want, so I was to pretend to be in love with him to drive Miss Chudleigh away. Somehow it went terribly wrong, and now they believe I'm his wife."

"True." The duke's eyes softened. "Under the circumstances, continuing that belief will be necessary to perpetuate. I will not have the family's name dragged through the scandal sheet over such a lie."

Matilda licked her lips. "For how long?"

The duke grunted, banging his fist onto the arm of the chair. "My grandson claimed that you are man and wife, and that is what you shall be."

Matilda stared at him, unable to believe what he might be suggesting. "Are you saying I will have to marry him?"

"If you do not, everyone will think you soiled goods."

"That is not true." Heat enveloped her cheeks beyond her power to prevent the flush. "I cannot marry him. I am to marry another man."

"Oh, so he chased after another man's woman too," he said, face contorting with disappointment. "I had assumed there was some partial truth to account for William's actions, but there you have it. He is exactly like his uncles. I will make arrangements for an expedient wedding immediately."

She grew very cold. This surely could not be happening. "I cannot marry Captain Ford."

"You are a spinster without means save your employment which you now cannot keep. How will you support yourself, eh? How can I allow my grandson to act without honor? I cannot do it," the duke said with rising passion. "The situation and scandal will be intolerable for the family. You must marry him. This other fellow, where is he?"

Matilda stilled her trembling hands. "I don't know."

The duke rolled his eyes. "Are you really going to turn down this generous offer to elevate yourself in society by marrying so well?"

Silence thickened around her. Was she really trapped, without means to protect her reputation from irreparable harm no matter the path she chose?

William entered the room at last, boots striking hard across the polished boards. "I won't be talked out of it."

The duke raised a brow. "Is that so?"

Matilda glanced behind him, but there was no sign now of Lord George Ford or the captain's sisters following behind.

"Yes, this is perfect. Maria can turn her scheming little heart elsewhere, and when she's married, we can go through the motions of announcing our fake marriage was dissolved."

"What do you mean, fake marriage?" Evelyn Ford suddenly made an appearance. "You said you were married to Matilda."

"And in love," Audrey said, her eyes accusing him.

"I did not say I was in love," William exclaimed.

"You called her 'darling' twice," Victoria chided. "Everyone knows that's just the same."

Matilda considered how likely it was that she might faint just to escape this situation. She'd never done it before. Perhaps if she held her breath a very long time she might swoon and wake up once it was all over.

Audrey Ford slipped into the space at her side and grasped her hand. "How could you toy with her feelings like this, William?"

The duke pointed to her. "Matilda was just telling me she has a betrothed. What were you thinking to involve her in such a lie?"

"What betrothed?"

"Harry Lloyd," she whispered. "He asked to marry me."

"When?" Captain Ford blinked, glancing at her with obvious surprise.

"A year ago," she confessed. "He left to make his fortune and went south to Portsmouth. He said he would try to join your ship as crew."

A muscle in the captain's jaw twitched. "He won't be coming back."

It took a moment for comprehension to come, then Matilda gasped and turned her face away. Harry was dead? Her eyes filled with tears that overflowed to spill down her cheeks.

"Oh, you are a beast, William. I am ashamed to call you brother." Audrey threw her arm around Matilda as she sobbed as quietly as she could.

She had waited so long for news of Harry, but she hadn't imagined she would never see him again. Her heart squeezed painfully in her chest.

"There will be no savaging of Miss Winslow's reputation through the scandal of a pretend separation," the duke insisted, "since there is not going to be any pretense of any kind. Contracts will be drawn today. I will handle the arrangements personally."

Matilda wiped her tears away, unable to believe they were discussing anything when her heart lay in pieces.

William's jaw clenched when they made eye contact. "I will compensate her handsomely for the inconvenience myself, as we had already discussed."

"I don't want to marry you," Matilda whispered.

"Marriage?" William frowned. "What are you talking about?"

The three Ford ladies groaned in unison.

"Grandfather, will you please explain the situation to our dear but dense elder brother," Victoria said with a sad shake of her head. "William has, quite sadly, been too long at sea to understand his duty. We'll resume making arrangements here while you talk."

Matilda was a little sorry to see them go. For a moment, she'd had companions who'd understood her sorrow.

Captain Ford crossed to her side and rested his hand upon her shoulder, firm and strangely comforting at such a difficult moment.

The duke rose to his feet and pointed to William. "You alone did more damage to this young woman's reputation, a servant in your home, than was necessary to thwart Miss Chudleigh's infatuation with matrimony. Your father would have eventually seen the error of his ways. Miss Winslow saved your life, and potential scandal is how you repay her? I will cut you off without a penny should you act against me in this. Did you not think your sisters would not suffer for it too once word of your lie spread among the *ton*? Don't think it won't because it will indeed get out."

Anger filled her that the duke would be so cruel as to force them to the altar, and that everyone was discussing her future with no indication she had a choice in their plans. She made to rise, but William held her still. Her soul rebelled against the idea of marrying a man she did not love or even want to be around. "I wish to withdraw."

"Of course." The duke soothed her, suddenly reasonable and kind as he smiled upon her. "By now my granddaughters will have had a guest room prepared for you. Please remain apart from society until you are both legally wed. "

That was easy for Matilda to do, but she shivered anyway before lifting her face to her employer. Captain Ford would not give in to his grandfather's illogical demand they marry. Wasn't Captain Ford wealthy in his own right? She had always assumed so. He surely would not give in to blackmail from his own grandfather. "Captain?"

His expression gave little away as he met her gaze. "You agreed, and I expect you keep to our bargain."

She couldn't have been more shocked than if he'd begun to sing a Christmas carol at the top of his lungs. "I agreed to pretend to be in love with you for one afternoon, not to lie and forced into marriage for the rest of my life. There is a very great difference between the two in my opinion."

A muscle flexed in his jaw. "Grandfather, would you excuse us a moment? Miss Winslow and I need to have a discussion."

"Certainly." The duke wandered away, leaving Matilda and William alone in the parlor.

"I cannot take the lie back now," he said, as serious as she'd ever seen him. "We have no choice but to marry. He owns this house; he has promised my sisters their seasons and has enhanced their dowries too. My father had too many children and wives for his income. Do not imagine my grandfather won't strike out at us by hurting them."

"But we can dissolve the marriage later so I can marry…" She shook her head. Harry was gone, but her mind still struggled with the loss. A fresh set of tears flowed down her cheeks at the cruelty of life that stole the people she loved. She drew in a breath and let it out slowly before rephrasing her response. "We can part ways later so I can live my own life."

"After my sisters are settled, we will have the marriage annulled or I will sue for divorce," he promised.

She blinked. Neither prospect would leave her with any sort of good reputation. "A short-term arrangement would be preferred. It could take years for them to fall in love."

"Or a season—if you help me with them." Captain Ford folded his arms across his chest as he swayed from foot to foot. "There are a number of things I need to know for the marriage contract. Your exact age, please?"

"I am not yet twenty years."

He grunted. "Do you have a relation or guardian I need to speak with to obtain permission to marry you?"

"I have no one." She pressed her hand over her face. Her mother, a woman with a restless nature, had discarded her years ago and run back to her Romani family. She could hardly care what she did with her life or worry what might have become of her only daughter now. "I had no one but Harry, and now he's gone."

"As I feared." He sighed deeply. "The season is drawing to a close, and for the ruse to work you must act the part of my wife immediately. There are gowns to be fitted, invitations to accept if we are to chaperone my sisters in society during the coming weeks. You cannot continue to weep over your former betrothed like this."

She dropped her hands. "I just heard he was gone."

"He left a year ago." His face set into stubborn lines. "You've had adequate time to forget him."

She shook her head stubbornly. "There will never be enough time for that."

"Then I suggest you weep in private."

"How can you be so unfeeling?" She clenched her hands until her nails dug into her palms, her anger giving her the courage to confront him. Something she'd never done before. "Don't you dare tell me what I may feel. You may think you control my actions because I am—was—in your service, but my thoughts are very much my own and always have been."

His jaw clenched and his arms unfolded slowly. "Be careful how you speak to me, Matilda. Do not forget who I am."

"How could I forget that?" But she trembled at the tone of his voice. "You care only for your own comfort."

"Which is how it is supposed to be when a man is a bachelor and lives alone." He sighed. "I have depended on you, trusted you above anyone else these past months. Trust me now. I will take care of you, I promise. You will have a very comfortable life ahead if you just do as I ask for now."

He sounded sincere enough that her temper subsided. Matilda turned away from him. "I will keep my heartbreak to myself because it is mine alone."

He grasped her shoulders, preventing her from straying far. "No one in London society knows who you are, so that is to our advantage. You've been by my side for months and understood my moods better than anyone, even when I could not speak. Given the depths of our acquaintance, I think you could fool anyone into believing we're man and wife. Acting as my wife would put me forever in your debt."

"You were not so complicated when you were confined to bed," she grumbled. Matilda had liked caring for him though, knowing he improved every day because of her efforts. But marriage was madness. She might have once been curious about

London society, having listened to the Fords speak so often about their friends and acquaintances, including all the wild and wonderful entertainments to be found in other houses, but she'd never expected to be part of that life. Not even for a little while.

Their eventual separation would cause scandal for his family. The duke would not be pleased. However, with William's sisters married off, would there really be no impediment to prevent it?

She turned when the captain remained silent for several minutes. Captain Ford's face was tipped downward, his attention lowered. With a start she formed a suspicion he had been staring at a part of her anatomy only he had ever seen.

His gaze rose very slowly; his lips were parted, and the tip of his tongue rested on his teeth. She shivered at the heated intensity of his expression.

Matilda drew herself up straight, determined not to be intimidated by him. "Was the prospect of marrying Miss Chudleigh so utterly terrifying, Captain, that you'd offer so much without limits?"

"There are limits. To my purse and my patience, as you well know."

She shivered at the mention of his temper. If she did something he didn't like, would he turn her over his knee again?

"Let me clarify my relationship with Miss Chudleigh because you need to know what I don't like about the woman. Our fathers are close friends. Because of that connection, my female cousins befriended her, an awkward girl who was never asked to dance. They eased her way into society. I was persuaded to stand up with her once, and since that day she has followed me around with melting eyes in the hopes I'd single her out again. I have needed to leave entertainments because she followed me relentlessly round and round the ballroom in the most embarrassing fashion. Enough so people were laughing about her infatuation and commenting upon it. She knows nothing of me except that I'm the grandson of a duke."

"You can be kind when it suits," Matilda whispered, concerned for the woman's state of mind. One dance was not enough reason to bind yourself to William Ford. "If your sisters do not make a match in two years will I be able to retire from society regardless?"

"You have my word this marriage is a temporary arrangement. If my sisters choose not to marry at all, we will discuss together what to do next." He frowned as his hands fell away; his fingers curled into a fist at his side. "Society will be easy to fool."

"Forgive me that I have not your confidence. I might know your nature, but you do not have the faintest idea of mine. I have no experience in being a lady."

"I will ensure you have everything you need."

The duke laughed as he rejoined them. "Is she not delightfully direct?"

"Indeed," William agreed. He stood stiffly now, as if he was annoyed by the interruption.

If she failed to please her husband, and she was positive she would at some point, would she be punished for it? And why did the idea of it not terrify her more?

"What is your answer, Miss Winslow?"

She blinked. "To what?"

His jaw tensed and then he bit out, "Will. You. Marry. Me?"

"Oh," she whispered. He was proposing with such bad grace. His attitude amused her. This was exactly how she'd picture the gruff captain proposing to anyone. She cast a quick glance at the Duke of Rutherford and saw his curt nod. Rather than risk aggravating the captain further, Matilda dipped her chin, sealing her reputation as a woman who'd tricked her employer into marrying her. After all, her other choices were just as difficult—a false life as a ruined woman living alone, or a false life as William Ford's unwanted bride.

None promised happiness. Only one offered security.

"Speak the words," he demanded, eyes boring into hers relentlessly.

Matilda bit her bottom lip and then squared her shoulders. "Yes, Captain. I would be honored to be your wife."

The duke crowed happily, but she was more concerned by Captain Ford's sudden smile. He seemed entirely too pleased with her answer, and that could not be good. Not good at all.

CHAPTER SEVEN

"WILLIAM!" Evelyn shouted as she dashed across the Newberry House drawing room to greet him and then threw herself into his arms as usual.

He embraced his sister quickly and set her back on her own feet, staring down into her eager face. His baby sister was growing up, but she hadn't lost her enthusiasm for the people she loved. He harbored hope that her exuberance might dim somewhat when in company once she was out in society. "How many times must I remind you not to run across these floors? The number of rugs on the Newberry House drawing room floor makes for a hazard to everyone's health."

"At least once more," Evelyn said, then her smile dimmed as her attention flickered to his scarred cheek. "It is a miracle you're here to scold me for doing it."

He grunted. She had a point. He'd prefer not to think about the past months. The future was much more interesting.

He glanced around the empty room, puzzled by that fact that his sister was by herself. "What are you doing sitting here alone?"

"Nothing in particular. I was reading." She twisted from side to side, making her gown float around her like waves lapping at the shore. "Victoria went to call on friends, and Audrey is"—piano keys crashed in the music room—"having difficulty with a new piece of music." She winced. "That's been going on for three hours actually."

He glanced toward the sound coming from the distant music room. Audrey's daily practice would usually span hours, but in the past the notes she struck had been much more promising.

"I've not heard Audrey play so badly for a very long time. It sounds as if she's not even trying," he said, frowning at the terrible noise.

"Audrey has been out of sorts of late." Evelyn shrugged. "Not to worry. She will come good eventually. She always does. You did not bring Matilda with you today. I was hoping to see her before the real wedding takes place."

"Ah, no. She is"—he'd not the faintest idea what she might be doing today, so he made up something on the spot—"resting, I imagine."

"Why? What has she to rest from?" Evelyn's expression turned sly as she looked up at him.

"Being employed as a maid," he suggested. "It is a very taxing occupation."

He considered Matilda's hand sliding into the glove yesterday. Her skin had seemed not as soft as it ought to be for one so lovely.

"Oh, I thought you must have spent the night seducing her." Evelyn giggled behind her hand.

He blinked and then scowled at the suggestion. Evelyn was growing up too fast to be speaking of such matters, and he was unwilling to be teased in such a manner by her. "Why would you think that?"

"Because you're going to marry her, silly." She waved her

hand. "Everyone knows couples in love do the most romantic things when no one is watching."

He set his hands to his hips. "Evelyn, your assumption was a mistake. We are not courting. We never were."

"And yet you will marry her." Evelyn blushed. "It seems to me that a man could not consider marriage without at least some courting having already taken place. Given the circumstances of your association with Matilda, the time the two of you might have spent alone, I imagine all sorts of improper moments might have occurred by now."

A wistful sigh escaped Evelyn as she turned to sit in a comfortable chair. "I do look forward to being an aunt one day and cuddling my dark-haired nieces and nephews."

Good God, his father's influence had over taken the girl's once-promising nature. "I assure you it was not like that. She has no romantic interest in me whatsoever. Nor I in her." He raked a hand through his hair and followed Evelyn to sit. "She bullied me to live—threatened me with all sorts of tortures. For God's sake, she changed bandages on my wound a dozen times a week and spoon-fed me all my meals."

Evelyn bit her lip as tears filled her eyes, but she shook her head, preventing their fall. "And in that time, I am sure she learned more about you than most new brides could ever dream of knowing about their real husbands after a long and entirely proper courtship. If caring for you—grumpy beast that you can be at such times—has not caused her to flee, then she must care for you a great deal."

"Evelyn, Matilda, and I made an arrangement that will ensure she is financially well-off so that I am free of romantic misadventures while you make your come-out. I do not want any nonsense this year."

Evelyn straightened a little. "She was always my favorite."

He stared at his sister in consternation. Who was this creature? "You have favorites among my servants?"

"Oh, always." She waved her hand airily. "Some dress hair better than others. Some share gossip, and a very few will never tell your secrets if they overhear them."

He peered hard at his sister. "Which one is Matilda?"

"The latter, of course." Evelyn blushed. "You made a wise choice in her."

He wasn't completely convinced he had any choice but to marry her given Evelyn's outburst yesterday. However, for the moment he had no complaints. "Matilda is why I am here. It occurred to me that as a servant she would not possess a great many of the articles a young lady in her new situation should have."

"That is true. I've only ever seen her wear two gowns. The gray she wore the other day and a muddy brown I utterly detest. As your wife, she should have a complete wardrobe of beautiful gowns made immediately. Jewel colors I think would offset her rich complexion."

That was what he'd concluded at midnight last night. He'd been musing about the changes he'd need to make in his life to accommodate a temporary wife. He'd spent the hours after midnight debating the merits of where to keep her after the marriage too. She'd left the servants' quarters already since she should act the part before the household staff as well as out in society.

There was only one bedchamber on the first floor. His. He'd eventually decided to keep her in the front guest bedchamber on the second floor after they married properly, so she would have a view over the rooftops of London. Her room was located directly over the drawing room where he liked to spend his evenings when at home. He would be able to hear her walking about her chamber in the late evening before he went to sleep. He would know when she was restless. He would know where she was at all times.

"I am going to need help."

Evelyn beamed. "For this I need Audrey. We would only be too happy to take care of Matilda's wardrobe for you."

"No." He wanted help, not to be pushed aside. "I want to have the final say on her wardrobe, but I would appreciate suggestions and company on a shopping expedition this morning."

Evelyn's brow crinkled. "You know women must be fitted for gowns in person."

"Yes, but I will choose the styles and fabrics today. Then you or Audrey can direct me to a competent dressmaker who can hold her tongue."

She stared at him in horror. "But William, what will Matilda say if you make all the important decisions for her?"

He expected her to accept. He had a vision in his head, an image of how he'd like Matilda to dress, that he would see come to pass. "I am confident she will comply." William folded his arms across his chest, unwilling to be turned from his decision. "She cannot be seen about town in her current garments, so we will have to expand her wardrobe a little until we are actually married, and then she may shop to her heart's content."

"That is a little cold, even for you."

"Not at all. Part of our agreement is that I fund her purchases for the next two years. She can hardly be discontent that I might choose some of it to begin with."

"I feel so bad. I made you get married." Evelyn winced, wringing her hands. "You don't say you are, but are you sure you are not very annoyed about the match?"

"No. I'm not in the least annoyed about it." He shook his head. It wasn't a marriage meant to last, so he had no expectations. No dreams would be dashed when the mistaken affair was over. "Matilda suits my purpose."

Evelyn punched her hands to her hips. "You are so utterly without romance in your soul. It is such a surprise to me that she said yes to you at all."

"It was indeed. She could have made quite a scene if she'd been anyone else." However, she'd hardly have a comparably comfortable life if married to that scoundrel Harry Lloyd—if he'd ever intended to do more than dangle a hint of a wedding ring beneath her pretty nose. William was confident he was saving Matilda from very disagreeable life indeed, which was why he'd not corrected her wild assumption of the other man's death. With William, their eventual separation might cause a bit of a scandal in the beginning, but she would have the funds to escape to a better life in the end.

It was done, or almost done, and they would wed soon. He was rather anxious that nothing should get in their way on this unexpected trip to the altar. Undeterred by his apparent marriage, Maria Chudleigh had passed by his home in a slow-moving open carriage twice that morning that he had witnessed. She had stared at the house, looking for signs of him or Matilda perhaps. The sooner he was squared away with Matilda as his wife, the sooner he could breathe easily.

"Better to be unromantic than a fool in love. Which reminds me, I understand you offered a vast array of advice for my recovery."

"Matilda told you of my letters," Evelyn said, beaming.

"She mentioned them in passing but was concerned about your state of mind in suggesting such actions. A gold crown over my heart? Where did you think a servant might acquire one of those? By stealing it from me in the first place?"

Evelyn only laughed. "How sad that she is as equally unromantic as you!"

"That suits me too. I am spared any nonsense with her." He held out his arm. "Come along, Evelyn. Shall we lure Audrey away from what troubles her?"

Audrey was only too happy to abandon her music to accompany them. "This would be more enjoyable if your bride was with us," Audrey insisted as the carriage rolled along toward Bond Street. "We could fetch her with no trouble."

"She is resting," he repeated for Audrey's benefit. "I will not have her disturbed today."

Audrey shook her head. "She must be lonely locked up in that house."

"She is not a prisoner." William squirmed though. He'd not thought she might become bored. "I am sure she is fine, and Dawson is on hand to see she has everything she might need today."

Audrey appeared unconvinced. "Still, the other servants could be difficult for her. They have their own way of doing things."

His conscience nagged him. He'd promised Dawson an interview last night. In the excitement of his upcoming change of status to husband, he'd not had time to see him. He'd thought the man wanted to discuss the running of the servants' hall and Matilda's employment. She was free of that now, wasn't she? "Difficult how?"

"The elevation of a servant can cause resentment within a household. Matilda was always one of the quiet ones and might have trouble giving orders. I often thought she was unpopular with the other maids before and now..." Audrey did not finish the thought, but he received a clear impression.

If any servant dared interfere with Matilda and what she might want done, they would be dismissed from service immediately. He had promised to look after her. "I will ensure her wishes are carried out."

The carriage stopped, and William stepped out onto the street before Cabot's Haberdashery—the first stop on this shopping expedition as a suddenly married man. His sisters always shopped at this establishment, and he tried to remember some of the items he'd noticed the bills for. Opera glasses, fans, coin purses, and a dozen other things he could not picture clearly. Everything a lady might need for a night out to make the right impression should be within this shop for him to purchase. He handed his sisters out and followed them inside, eager to reward the woman who'd saved his life.

A middle-aged gent swooped on his sisters. "Miss Ford, Miss Evelyn. What a lovely surprise to see you today."

Evelyn grasped the man's hand firmly to shake it and held it a little too long for his comfort. "Mr. Cabot. We were all so very sad to hear the news of the passing of your wife. How have you been?"

The man paled a little and retrieved his hand quickly. "As well as can be expected, but happier for seeing you both again."

Evelyn nodded, full of sympathy as usual, and turned to perform introductions. "Mr. Cabot, might I present my brother, Captain William Ford. He has recently returned from duty at sea."

Cabot bowed. "A pleasure to make your acquaintance at last, Captain, and thank you for all you have done for our country."

William had never been comfortable with compliments, but he managed a curt nod. "Sir."

Cabot took a pace back and gestured to the shop. "My shop is yours, ladies."

Evelyn and Audrey beamed. "Thank you."

They wandered off in an excited, chattering rush, leaving William alone with the widowed proprietor and feeling decidedly out of place. He had thought perhaps he might find a place to sit while his sisters shopped, but clearly this was not an establishment where a man could linger with any assurance he was meant to stay.

Cabot cleared his throat. "Is there anything I can help you with?"

"I think I will simply look around while my sister's shop." He nodded. "My condolences."

"Thank you, Captain. If I can be of any help, please don't hesitate to ask."

The man returned to his counter and almost immediately started accepting items from Audrey and Evelyn. His sisters wasted no time in collecting gifts for Matilda, and he hoped they chose well because she deserved the best money could buy. Matilda would need many things if she was to present herself anything like his sisters were accustomed to. He wanted her to feel part of his life for the little time they were known as a couple. Hopefully she might find some enjoyment in their ruse too.

He considered Matilda and what she might like to receive from him. The comforts of home was what she needed most, but perhaps he should give her something more personal, as thanks for her care. She had lost a great deal of sleep watching over him. Not to mention the inconvenience of their temporary marriage. She *had* come to his rescue and saved him from an awkward meeting with Miss Chudleigh. That deserved silk to go with the gold wedding band he would place on her finger in the next few days.

"Actually, there is something," he called out to Cabot. "I am in need of silk undergarments."

His voice carried, shockingly loud in the room. He cursed everyone that turned to stare at him. Cabot bit his lip, and several patrons snickered at his request.

"For a gift," he clarified, rolling his eyes. Dear God, London hadn't changed while he'd been gone to sea. "I am married."

Cabot hurried over, full of congratulations for his happy news, and ushered William to a corner of the shop he'd yet to explore. Folded carefully on the table was an array of delicate garments. Cabot pointed to each pile. "Nightgown. Chemise."

Stockings. His hands itched to touch the delicate items. He yearned to glimpse them upon Matilda's legs. To place them upon her limbs himself just before he disciplined her again. He swallowed the urge to reach out and snatch them up. "Two."

"Of what, Captain?"

"Everything."

"Of course." Cabot made a small pile between them of frothy white silk. "Garter ribbons too?"

"Yes," he whispered. He knew the perfect color. Something bold. Something unexpected, as a reminder of the past that drew them together. "Red."

CHAPTER EIGHT

THE MARRIAGE by special license was expediently arranged, and the rushed event occurred four days after Captain Ford proposed. Thirty minutes and a great deal of embarrassment after that, Matilda Winslow became the legal wife of Captain William Ford and a woman with responsibilities. A wife with a house to manage and vast wealth in her future.

Without ever being courted.

Never even receiving a single flower as proof of any affection.

She was married before the Duke of Rutherford, Captain Ford's sisters, a close friend of William's—Mr. Percy Cobb of Vere Street—and surprisingly, Mr. Dawson was asked to attend and give her away.

Congratulations were subdued, but Matilda tried her best to appear merry despite the unexpected nuptials. She had to convince everyone that she was happy for however long they remained a pair.

Captain Ford expected her to keep to their bargain and be in love with him, so she did her best to seem so. A baffling undertaking. She was utterly terrified of disappointing him and of ruining her new gown, a bronze sheath of silk and fine lace that fitted her curves so perfectly she'd not been able to hide her astonishment at how good she looked in it.

Yet for all the good will and gifts that had come her way, Matilda could not remember a time she had ever felt so uncomfortable. She had no one she could confide in that would not think she was strange to be having doubts about the marriage after the fact.

Captain Ford's three sisters had been giddy with excitement all day, having delivered the dress at dawn and remaining to help her bathe with scented soaps and oil her skin, then assisted her to dress an hour too early in readiness for the ceremony. She had never felt so beautiful or cared for, but the idea of putting a foot wrong horrified her. Even her stockings and red ribbon garters on her legs made her feel elegant and strangely on edge.

"I am glad that is done and out of the way," William murmured as he delayed by her chair. He slipped his hand over her collarbone, a light caress that almost tickled. Her new husband had been quiet all day, watching her closely for her reactions as he'd placed his ring upon her finger. She fiddled with the gold band as he lingered, teasing her skin with a surprisingly gentle caress from such a grim man. "Now it is not a pretense at all, Mrs. Ford, my dear and beloved wife."

He'd called her beloved? Matilda stared at him for half a beat. Surely, he could not mean it. The last thing she'd ever expected was to marry a man so distinguished and for him to be happy about the circumstances. Becoming William Ford's wife was utterly beyond her ambitions. They had nothing in common and never would. No one was ever going to believe them in love. Getting used to her new address and elevation would take a great deal of time. Becoming accustomed to his endearments, even pretend ones, might take the rest of her life.

"So it is final."

A brief smile flickered over his lips. "Are you comfortable there?"

"Yes, Captain." But it was a lie. Sitting in this room, at the captain's side, didn't feel proper. Any moment she expected Mrs. Young to drag her back to the servants' quarters and give her greasy pans to scrub as penance for her presumption in returning his smiles.

His brow creased as he took a place beside her. "William would be preferred among family and friends."

"Yes, William." She almost choked saying his first name and blushed yet again. She'd lost count of the number of times she'd done that since his scandalous proposal.

Footmen came and set out course after course of an elegant dinner to celebrate their marriage. Each frowned at her a little before shaking their heads in consternation and moving on to the next guest as if they could not believe she was to be waited on. She shuddered to think of what was being said of her downstairs.

Lobster soup and quail eggs, syllabub followed by meringue tarts—it all looked so delicious her mouth watered with each course. So much had been prepared that she was embarrassed to be the cause of such effort in the kitchens. After two hours of eating and smiling, Matilda was exhausted. Mrs. Cowley would have been run off her feet to have done all this at such short notice. Matilda felt she must eat every morsel placed before her so she could thank her for the effort later.

From time to time, William glanced her way and smiled but was soon drawn back to the duke's rather more important conversation about society goings-on and politics. The food was excellent, far better than she'd ever had in the servants' hall, so she did not long for any attention.

Matilda was already so far out of her depth her heart fluttered in panic every time William looked her way. She glanced toward the three young women chattering as if such a marriage was commonplace, a wanted event. She knew each girl well in a strange fashion.

Victoria, the eldest sister, liked to breakfast in bed, Audrey, the middle girl, charged out of her room very early and jumped about in the stable block, exercising—she claimed—to maintain her figure. Evelyn was the tardiest riser, but could often be found with a book in her hand instead of eating from the tray she'd requested be brought to her room. She had been waiting on them for three years but had never presumed them friends.

Despite their knowledge of her background, they had accepted her with surprising kindness so far, seemingly unperturbed by the early lie, though she was often overwhelmed at times by their conversation and plans for the future. It seemed her husband's family did a great many things together through the year. Picnics and holidays and grand balls. She was very glad the girls were not staying in William's home at present but lodging with the Duke of Rutherford until the matter of her and William's marriage was settled. It gave her time to grow accustomed to the idea of future travel and going out so much on William's arm.

"We are so very pleased to have you as part of the family," Evelyn gushed as William leaned away. "It was the coin over his heart that made my wish come true."

"Your wish?"

Evelyn's smile was very wide. "To have William fall madly in love before he died."

His sisters all nodded enthusiastically.

"I see," Matilda said slowly although she tried not to wince. Receiving William's love was sure to be a memorable moment for some woman in the future. He wasn't in love today, and neither was Matilda in love with him. Everyone knew that. But Matilda nursed a private heartbreak. She was distraught over Harry

Lloyd's death. However, she couldn't let this girl continue her delusions because she might be hurt if she should try to capture a man's attentions that way. She might become embarrassed when the plan failed to procure the fellow's love. "I never actually placed those coins on his chest."

"Oh, I know that." Evelyn sipped her watered wine slowly. "However, since William mentioned the treatment as being blatantly false a few days ago, you must have found time to discuss it with him. I am glad to have been the impetus for your growing attachment."

"That wasn't the moment," Matilda muttered under her breath. Thankfully none of the Ford sisters heard. Fear had been the cause of this marriage—William's of Miss Chudleigh's infatuation, Matilda's of being destitute.

Evelyn leaned close. "My brother has always been particularly reserved and unromantic, which irks my sisters and I greatly. We once feared he would never marry. He hardly speaks to anyone we like. With him being away at war so long, hardly ever at home, it has been so difficult for him to form close connections beyond men."

Matilda nodded slowly, seeing his sister's point easily. William was not exactly the warmest man, and his callers had been few and far between in the past months.

"We did fear he'd never marry," Evelyn whispered, "until you came along and turned his head."

Matilda blushed with embarrassment. William's youngest sister was an utterly baffling creature. She really believed they loved each other and that they had a future, despite knowing the truth of their financial arrangement. Evelyn alluded to that future often, but forever couldn't be further from William's plans. Matilda had spent the better part of the past three days weeping over Harry Lloyd's death. What William had done during that time—she had learned he'd gone out at most nights—was his own business, and she had no right to ask where he'd gone and who he'd met with.

Matilda cast a discreet glance at her new husband. His scar was a stark reminder of the scope of their limited history. William was talking with his grandfather, but there was tenseness about his posture that concerned her. During his illness, when he couldn't speak of his needs, she'd developed a sense of his moods by the way he'd held himself. He wasn't happy. Whether that was with his grandfather, their marriage, or something else entirely, she wasn't sure.

William glanced her way when the last course was cleared away. "Perhaps you and my sisters would like to take tea in the parlor."

"Oh, of course." She should not have needed the reminder, but she was grateful for the nudge. She had three books on etiquette on her bedside table, but memorizing all the social rules of proper society in four days was proving a challenging undertaking. "Ladies, shall we adjourn?"

"Actually, we feel we should be going," the eldest sister said as she stood.

Victoria came around the table, caught up Matilda's hands, and kissed her cheek. "The newly married do not need a trio of little sisters lurking around and spoiling a perfectly romantic evening, do they? Good night, dear sister."

Matilda's breath caught at the remark, caught her off guard by a truth she'd not considered. She had not only a husband, but had received sisters too through this marriage. A week ago she'd been hoping simply to keep her position. It was disconcerting how quickly her life had changed. "Good evening, Miss Ford."

"Victoria, please," she insisted. "We are family now."

The other pair hugged her tightly with a few whispered

words of congratulations and promises to visit and then hurried the duke out of the town house. He might have grumbled a little at their haste to depart, but they made a happy group as they left.

Matilda experienced a moment of longing that her father could have witnessed her wedding today. He would not have cared for the terms of her marriage, certainly not their intention to separate later, but she thought he would be happy she was no longer in service.

"I will be on my way too," Mr. Cobb said. "You definitely do not want a bachelor like me underfoot on this most important of evenings."

Matilda blushed furiously but still managed to meet his gaze. "I look forward to seeing you again, Mr. Cobb."

"Thank you for coming." William clapped his friend on the shoulder and walked him to the door, talking quietly. When William returned, he was smiling. "Wife."

Matilda dipped a curtsy. "Husband."

He drew closer, eyes lingering on her bustline. It was lower than she'd worn before, but not indecent enough to account for his interest. Still, she struggled with a blush. This man had the right to look all he wanted.

For that matter so did she.

Captain Ford looked very handsome. He had dispensed with his naval uniform today in favor of a new chocolate-brown coat, cream waistcoat, and fawn trousers, reflecting his usual reserve. But there was an air of prosperity about him that had been absent before—a signet ring he'd not worn before today graced his left hand, a heavy silver chain attached to a pocket watch hung across his waistcoat, and an amber pin that matched the lightest part of his eyes was threaded through his cravat. The color matched her gown perfectly too.

He appeared every inch the aristocrat. A man she'd been in awe of when they first met and to a degree still was.

"Mrs. Ford, do you dance?"

"Yes," she murmured. "But not since I was a girl. I will probably bruise your feet with my stumbling."

He held out his hand despite her warning. Matilda stared at him a moment, then placed her hand in his. He drew her close, and for a change he held her fingers rather than her wrist. It felt odd, almost too intimate to stand so close in his grasp, especially in this room.

"There is no music," she said, fighting a blush that threatened to consume her.

He shrugged away the problem. "Do you waltz?" His question was soft, almost breathless.

She shivered, catching a glimpse of eagerness in his gaze she was not used to seeing. "Not at all."

"That is unfortunate, for I am fond of it." He drew one of her hands to his shoulder and then settled his fingers at her waist. He slowly slid his hand around her body until he covered the fastenings of her gown.

She struggled to breathe as he drew her closer still. Her face was burning up with embarrassment. He was her husband. There was nothing to stop him touching her, no chaperones, no family, and no excuses not to hold her as close as he wanted.

He tapped his fingers over the knotted bow at her back, and she glanced up quickly, afraid he'd undo the bow.

His eyes were wide, growing dark and deep with an emotion she couldn't name but had glimpsed before. He swallowed, and then turned his face so his scar was hidden from view. "I will have to instruct you soon so we might dance together in public."

Matilda nodded but her heart raced. That look in his eyes unsettled her. This husband of hers, a man so worldly-wise, knew things she did not. She had seen enough of his nature to conclude he had experienced other women, and now, bargain or not, according to the vows she'd spoken, she'd agreed to obey him in everything.

Her legs trembled at what he might ask for.

He lifted his chin toward the staircase as he released her. "It has been a long day. I want you to go upstairs and get into my bed."

Her heart hammered against her ribs in panic. "But I thought I was to stay in the guest bedroom."

"You are my wife now. It is expected that you spend some nights in my bed. Especially tonight."

Matilda swallowed her fear. She'd been trying not to think about tonight and what would happen when they were alone. Captain Ford had said nothing about wishing for intimacy between them, but it was his right as her husband to take his pleasure with her. "Yes, Captain."

"William." He nodded and took another step back.

"William." Matilda dipped a curtsy and then fled to his bedchamber.

In something close to blind panic, she rushed through undressing and redressing into a modest nightgown that had been laid out on the bed. The new, soft garment covered her from neck to toes, but she felt exposed and altogether naked by changing in this room. She scurried into his bed. Glanced around swiftly, then darted back out again to the candle, and blew it out before scrambling under the covers once more, heart thundering.

She lay still, clutching the sheet to her chin as William's footsteps echoed in the adjoining dressing room. He was not alone; his voice was a soft murmur as he spoke with another man, most likely Dawson as he readied for bed. She blushed thinking of him removing his elegant attire, stripping down to even less than when he'd been abed during his recovery.

She lifted her head to peek over her toes as a door closed, but it was not her door. The faint outline of light under the bedchamber's heavy oak door flickered, and then darkness fell in the adjoining room. She could not hear William moving about anymore, but surely, he was coming in.

After a few minutes of silence, she sat up in consternation.

She couldn't hear anything beyond her own frantic breathing.

Matilda took a steadying breath, reassured but confused since she could hear no sign of her husband moving about.

Her husband.

When it became apparent William wasn't coming tonight, Matilda lowered herself to the bedding and glanced dispiritedly around the dark room. This was her wedding night. The night she'd expected to give her virtue to Harry Lloyd.

In his place, William had the right to sleep with her.

She swallowed as new tears filled her eyes. He would come to her soon and then... She had no idea.

It might be true she'd done very well for herself in marrying Captain Ford, but she was quite terrified now. His family was one of the most distinguished in society, accepted anywhere they wanted to go. The man was wealthy and, so far, he'd not stinted her any comfort. The terms of the marriage contract had been very generous indeed. He'd brought a legal man into his home to study and explain to her the document he'd drafted, explaining what her portion would be upon his eventual demise, as if there was not going to be a separation between before then. It had been rather strange to think of the moment of William's death again, which was surely far removed now that he was out of harm's way.

She would be well supported, financially, for the rest of her life. They had not discussed their eventual separation in any detail, but William had promised they would as soon as his sisters had found husbands.

But he was a stranger. Her husband.

It was a great step up for the daughter of a medical man and the wild woman he'd married out of lust and been deserted by as soon as Matilda had been born.

This was not the future she'd expected to have. It wasn't bad, but a life without love wasn't at all unfamiliar. She'd never known a love beyond her father's infrequent affection. Even the memory of Harry's regard was a distant and fleeting memory. She didn't know how to react to William and his occasional kindness.

It took a long time to fall asleep that night, and when she did wake at the usual hour the household came to life, she was still in bed and still alone.

CHAPTER NINE

MATILDA WAS A DEEP SLEEPER. She slept curled on her side, her long dark lashes fanned over her olive cheeks, her slender arms stretched out but kept modestly covered by the bedding. She looked striking in his bed. So innocent and tranquil. The perfect relief for his darkness. He would love nothing more than to wake her from her slumber with his touch, to draw the bedding back and make love to her for the whole of the day.

He wanted to explore every curve of her body usually hidden by her gowns. Touch and be touched as if their marriage was real.

Instead, William remained seated on a straight-backed chair, his hands clenched tightly on his thighs.

Being married to the woman was proving difficult. It had only been a week since they'd spoken their vows, and the urge to control her, urges that plagued his every thought every day of this marriage, were becoming difficult to placate. He was grateful that society did not expect newlyweds to socialize very much in the early days of their marriage and their invitations so far had been few. Matilda had needed this time to accept her elevation from maid to lady. And for himself, he struggled to understand the intense relief and contentment he felt every time she drew near.

He was married. His bachelor days were behind him. He'd expected to eventually resent his grandfather's interference.

But he did not.

Matilda sat up suddenly. "Oh," she whispered as she spotted him sitting beside the bed.

William got to his feet slowly and approached her. "Matilda."

She pulled the sheet up farther to cover her chest the closer he came. "Captain."

How long might it take her to grow accustomed to him? He hoped sooner rather than later. "I answer to William when we are alone."

She licked her lips nervously and glanced around as if seeking escape or her robe. He'd taken her robe away while she slept, tossing it back into the dressing room where all unworn clothing belonged.

"Yes, William." Her grip on the sheet tightened.

"Time to get up," he told her, casting a glance at the windows where the light of midmorning shone through the gaps.

Matilda usually wept in the mornings, he'd heard her several times and had allowed the behavior, but as he'd waited for her to wake that day, he had decided enough was enough. He couldn't bear her sadness over Harry Lloyd, a liar and scoundrel, for one more day. She deserved a better man to look after her.

He meant to be the man she turned to in future.

Lloyd could never spoil her as he was doing; even if their marriage was temporary, she was better off with him. Better for Matilda to believe the man dead than discover the truth of his character and be disappointed.

"Come." He held out one hand to her, a test of her trust.

When she placed her fingers over his, he assisted her out of bed, receiving a lovely flash of slender leg for his viewing pleasure, and lured her into the dressing room while she wore nothing but her nightgown. The fire was burning, pleasantly warm, and tea, cheese, and bread to toast, enough for two, had been brought up at his request.

He placed her in the center of the room and surveyed her. She had the makings of a perfect wife for him. Beautiful, clever but modest. However, modesty was only preferred outside their private rooms.

"I am going to take off your nightgown," he warned her.

She sucked in a sharp breath, eyes widening. "That is indecent."

"We are man and wife." He met her gaze directly. "You must grow accustomed to obeying me. Turn and face the mirror."

She swallowed, and then her chin lifted. "So you can spank me like last time?"

He admired her defiance, even if it was misplaced. "Perhaps if you are very lucky I will."

He smiled at her shocked expression. He drew closer, reaching for her gown to lift it over her head. He did not intend to touch her intimately, but he would know her as much as his conscience allowed. A glimpse of her nakedness would go a long way to satisfying his hunger to understand her better. He waited for her decision. "Well?"

She seemed torn but eventually nodded.

His hands trembled a little as he lifted her gown. She had lovely, slender legs, and his heart raced as he moved the garment higher. The spanking last year had only revealed so much, and he devoured her with his eyes now.

Her gently curved back was a work of art, long and delicately muscled, no doubt from her recent years of service. Matilda was exquisite, beyond anything he'd imagined. He glanced at her face to convey his appreciation but discovered she'd closed her eyes. A pity she could not revel in their first truly intimate moment together as he was doing.

Her skin was golden, even beneath her clothing where he'd imagined her paler. The shade hinted at foreign ancestry he couldn't place. Her breasts were small and tipped with plum-colored nipples. Her waist was tiny and flared to generous hips, and at the apex of her thighs a nest of dark curls covered her sex. Her bottom, as he remembered fondly, was round and full. Perfect for his hand.

"Tell me about your mother."

Her lashes fluttered and she met his gaze. "My mother?"

He smiled as her cheeks reddened with a blush. She blushed so frequently around him that he often wondered at the direction of her thoughts. Was she wicked of thought under her proper facade? "You've only spoken of your father and his career."

"I, um." Her long lashes fluttered again, not a coquettish flirtation but actual distress. Her hands twitched to cover her breasts and lower.

"Don't do that." William gently returned her hands to her sides. "Please continue."

"I never knew her. She died when I was very young."

"So did mine. I was barely six years old when Mama passed away. I remember her hands were gentle, but no more than that." When Matilda failed to share her own confidences about her mother after a lengthy interval of silence, he concluded her late mother was something of a delicate subject or utterly unknown to her. He let the matter drop, not wishing to spoil the morning with unpleasant remembrances. She would speak of her mother eventually if she knew anything at all about the woman.

He circled behind her as she shivered. "You are so beautiful."

There was a very long pause before she found her voice. "Thank you."

He smacked her left buttock once, gratified by her shocked gasp. His fingertips tingled from where they'd touched her, and he rubbed them together, savoring the sensation. "Next time, don't hesitate to answer me."

"Yes, Captain."

He took a stance behind her, admiring the slight reddening of her skin from his slap. "Three more for not using my given name in private as I have asked you to do," he whispered.

Matilda gasped each time he flicked his hand out to administer a gentle discipline appropriate for her lapse, but only swayed a little. Four was enough to begin a day with. Too many and she might be overcome with fear as she had been on their wedding night when he'd suggested she share his bed. He needed her to understand that her virtue was safe with him, and punishments were not lasting.

William moved to the chaise where he'd been sleeping this past week and lifted a fine and very sheer chemise that he'd chosen from the Cabot's Haberdashery shelves. He carefully slid the garment over Matilda's head, lifting her hair out of the way gently, and then found a cotton-and-whalebone corset to bind around her chest. He tightened the laces firmly, then had her sit on the edge of the chaise. She bounced up a little as the firm surface pressed against her tender bottom.

He knelt at her feet to hide his grin, covered her slender legs with new stockings, and tied the ruby-red garter ribbons beneath each knee briskly. When he was done, Matilda swiftly brought her knees together before he could glimpse more than the top of her thighs.

"Are you hungry?" he asked.

"A little."

He gestured to the table. "Then sit and pour tea for us both please."

Matilda fled across the room to where a table had been set for them earlier, and while she poured, William toasted bread. "Did you sleep well?"

"Yes, thank you. And you?"

He sighed. "The chaise is too short."

"I'm sorry."

"For what?" He turned while the bread finished toasting and admired his wife's proportions for a long while. Exquisite, but out-of-bounds. A pity. He carried the first slice to her plate when it was ready, then returned to toast another for himself. "Keeping your virtue intact was my idea, hence the separate sleeping arrangements."

Matilda frowned as she tugged the sheer chemise a little farther down her legs. "I appreciate that."

"But we cannot be strangers," he said as he lifted his gaze slowly up her body. Her corset-bound breasts practically spilled out of the garments. He grew heated as he recalled what lay beneath. "For better or worse, you are my wife, and I can only sleep on that chaise so often before a servant catches me there."

A deep frown line appeared on her brow. "I would not like to be gossiped about any more than we already are. I could easily return to the chamber upstairs."

"No. I don't care for the separation," he said quickly.

William liked knowing Matilda was far from the servants. He wasn't at all worried about any gossip they stirred up. If there was talk about his sudden marriage, the scandal would blow over soon enough.

One only had to look at Matilda now, or when she was properly dressed, to see her appeal. He had the luxury of not caring that such a choice was unpopular since it was to be as brief a marriage as possible. He had Rutherford's support, and that meant his sisters would not suffer any slights during the season. He was content with his and Matilda's chaste arrangement, especially since the alternative was being pursued by Miss Chudleigh. Matilda did not chase him at all.

"I would have you grow used to me touching you, seeing you uncovered like I have this morning. I did not like the way you held the bedsheet to your chest as if I were about to impose on you. I assure you I will not try to steal your virtue, but I would like to dress you each day in place of a maid."

"You startled me this morning." She licked her lips. "I had not expected to see you when I woke."

"You will see me every morning now." He nodded, deciding to deny himself such a simple pleasure no longer. He would break her of her hesitation eventually, allowing her time to come to terms with his presence and her place in his life. "I will dress you, and we will take breakfast together."

"And at night?"

"We will share the same bed from tonight. We can discuss our day and fall asleep together, side by side," he told her, tipping his head to the side as she worried at her lip. "We have done that before, many a night in fact, during my recovery."

"Except that I did all the talking. You never said a word even when you could." She pointed her finger at him and then attempted to hide the gesture behind her back. "I only fell asleep near you a few nights by accident."

"I did not mind. I have missed your reading to me though." He grinned. "The chaise was acceptable for the first nights of our marriage but no longer. Agreed?"

"Yes, William."

He smiled widely at hearing his name, but he noted she'd

dropped her toast to her plate while they conversed. "Eat. We have errands to run today."

She picked up her toast again but spoke before taking a bite. "What sort of errands?"

He supposed he'd have to grow used to explaining everything in detail. One of the facets of marriage every man must accept if he wished for a congenial home life. "My grandfather has offered a town carriage for our use this season. I will, of course, order one bespoke, but until that task can be completed, we will make do with one of the Newberry conveyances on loan."

She paled a little. "If you think that best."

William leaned his head on his hand, cradling his scarred cheek in his palm. "I expect you to answer me immediately Matilda, but if you agree with everything I say then our conversations will grow dreadfully dull before too long."

She glanced away, frowning. "Do you really need a town carriage?"

"*We* need one, yes," he corrected her. "The carriage in question will be on loan from Newberry House and is largely used by my cousin Sally when she is in Town. Since Sally remains at Newberry Park with her new husband, it has been offered to us until we can acquire our own. I have a larger landau, but it is better used for long journeys rather than the tight confines of London's streets. I never got around to purchasing a smaller carriage for myself. I've hardly been ashore long enough to need one before and have most often hailed a hack for short journeys about Town."

"That is very sensible."

"I will not allow you to hail a hack," he said in case she ever entertained the idea. "You will have your own carriage and the protection of our staff whenever you go out."

"I see." She swallowed. "You come from a large family."

"I do." He smiled. "Does the idea of meeting all of them worry you? Don't let it. They are not unkind people, but I did choose to live four blocks away from everyone quite deliberately. They are loud and often meddlesome. I am sure you will come to agree with me by the time of our separation."

"You do not like a fuss," she whispered, eyes dropping to her lap.

"Obviously. I prefer a quiet life," he reminded her. He sipped his tea and finished his toast. "If the war has taught me anything, it is to cling to the familiar and value what I have. Peace, routine, and all the comforts my wealth can provide for us. I used to keep dogs as a boy. Do you care for them?"

"I had a black spaniel until I was fourteen," she confessed. "Blackie. I was terribly unimaginative as a child to name him so."

Her nose wrinkled, and he studied her warmer expression with approval. "I probably should confess to having been an equally unimaginative child. I had a terrier. I called him Blackie as well." He frowned, recalling that long-dead pet and his sadness at being told it had been shot by mistake by a guest at Newberry Park. He shook his head. How long ago must that have been?

Matilda gazed at him with sparkling eyes and then leaned forward, at last appearing to forget she was sitting down to breakfast in her unmentionables, to touch his arm. "How clever of us to have picked the same name!"

A little thrill swept through him. That was the first time Matilda had referred to them as a couple, and he liked the sound on her lips. He also liked that she'd reached for him. It was the first time since their marriage. The first time even since he'd left his sick bed.

Since Matilda appeared disinterested in eating, William took her hand and raised her from her chair, then returned her to the center of the room where she could see her reflection well. He collected her new gown, a soft green muslin with yellow flowers embroidered at the neck, sleeves, and hem, and buttoned her up in it. Even though the gown was of a modest design, dressing her aroused him enough that his cock swelled inside his breaches.

Only the faintest hitch in Matilda's breathing suggested she'd noticed his state, but he ignored his condition and her reaction.

They were not going to remain married, and he believed taking liberties would only cause problems for both of them. The complication of a pregnancy would extend the duration of their arrangement. If she birthed a boy, the child would be his heir and their arrangement might have to continue indefinitely.

Matilda wasn't meant for a life with him. But he wanted to educate her in the ways of his world, and perhaps if their natures aligned the way he hoped, he might tempt her to enjoy what they did together.

When she was stylishly dressed in the manner he preferred, modest chain about her neck and blushing deeply from his attention and compliments, he grinned. "Wife."

Her answering smile was just a little embarrassed. "Husband."

He held out his arm. "Let us go inspect this carriage of Sally's and, if it suits, we can move on to the second task of the day."

"What might that be?"

"There is a litter of puppies waiting for our inspection in the adjoining mews. They are too young to be taken from their mother today but in a few weeks, if you like, we can bring one home with us. Shall we walk?"

Matilda had kept to the house and the drawing room a little more than he considered healthy. He wanted her seen on his arm. He wanted her to want to spend time with him.

"I would like that," she agreed, a hesitant smile blooming on her lips.

He paused to add a stylish bonnet to her head, passed her

short kid gloves to slip on while he collected his own possessions and a few coins. He escorted her down the staircase and out onto the street, well pleased with how the morning had gone between them.

Dressing her had been both arousing and comforting. He could stand a little more togetherness if she would only agree.

Matilda, however, let out a shaky breath as soon as they were out of sight of home.

He clasped his hands behind his back as they strolled along side by side. "You have nothing to be nervous about."

"Surely you must regret your grandfather's interference. You've only just recovered, and now you are saddled with a wife. I am afraid I have not been a very good wife to you."

He wasn't concerned, but he was curious about her opinion on marriage. "What sort of wife should you be?"

"I don't know," she said, clearly worried. "I never imagined marrying a stranger."

He raised a brow. "Would it surprise you to learn that you know my nature better than anyone? I'm not the sort of man to reveal my habits to just anyone."

She blushed again. "I do know your nature, but you do not know me."

"You might not have noticed, but I was attempting to fill in the gaps of my knowledge this morning over breakfast." He fell silent as they strolled side by side for a while. They kept pace easily enough, and he was pleased he did not have to shorten his strides very much at all to match hers. "Many marriages among the *ton* are hardly ever more than a business arrangement." He shrugged. "As is ours to a degree, I suppose, but I hope that we might become friends."

"Friends?"

"Well, yes." He leaned toward her. "It will be a long and trying affair if you keep avoiding me."

Her hand rose to her lips guiltily. "I've hidden from you this week."

"I did notice that, but no more. Agreed?"

"Yes, William."

He took her arm to help her across the street and then decided to keep it, steering her around people and obstacles in their path.

Miss Chudleigh's carriage was also approaching them. He ignored the woman whose face was pressed to the glass and smiled at Matilda as they carried on at an unhurried pace. "Can I ask you a question?"

"Yes, of course."

William stopped once Miss Chudleigh's carriage was out of sight. "How did you feel after I spanked you last year?"

Her eyes widened in shock. "I... I cried," she whispered, glancing around to see who was nearby.

He patted her hand and drew her along the street again. "You did not cry this morning?"

"No. It did not hurt as much."

Holding back had been quite deliberate. "Did you tell anyone what we did last year?"

She shook her head quickly. "But I think Dawson might have heard us."

That was what he'd suspected too. "Why didn't you tell anyone?"

"I was sure no one would believe me," she admitted. "I have not been spanked since I was a little girl."

He moved her away from a hawker selling pigeon pies, keen to keep their conversation going without distractions. "I enjoyed it, you know. Spanking you then, and this morning too. I find discipline pleasurable."

A shocked gasp left her pink lips. "You like hurting me?"

He had indeed. The memory of her red bottom had warmed many of his evenings while he'd been away. "What I did to you caused no lasting harm."

"I felt pain the next day every time I sat down, and this morning."

He chuckled. "That pleases me."

She stopped then, slipping from his grip. "Why?"

"Because I am ashamed to say I wanted you to remember me when I went back to my ship. My hand on your skin, my attention on you. I was brought up to believe a gentleman is not supposed to dally with the hired help. You have been my greatest test and greatest failure. There must be a reason for that." He considered her. It was strange how much he was drawn to her. "Do you remember everything I did last year?"

She blushed again and glanced left and right.

Was she too shy to admit what had occurred after the spanking even now they were married? He leaned close, close enough that his breath would tickle he ear. "I wasn't the only one aroused by the spanking, was I?"

She closed her eyes as he drew back, as if that action would deny the truth of what they had enjoyed together. When he'd spanked her bottom red last year, the quality and volume of her moans had tempted him to slip his hand between her legs. She'd been so wet with arousal that he'd rubbed her clitoris until she'd cried out in pleasure a few short minutes later. Some women truly enjoyed punishment, and he'd felt extremely proud he'd discovered Matilda's secret delight and brought her fulfillment that day.

It had been a memorable moment with her, and he wanted more of that. When she was a servant, he shouldn't have done it again, but with her being his wife, they could indulge their passions in private as long as he remembered not to ruin her.

But only if she agreed.

"You didn't ask me to stop; you didn't ask to be released. You lay across my knee, moaning to every beat of my hand against your skin." He captured her hand. "And when I judged the pain enough, I rewarded you with pleasure."

Matilda trembled. "You shouldn't have done that."

"I couldn't have left you in such a state of arousal and not provided complete satisfaction. That would have been callous and unkind."

A hot blush rose up her cheeks, warming her skin as much as it had been that day.

"You like it," he whispered to her after a couple had passed them by. "There are many women who enjoy a strong hand and direction. There is nothing to be uncomfortable about. You like how I make you feel, and I like taking care of you."

She shook her head. "I was innocent until that day."

"You are innocent still, Matilda. I don't intend to change that fact no matter how many times you spill across my knee. I can pleasure you without taking your virtue. I would like to touch you intimately very much." He glanced ahead, noticing Miss Chudleigh's carriage had somehow circled around the block very quickly to roll past them again. He set his arm about Matilda's back, and turned her toward the adjacent buildings so she did not notice the woman was watching their every move. She might find it as unnerving as he did. "Ah, here we are. The Duke of Rutherford's London residence, Newberry House. What do you think?"

Matilda glanced ahead at the massive structure, but he could tell by the way her breath was rushed that she was fighting with herself, struggling not to be affected by their frank discussion of pleasure and pain, all while his arm remained curled about her body.

"Impressive," she whispered.

"Yes, you are. The house also to a lesser extent." He grinned when she spluttered in shock at his words. He might not always be a charming conversationalist, but when the time was right, he could utter honest compliments. Matilda challenged him in a way he'd not expected. There was more to her than met his eager eyes. She had strength and courage, two traits utterly necessary for any real wife of his to possess.

She made him want to discover her depths, valleys, and limits. "We will discuss the matter of satisfying your desires at a later time when we can speak freely again. Agreed?"

She stared at him and then slowly nodded. "Yes, William."

CHAPTER TEN

MATILDA HELD her breath as the announcement of their arrival was made to a full room. "Captain Ford and Mrs. William Ford."

Her first ever ball.

Her first evening out as William's wife.

Matilda's heart began to pound in time with the thrumming of a dozen dancing feet as her husband led her into a room lit by a hundred candles at least. The light reflected off four enormous mirrors that hung on the four walls of the Cavendish ballroom and dazzled her eyes. The sparkling windows were shrouded by an abundance of heavy burgundy drapes, and gold braid held them back to reveal the darkness of night beyond.

She grew weary thinking of the work involved to keep this room clean, only to notice a heartbeat later how many disapproving stares were aimed in her direction.

A tall man of middle years swung around. "You're late," he complained to William. He held out his hand though. "I thought you would miss my ball altogether."

"Forgive me, Cavendish." William glanced her way. "I lost all track of time."

The man—whom she finished cataloging at wearing three rings on each hand, one obscenely large ruby cravat pin, and gold-headed walking stick—glanced her way with a raised eyebrow. "You should speak to her about that."

William muttered softly. "Later."

"I would advise not to delay."

"Matilda, darling." William released her. "Might I present His Grace, the Duke of Cavendish?"

Matilda dipped a curtsy to their host, remembering William's instructions on the length and depth that would be required for meeting this particular man. He was not of royal blood, but he was extremely important in society. William expressed a wish that of all the instructions, she must pay most attention to this one. "Your Grace. It is an honor to meet you."

Apparently appeased, the man bowed. "Madam." He clicked his fingers, and a younger but elegant gentleman appeared almost immediately. Not dressed as flamboyantly as the host but very impressive just the same. "Lord Fox. Captain Ford. I trust you remember each other."

"I do indeed. A pleasure to see you again, my lord," William said.

The younger man, much warmer in manner than their host, grinned widely. "Captain and Mrs. Ford. I have looked forward to this meeting most eagerly."

The fellow took her hand and squeezed her fingers. "Welcome among us, my dear woman. I hope you will allow me to introduce you to my wife very soon."

"I should be very pleased to make her acquaintance." She eased closer to William. Such a warm greeting after the frost of their host was just a touch disconcerting.

"Fox, see that my guests are comfortable." The duke moved away without waiting for a response.

Lord Fox drew them deeper into the room, signaling to a nearby waiter. After William had handed her a glass of punch, they drew closer together to speak. "Everyone is talking about the shock of your marriage," Lord Fox said in a low tone that reached her ears too.

"Let them." William scowled.

"I just wanted to warn you that Cavendish is very concerned you have made a grave error in judgment." Lord Fox glanced her way, frowning. "You know how he feels about misalliances."

William straightened, capturing Matilda's arm to wrap about his. "I know what I'm doing."

Fox appeared ready to say more but suddenly glanced around. He grinned, a look of pure joy crossing his features. "Ah, here comes my one and only to say hello."

A voluptuous woman a little older than Matilda, eyes bright with excitement, approached and held out her hand to William. "Darling."

Matilda stared at William in shock as he returned the affectionate greeting. "It is good to see you again, Lady Fox. I have missed our discussions."

Coldness filled Matilda as she was introduced. The woman was exquisitely dressed and had a pampered air about her. She also knew William very well. Matilda managed an adequate curtsy. "My lady."

Lady Fox glanced away to William. "So this is the woman who replaced me in your affections."

William coughed, glancing at the still smiling Lord Fox. "You've been married many years, pet."

She shuddered and pasted a smile on her face. "The happiest five years of my life, Billy."

William's entire body tensed at the nickname, and the pair

engaged in a staring match. Matilda grew uncomfortable after a few moments, but Lord Fox only smiled.

Lady Fox was the first to break eye contact. She met Matilda's gaze again. "A pleasure to meet you, Mrs. Ford. I wish you both every happiness."

"Thank you."

William turned to Lord Fox. "How are your children?"

"Thriving," Lord Fox exclaimed, then spoke expansively about his offspring for several minutes.

Lady Fox assessed Matilda again through narrowed eyes until Matilda shifted uncomfortably toward William. The corner of Lady Fox's mouth quirked a little in response, which brought a blush to Matilda's cheeks. She fought it, remembering William's admonishment that she must behave like she belonged. Matilda did not like to be stared at. She did not feel comfortable around this woman or like the way she spoke to William so intimately. She never wished to meet the woman again.

"I am very pleased to hear it," William replied. "Ah, I see my sisters. I had better go greet them before they make a mad dash along the length of the ballroom to reach us. I hope to see you again soon."

"And you, too." Lady Fox nodded. "You must come to dinner, Billy. It shall be like old times."

William nodded. "We look forward to it, pet."

Steered across the room by William's guiding hand beneath hers, Matilda silently fumed. The woman was outrageous. The pair had been flirting right under her nose. She would not go to any dinner that Lady Fox hosted or attended. She would plead a headache or any other nonsense just so she might never have to see her again.

"Sister dear," Victoria gushed, embracing her gently. Matilda appreciated her caution. She liked this gown too much to wish it to be crushed so early in the evening. "You are stunning. William apparently does have good taste."

"Of course I do." He grumbled, then moved to greet a group of men nearby. Matilda noticed Mr. Cobb whispering in William's ear again. Her husband shook his head firmly. "I cannot tonight."

Audrey frowned at her brother. "We worried you were not coming."

"I... ah," she began. Being late was not exactly her fault. "I was not sure which jewels to wear, but William insisted on his first gift in the end," she whispered.

"His mother's pretty pendant has always looked very well on you," Evelyn said softly.

Matilda covered the piece with her fingers. She had not known she was wearing a family heirloom. If she had, she would have insisted on not wearing it all the time. She would have given it back. "Did this belong to his late mother?"

"Oh, yes. William would never allow us to wear the piece, even though we begged him often," Victoria said and then grinned widely. "He trusts you more than he ever did us."

Musicians announced a dance, and William turned to her. "Will you dance with me, Mrs. Ford?"

"I'd be very happy to, Captain."

He took her hand and led her onto the dance floor. Out here among the other dancers, she was uncomfortable. It was as if she'd stepped onto the stage of a great performance. And perhaps it was. Tonight she was meant to be in love.

She met William's eyes, placed her trust in him to guide her safely as they stepped off into her very first waltz before witnesses. At home, she'd feared she'd stumble, but with William's hand firm on her back and his attention fixed on her, she soon became lost in his dark gaze.

Her pulse sped up with every turn, every brush of his legs

against her gown. He was a very good dancer, his grip sure and comforting. He seemed very skilled to keep their spinning tightly controlled. When the dance came to an end, Matilda was so wrapped up in him that she barely registered they'd stopped moving. He smiled down at her a long moment. "Lovely. Thank you for the dance."

"It was a pleasure, William." She looked away from him when his eyes widened a little. Was that wrong? It had felt right to use his first name after such a dance.

He led her back to his grinning sisters and eased away a few moments later to return to his conversation with Cobb. She was glad he had such a good friend, but he shook his head so often she wondered of what they were speaking.

"They've been friends a long time," Audrey said. "Thick as thieves. Of course, it is different now."

"Why is that?"

"Well, William can hardly want to spend his every evening with Cobb as he did once. He has you to come home to. His own woman to devote his attention and love to."

Matilda swallowed nervously. She did not want to come between William and his friends. Not when their marriage wasn't going to last.

As she was about to remind Audrey of the real situation, the young woman's eyes widened. "Oh look, there is Lady Rothwell. I did not know she was in town. I am so glad you will meet her tonight, Matilda. She is simply wonderful. So kind and funny. You must meet her now," Audrey gushed, dragging Matilda up to William's side for yet another introduction to be accomplished.

"I simply cannot get away," William told Cobb for the third time that evening.

Cobb's jaw jutted mulishly. "It's been a year. Are you not feeling the restriction?"

He and Cobb had discovered a mutual affinity for dominance many years ago. They had frequented the same brothels as younger men until they'd found the perfect one. Discreet, clean, and it was a place they were assured of absolute secrecy for their evening of activities. Owing to his career, William had never attended quite as much as Cobb and had yet to indulge all his fantasies.

His friend had a very singular mindset and deep pockets. He attended on a weekly basis. He stinted himself no pleasure.

William checked his wife's location before replying, making sure his sisters were keeping her amused and distracted from his conversation. There were some aspects of his life Matilda should remain unaware of. "Not a year. I went before I married. We're not quite that similar either. I have often preferred the anticipation to the act."

"We're the same," Cobb claimed stubbornly. "You just won't admit it."

William smiled tightly. "Let's not speak of this here."

Truth was, he and Cobb had too much in common. They both liked compliant partners in the bedchamber, but he suspected Cobb was much more focused on delivering pain than pleasure. He'd noticed the state of the women Cobb used afterward. William preferred that his lovers could smile as he left. Cobb preferred his partners weeping.

Cobb grunted. "What does the admiralty say?"

"Nothing new. The peace is holding. My services are not required."

"So you do have the time," Cobb insisted.

"I have a wife now, man. She needs me not to desert her. It was my idea to drag her into this marriage."

Cobb took a long drink and claimed a passing waiter's attention for another. "Next week then."

William sighed. "Visiting a brothel again is not high on my list of priorities. The last time did not go so well."

"Pay them enough and they'd kiss that scar, and anything else of yours, without complaint."

William stared at his friend with growing annoyance. He didn't need the reminder that his face scared some women witless. "Excuse me."

He walked back to Matilda's side.

Matilda laid her hand upon his arm immediately. "Is everything all right, William?"

"Yes," he answered quickly and saw disbelief cross her face. Her expression remained wary, as if she did not believe his answer. She had always been too good at reading his moods. He couldn't tell her what was wrong with him, so he turned the conversation back to her. "Are you enjoying the evening?"

Another frown flickered over her features. "I enjoyed dancing with you."

He smiled at how she singled him out. She did not dwell on the worst of things but always mentioned what pleased her. He was glad he was one of her pleasures tonight. "I enjoyed the dance too. Thank you for letting me teach you the steps this week. I know I was very particular about your practice."

"You almost always are about everything," she replied and then laughed softly. "I was so afraid I would trip over my own feet and embarrass you."

"I never imagined you could ever do that to us," he replied as a grating voice buzzed in his ear.

"I swear I almost fainted when I saw him again," a woman

exclaimed in a shocked tone somewhere behind him. "That scar. That handsome face. Gone forever."

He turned slightly, belatedly noticing the French doors behind him were ajar, allowing a current of air to cool the room and voices from outside to carry in.

"I'd pity the woman," another voice claimed just as loudly, "except she made her bed. Now she has to kiss him when she goes to sleep at night. A maid of all things marrying into that exalted family."

The pair burst out laughing cruelly, heedless of his standing a few feet away. They could not know he could hear them, or perhaps they did not care that he might. His temper rose; his hands clenched. How dare they insult his wife? They had no right to judge her for what he'd set in motion.

Matilda eased against him, and he caught her wrist tightly in an effort to cool his head. She turned back to him, startled. "I was only looking for a footman. My glass is empty, and I'd like to return it."

"I'll get you another."

"Thank you. It is so very warm tonight," she said as she beat a fan before her face. She glanced behind him and smiled. "I wonder if they will open the doors wider to let in more of a breeze soon."

Had she not heard those women lurking outside speaking of them both? He took comfort in her ignorance, relieved she'd not heard them talking of her. There would always be gossip, but he would not like her to hear it directly and become upset. "I'll see to it. Wait here."

He spun around, moved to the doors, and threw them wide, startling both Lady Charlton and Lady Poole completely from their intimate conversation. They were both widows with nothing much to recommend them but that they had daughters of marriageable age.

He smiled coldly at them. "Will anyone be kissing you tonight? I doubt it very much."

He smiled widely just to alarm them a little more with his appearance but turned away before the stretch of his skin became too much for him to bear. The right word in the right ear could ruin their daughter's prospects, and they knew it. He had that power within reach; their host was a very good friend, though he'd never thought to ever need to use his connections for revenge before.

But he would protect Matilda.

He returned to his wife's welcoming smile, and that soothed him, but she frowned when he rubbed over his scar. "What have you done to your face?"

"Nothing more than smile."

Her shoulders relaxed. "Good. You must still be very careful."

"I am. Don't worry so."

Her brow arched high. "Is it not my right as wife to concern myself with your health?"

"Not now, Matilda. Do not fuss at me tonight."

"Yes, William," she whispered, and the playful light in her eyes died. He had not meant to provoke that reaction. Damn them. Society didn't matter. Matilda's happiness did. "I did not mean to snap."

"Why did you?"

"Not now." He wrapped her arm about his firmly, then steered her into the crowd in search of a footman and more punch for her, determined never to react so badly to anyone's opinion about his looks. Matilda liked him as he was, and that had to be enough.

CHAPTER ELEVEN

MATILDA KICKED off her shoes and shrugged her shoulders to shift the unease that was building inside her. Her first night out in society as William's wife had been all too revealing of how ill prepared she was to live in his world. Their arrival had caused a ripple of conversation to sweep the ballroom ahead of them and for people to turn and stare. The whispers had started almost immediately and continued all night. As a consequence, she had been wary of everyone but his family.

His friends had smiled too broadly at her, as if they knew a secret she did not, and were always watching everything she did and said. She had never felt so self-conscious before.

When William had left her alone for a short while, a woman had pressed for details of their love affair. Then later she'd been discreetly offered a *real* man in her bed as she'd danced mere feet away from her glowering husband. The idea of betraying William had shocked her speechless for the rest of the dance, and she'd been relieved to leave the entertainment somewhat earlier than expected.

She had no idea what she was doing anymore, but she felt she was waiting for William's next request.

He had never continued the conversation regarding her enjoyment of spanking, for which she was profoundly grateful and suitably chastened. After all, he was paying her to continue the charade of being in love with him, not to be intimate with him.

She'd no idea what he thought most of the time, but she knew his moods. Tension was building in him. She had thought he was softening until tonight. Not that the captain was ever completely gentle where she was concerned. Once they were out of the spotlight of attention, he usually sent her to this drawing room where she sat alone, idly reading a novel, or watching the sunset. It was a nice room but far too empty for just herself.

"Are you going to stand there all night or come to bed?"

Matilda shrugged, shivering at the annoyance in his tone. "I thought you had already retired. I wasn't sure what to do."

William stood in the doorway to his dressing room, severe and yet oddly comforting in his beautiful clothes and scowl. The scar on his cheek puckered whenever he clenched his jaw, a premonition of his unstable mood. It was just a part of him, like his usual gruff temper, but she still felt apprehension.

She took a step and winced. "Ouch."

Matilda hobbled to a chair, sat down, and inspected her toes, abused by an earlier dance partner.

"What is wrong?"

She flexed her toes, wincing at a spot of blood on the tip of her fine silk stockings. She eased the material away and hissed at the stab of pain. "Mr. Cobb stomped on my foot harder than I suspected."

"Let me see," he said as he crossed into her room in three long strides and sank to his knees at her feet.

He slid his hands under her skirts and tugged, dragging down her stocking by force, ignoring the ribbon tied beneath her knee. It hurt.

"William, you'll ruin them."

"Purchase a replacement tomorrow," he bit out.

However, he gentled as he finished drawing off her stocking. He caressed her skin, then lifted her foot into the light. He swallowed and tightened his fingers around her ankle.

"It's nothing," she promised him as she attempted to pull her foot back.

He released her to stand, punching his hands to his hips. "Do not dance with Cobb again."

Matilda was only too happy to comply. Mr. Cobb's conversation had made her uneasy. "I will try to avoid him, if possible, but he is your friend."

"My friend should have learned how to dance properly by his age." He stood quietly a moment, then glanced around, and knelt back down at her feet. He removed her other silk stocking with less haste and far more care. "What did Lady Fox say that unsettled you so much?"

"Nothing." Matilda tucked her feet back under her seat when he was done.

He rubbed her knee slowly. "You were pale after you met her."

Matilda winced. "You know her well?"

A muscle in his jaw twitched. "Yes. We met a long time ago."

There was a strange gleam in his eye as he slid his hand down to her leg and tugged her bare feet into view again. He held her ankles, and her breath caught. His fingers were warm as he tightened them around her limb the way he often did with her wrists.

She was curious about him and risked a question that he might not like to answer. "Did you court her?"

His brows rose. "Why do you ask that?"

"She seemed very pleased to see you. She invited you to dinner."

"She invited us."

Matilda shook her head. She had not mistaken Lady Fox. "She invited just you."

"She likes to make an impression." He glanced up at her, a wry smile on his lips. "She was testing you. Seeing how you react to a rival."

So there was something between them. Matilda's heart sank at the discovery that William was involved with a married woman. "Lord Fox didn't seem to care that his wife was arranging an intimate dinner with you." Matilda stared. "Is this how you always behave with other men's wives?"

"Not since... Not for a very long time." He nodded slowly as his palm moved up her leg beneath her gown, and his fingers teased the crease at the back of your knee. "The Foxes are a very liberal couple and quite the reverse of most marriages in terms who has the authority."

"I don't understand."

"Lady Fox is the dominant one of the pair. It works for them. Lady Fox and I clash often." He tilted his head. "A woman like Lady Fox could never suit me. We are too similar in temperament."

"I can see no similarity between you at all," Matilda insisted.

"Lucky me." His lips quirked a little as if he was highly amused. "I have a favor to ask."

Matilda glanced down at his hand where it caressed her leg. She should stop him, but her heart was racing very fast all of a sudden. He had not touched her in this manner before—nor so gently. "Of what nature?"

"It is most likely something you will not want to do." He shook his head then and found his feet quickly, putting a distance of half the room between them. He was almost to the connecting door before he spoke. "Forgive me. "

He started to leave, and with a start she realized he was too uncomfortable to continue. Matilda was so tired of whatever great secret her husband meant to conceal from her. She called him back. "What is it you want from me now, William?"

"A friend said something tonight that annoyed me, but afterward I couldn't help but wonder if he might have a point. It is something I had not considered might be a problem." He touched the scar on his face. "I don't know if I can kiss well anymore."

Her lips parted. She could not help but stare at his lips. Was that the reason he'd never tried to kiss her?

"I've shocked you," he said, nodding to himself.

"Well, yes." Matilda shook her head. "I knew you harbored concerns about resuming your old life after your difficult recovery, but I had never considered you could have doubts about such a personal thing. Of course you can kiss."

"Soup is problematic, and I cannot whistle, though I could from when I was very young." He drew close again but stopped behind a chair facing hers. He leaned onto the back, clasping his fingers before him. "I want to know if kissing is something a woman would still enjoy with me. I would not like... I do not wish to horrify the one I kissed if I am bad at it."

Matilda faltered. She'd bullied him back to life, forced him to accept the reality of his altered looks. Helping him relearn how to kiss a woman had never occurred to her. She didn't know how to answer him. She'd never actually been kissed before, and that one excuse gave her a valid reason to refuse. "I would not know what constituted a good kiss."

His eyes widened and he straightened. He gripped the back of the chair until his knuckles turned white. "Why is that?"

She glanced toward the fire, blushing furiously. "I've never."

"Not even one stolen kiss, Mattie?"

She pasted on a smile, wishing he would go to bed and leave her to undress herself. He would mock her. Harry had teased her about her inexperience too, and she'd still refused to oblige him. She had told him that kissing was personal and only something she should do with a husband. She had waited for Harry's return for that. "Never on the lips, so you should probably ask someone else for their opinion. I learned tonight that Lady Piper was very interested to discover if your skills in the bedchamber had waned."

"And she would tell everyone about it, especially if I fail to please." He moved to her side and held out his hand. "You would not embarrass me that way. I would like to try with you."

"Why now?"

"The conversations we have shared about our desires occupy my thoughts. They distract me. Consume me. If you have never been kissed, it explains so much of your reactions to me. Having never been tempted before, you would of course consider what I did to you last year very wicked and wrong." He swallowed. "You seem to have skipped several important experiences with intimacy. Understanding desire, the comfort and excitement of being touched, those should have been your first experience of passion, and I am sorry that you were not ready for me. But I can rectify your inexperience now if you would allow me the privilege of a kiss."

He slipped his hand under her chin and lifted her attention from the flames. He left her chin in his palm, studying her face. "If I'm to kiss anyone, it should be my wife."

He leaned down, and his lips brushed hers before she could talk him out of it. Matilda froze, uncertain of what to do. Having never been kissed before, it seemed a momentous occasion, except for the fact that her unwilling husband was experimenting on her mouth. He drew her to her feet and gently pressed their lips together.

The impact of the dry brush of his skin against hers, a soft kiss, was quite unlike anything she'd expected. There was a gentleness to William now that made her breath catch. The support of his hand around her face made her skin tingle with warm sensations.

"Part your lips," he ordered when they separated briefly.

His voice came out as a gruff command, and she knew that tone well. It was the same one he'd used before spanking her, and the tender moment changed instantly. She opened her mouth, and her husband's tongue brushed over her lips. She swallowed quickly, tasting him, then pushed her tongue forward to brush his.

A moan escaped her.

William caught her head by her hair, dragged her body flush against his, and plundered her mouth, brushing his tongue against hers. She squirmed under his passionate assault, pressed her hands against his chest for support. He growled but then gentled and drew back enough that kissing him wasn't so overwhelming. His tongue and lips worked against hers and she whimpered, not afraid but definitely uncomfortable with what they were doing. This was more than she'd ever bargained for as William's temporary wife. She felt herself utterly overwhelmed with feelings and sensations she couldn't begin to describe.

She clutched at his expensive waistcoat. The scarred part of his lips was just a little rough against hers, not unpleasant, but noticeable when she thought about it.

He lifted one of her arms to encircle his neck and drew her in closer as he continued to experiment with her mouth.

She held on to him firmly, feeling the muscles of his shoulders shift under her hands. He groaned and slipped his hands down to clutch her backside. He was warm and utterly, overwhelmingly male, something she'd been able to push to the back of her mind while he'd been ill. Now, though, his masculinity was shockingly obvious. He was clearly skilled at seduction and comfortable with desire. However, given their arrangement, he had no business kissing her like this. Actual intimacy was not part of their deal, and they both knew that.

She pushed against his chest, and he eased back even more. The kiss lightened, and his lips clung to hers as if he did not want to stop kissing her. She shivered as just the tip of his tongue lightly skimmed her lips in a fleeting brush, so gentle and so wicked that she grew flushed.

Matilda closed her eyes as he did it again, and that time she grew aware that her response was more than she was prepared for. She had become aroused by him.

Eventually he ceased kissing her, and she opened her eyes to a broad smile spreading over his face.

So that was kissing. That was what a kiss from William Ford felt like. Not quite the dry claiming she'd imagined a kiss could be, but something entirely more eloquent. Everything about William's nature had been in his kiss. He demanded, he took, unless she stopped him.

He swiped his thumb across her lips from one side to the other, and again that strange sensation between her legs returned. "Well?"

The man could be gentle, but he could also be cold. How could he turn on his emotions so quickly? Would he be so open with her tomorrow?

She put her hand to the base of her throat over the necklace he'd given her, uncertain how to answer him. She never knew from one moment to the next which side of him she would meet—the man who spoke of being her friend or the one who would punish her if she displeased him.

She chose her words with care. "As I said, I have nothing to compare your kiss to. You should kiss someone else next."

"I might, but would I enjoy it as much, my Mattie?"

She flinched hearing the name again. Her mother had called her that. It was the only thing she could remember about the woman who'd given birth to her. "Please kiss someone else next."

He studied her a long time, eyes dark and blazing with strong emotion. Matilda trembled with anticipation for his next decision. Had she displeased him enough to be punished, or would he allow her to maintain the distance between them? He'd promised not to take her virtue, so he should save his kisses for his real wife. He should kiss the woman he could give his heart to.

That wasn't going to be Matilda. He nodded, a sharp dip of his head. "I'll consider it."

He turned on his heel and left, slamming the dressing room door closed behind him. He did not lock it, but Matilda knew better than to follow him in. Trust and distance had become the currency of her life with William Ford.

That was why she'd felt safe enough to allow that one favor, because deep down she knew he would stop if she asked him to. But if she was stripped of her clothing and then climbed into bed with him afterward, she would have to contend with the change between them, and she wasn't sure what her response to him would be.

That feeling William had roused in her body last year, when he'd spanked her and touched her intimate places, had returned.

She turned toward the drawing room chaise, sank down onto it, and then curled over on her side, clutching William's discarded coat for a pillow. She ached between her legs, a sure sign she was not in her right mind around him.

She desired her husband to touch her there again.

She should not encourage that unless she was prepared for what might follow.

A little time apart was probably a good idea after kissing him. She could sleep here in the drawing room, so he was not tempted to make further advances. She had agreed to be his temporary wife, not his temporary lover. She shouldn't encourage more between them than an affair of short duration.

She rubbed her cheek against the rich fabric of his coat, more than a little disconcerted by her longing for William's touch. He was a pleasant husband, except when he was spanking her. And even those times were not quite the deterrent to comfort that they should have been. Any more kisses from him like that and she was sure she was asking for trouble. She was already in too deep as it was.

Marrying William had given her a great deal to think about. She could grow accustomed to the finer things in life, but she would eventually have to move away from London to where no one knew her past with him.

How she would live after their separation, live alone with only her own company, concerned her. She was often lonely in this house, but to her surprise she was never unhappy when William had his hands on her.

CHAPTER TWELVE

ANOTHER NIGHT, another round of appearances to cement the belief in his happy marriage, which it surely was not since they had spent last night apart. At dawn William had woken to find himself alone in their bed, and he'd been furious with himself ever since. That Matilda had spent the night in the drawing room with only his coat for a pillow had made him ashamed that his disappointment had gotten the best of him.

He'd carried her to their bed, tucked her in without waking her, and quietly left to remove the evidence of her temporary sleeping arrangement before a servant discovered they'd fought—if he could call his childish snit any sort of argument.

Matilda had slept for most of the day and kept her own company once she'd risen. William was still trying to decide whether he should apologize for the bad kiss or not, but he had accepted he wouldn't try to kiss her again anytime soon.

He didn't like the way she looked at him so warily now.

William escorted Matilda into the Hamersley ballroom, feeling just a little unsettled by the tension between them and the loud crowd. He held tight to Matilda's elbow as the noise of the ball washed over him, attempting to guide her through the throng. The walls seemed closer than usual, the colors and sounds brighter. Harsher. It was a crush, but he should be used to large gatherings. He'd enjoyed a very active social life during his shore leave and recognized many faces he knew well.

Lord Deacon appeared before him suddenly, almost out of thin air, grinning from ear to ear and laughing. "By the devil, if it isn't itty-bitty Billy Ford. How good to see you again."

That bloody nickname! Gods, he'd hated Deacon for that. He ground his teeth as he held out his hand, determined not to show his annoyance.

They shook hands, and Deacon stared at his face. "Damn, but that's a horrific scar."

"It is." He turned his face slightly to show it, and for the first time he was glad to address the worst of his alteration. Deacon might be a bull in a China shop when it came to diplomacy, but he was always honest. William's appearance caused everyone he met to pause, but few came right out and mentioned the change in his face. "But as a beautiful woman once insisted, *better disfigured than dead*. So here I am."

Matilda shuddered, and he patted her hand in an attempt to soothe her. Her remark as he'd lay dying had been the turning point. There were good reasons to fight for his life, one of them stood at his side.

"And that's a very good thing too. I would have missed you." Deacon clapped him hard on the shoulder, and then his gaze shifted to Matilda, brows rising in expectation. His expression conveyed his appreciation of his view—Matilda's quiet beauty never failed to turn heads, much to William's annoyance. "So this is the woman who tamed you? I had heard the rumors of the marriage but could not believe it until now. Introduce us, you oaf."

He unclenched his teeth. "Matilda, darling, this is Thomas

Bastrum, Earl of Deacon. We roughhoused as children on his estate and in Essex, but unfortunately, he hasn't grown up enough to learn some manners yet."

Deacon bowed deeply to Matilda. "Don't listen to a word he says. He's just jealous that now there's no question who's the better-looking gentleman of the pair of us."

William snorted. "He claimed that before the scar."

"Then he'd better hope not to meet anyone with as long a memory as mine." She smiled shyly and then leaned forward a little to add in a softer voice, "My husband's looks haven't changed that much to force him to second place to anyone."

William choked back his surprise at the praise while Deacon laughed. Damn it all! Matilda could say the most flattering things in public. Word was sure to spread of her admiration too, which would make the eventual news of their parting so much more shocking to a scandal-loving society.

It was all an act of course, flattery designed to encourage public belief in their happy marriage, but her remarks of indifference to his injury never failed to stroke his ego. His scar was hideous, his whole face twisted to one side, and he had noticed more than a few women become distressed at the sight. Not Matilda though. She barely paid it any attention and always looked him in the eye.

"I'd be honored if you'd grant me the pleasure of a dance, madam," Deacon asked of Matilda, his eyes glowing with good cheer and innocent friendship.

William nudged Matilda softly so she would accept. He'd talked to her about dancing with other men. Although she was nervous about putting a foot wrong and having her feet crushed time and again, he'd promised that he'd be watching so she'd never feel alone. Dancing with Deacon should pose no problem to her toes. He was a decent sort, and not one to overstep with a man's wife, and by all accounts he danced well.

"It would be a pleasure," she murmured. Matilda turned to him and smiled warmly. "Excuse me, darling. I will return soon."

"I'll be waiting." *And watching.*

He always watched her. He couldn't seem to stop. Since the first night he'd held her in his arms, he'd been unsettled whenever they were apart.

They left him to line up on the dance floor. Deacon was well over six feet, and next to Matilda he appeared a veritable giant. Matilda swirled her skirts a little as the musicians tuned their instruments. A cotillion began, and William moved closer, keen to watch how Matilda did with the dance. She fascinated him. She was very graceful, which had at first surprised him. When they had practiced at home, he had quickly come to the conclusion she might have taken lessons before entering service.

About her former life she was reluctant to speak. Anything he found out he'd had to pry out of her carefully.

Even with Deacon she was light on her feet, graceful and charming to watch. Her lithe movements made his heartbeat quicken.

They moved farther away, and although he'd prefer to follow, a new wave of guests arrived from the direction of the card room, and he was blocked.

Annoyed, he tried to push his way through to no avail. He was jostled, and the noise of hearty greetings rose around him. The stink of cigar smoke and alcohol filled his nose, and he fought a sudden wave of nausea.

He lost sight of Matilda and Deacon as his heart raced.

In fact, he couldn't see anyone he knew around him, and the idea that he was left behind, abandoned, rolled over him like a breaking wave in a high sea.

He broke out into a sweat as he gasped and mopped his brow with his handkerchief. A woman brayed like a horse right behind him, causing him to jump, but the hubbub kept rising until he could only hear the sound of his own desperate breathing and quickening heartbeat.

William dug his fingers under his cravat, desperately trying to gain some air, frantically trying to see where he was headed, determinedly trying to reach his Matilda again.

Although he tried to move forward to where he thought Matilda might be by now, he was utterly surrounded by a wall of strangers. A glass smashed to the floor, a man shouted, and William gasped out loud. Panicked. Afraid.

He saw an opening in the crowd and shoved his way through it, not stopping until he reached the empty terrace and the fresh night air beyond. But even out here, there were hidden dangers. He heard whispers and moans from the darkness. There was no escape from people with prying eyes, lurking in the shadows with their lovers.

He dragged in huge breaths as his pulse raced. He needed...

From within the ballroom, noise continued to drown out all thought he might have had of going back inside. He stumbled into the darkness, desperate for a moment alone. He didn't want to be seen like this. He reached the shelter of a low stone wall and rested against it as his ears began to ring and a second, hotter fever broke out all over his body. He stood again and managed to walk away, allowing the cooler night air to slide across his face.

He ran.

Running for safety.

William clutched his head, covered his ears, overwhelmed by sounds that had no right to be heard in this place or time. Weapons clashed, pistols boomed as if he was in the midst of battle, commanding a ship of doomed men with no hope of winning the day. Just as in his nightmares.

He kept moving as the onslaught continued. He ran for his life, fleeing before the pain began again.

He burst out of a gateway but couldn't break free of the memories. The stink of battle enveloped him, and he ran until a wall stopped him. He clutched at the brickwork, then sank to his knees, covered his head, and prayed for death to take him quickly this time.

CHAPTER THIRTEEN

MATILDA SHOOK WILLIAM. She shook him harder than she ever should and tried to lift his face from his bent knees. She was so afraid. It wasn't natural for a grown man to be huddled against a crumbling wall like this, cowering and muttering to himself. He made no sense.

"Billy. Billy. What has happened to you?"

He sucked in a shuddering breath suddenly and blinked up at her. His eyes narrowed. "I've told you not to use that name."

Matilda dragged him into her embrace. "I've been calling your name for so long. Why didn't you answer me?"

He put his arms around her and squeezed her. Then he shifted to lean against the wall. He glanced around, blinking at his surroundings in the weak moonlight. "I don't know."

"Is he all right now, Mrs. Ford?" Lord Deacon whispered with a nervous glance for their surroundings. "Is there anything more I can do to help?"

Matilda was grateful Deacon wasn't the sort to draw attention to them right now. She didn't want anyone to see William like this.

She did not know how to explain his behavior. She stood and faced the man. "No, I think we'll be fine now."

Deacon checked the lane and then came back. "Are you sure?"

William clutched her gown and tugged.

"Thank you for all you've done, but I can manage him now." She kneeled down and pressed her hand to William's brow. She discovered him warm but not fevered. He caught her fingers and held them lightly in his but said nothing more. "Would you mind leaving us and returning to the ball, my lord? We will rejoin the party shortly."

Deacon glanced around, eyeing the shabby surroundings with distaste. "I'm not sure I should leave you both out here. We are very far from the ball. It could be dangerous."

Matilda had grown up in such a place. For now they were perfectly safe. She could hear nothing but the occasional rat or mouse shuffling through the straw to the left.

"I remember the path back." The last thing William would want was a fuss or for a friend to see him so unlike his usual self. "Everything will be fine now. We will be along in a little while. I promise. Please."

William clutched Matilda's wrist as soon as Deacon left them. "I'm sorry."

Matilda crouched down at his side and cupped his face, drawing his gaze up to hers. He seemed so bewildered that her heart was moved. "It is all right, I'm just glad I found you. Lord Deacon saw you go and stayed with me until we discovered you hiding here."

"He's a good friend." William's fingers slipped slowly from her skin. "I hate to imagine what he thinks of this."

"Don't worry about Deacon." She listened to his breathing, which thankfully had slowed down quite a bit since she'd roused him. "I'm just glad you came to no harm out here in the dark."

William studied the darkness around them. "Where are we?"

"I'm not entirely sure. You fled the ballroom and the garden too and traveled a distance along the rear lane. We are outside someone's abandoned stables."

He stood quickly, mopping his brow with a snowy white handkerchief. Matilda stood too so she could brush his hair back from his face. His skin was damp, as if he'd been running for hours. Quite frankly, she was baffled by his behavior tonight. She had thought nothing but the idea of making a match with Miss Chudleigh had ever bothered him.

He held out his hand. Matilda placed her wrist across his palm, smiling as his fingers folded around her limb. His fingers drummed over her pulse a moment, then tightened.

"We should go before we are seen," he said softly.

The discomfort in his voice stilled her tongue from asking any more questions about his flight from the ball for the time being.

"Of course." Matilda brushed at her skirts feebly and then tugged him along. If she was dusty from the straw-lined floor, then hopefully by the time they returned to the ball it would have fallen away. "Perhaps a slow stroll back to the ball to cool you down."

He adjusted his grip and squeezed. "I am sorry I broke my promise. I left you alone with Deacon at the ball."

Matilda threaded her fingers with his and squeezed. She couldn't quite believe he was apologizing for leaving her. If not for Deacon's greater height, she wouldn't have found William at all until he returned on his own. She had once imagined how awful being abandoned among the *ton* would have been. Seeing William whimper had been ten times worse. "I did not mind. He had nothing but good to say about you, I assure you."

A bitter grunt left his mouth. "He always did have a way of buttering up the ladies."

"You are two of a kind." She smiled warmly, determined to set him at ease. In the weeks he'd been her husband, she had discovered William Ford had qualities she'd not expected. He was kind, thoughtful—bossy every other moment though. She occasionally wanted to laugh at his dry humor and self-deprecating comments. "I recognized him as soon as I saw him tonight, so I wasn't worried. He used to call at the town house and was a great source of amusement for your sisters, but he acts like he doesn't remember meeting me. He has a kind heart, and it shows."

William wrapped her arm about his. "He's not the type to embarrass anyone."

"Well, even so I will be on my best behavior around the earl." She glanced at her husband, more than a little worried about him. "You have more to lose after the separation than I do. Ah, here we are. We are back at the ball already."

She stepped up to the open gate and glanced ahead, scanning the path for other people. The gardens were thankfully very quiet. The Hamersley's guests must be inside, still soaking up champagne and making merry in the house. Anyone who saw them would think they'd come outside for peace and a quiet stroll together.

"Your reputation means as much to me," he said as she passed him.

Matilda locked the gate. "But these are not my friends. When it ends and we part ways, they will sympathize with you and hate me. I can live with that. I don't think you should have to."

His gaze was direct. "I don't think I would like that outcome for you."

As they made their way through the garden, William slipped his arm behind her back. She leaned into him, wondering what had happened to him earlier that he could have acted so afraid. William did not like her to pry, but it had been obvious he was beset by a spell of some description. She'd been calling his name in that dusty stable for several minutes before resorting to using *Billy* just to break through to him.

She stopped him and then quickly inspected his appearance. There was straw sticking to the tails of his coat, so she quickly flicked the pieces away with her hand.

"Are you attempting to punish me?"

"No. I leave that sort of thing entirely to you." The flippant remark sparked an unexpected twinge. So far, they had not returned to the subject of spanking. But to bring it up now wasn't the best time for her nerves. She shrugged and brushed his shoulders one more time. "There now. Perfectly handsome once more."

He looked toward the ballroom and tensed. "I need to go home," he whispered.

Matilda nodded, thinking that a very good idea. "I'll speak with your aunt and claim my headache takes us away. I'm sure she can manage your sisters for the remaining hours without us as chaperones."

"Thank you."

They returned to the ballroom, William's grip on her arm tight. She said their good-byes, explained she wasn't feeling well, and hurried William out to await their carriage in the hall. On the way through the crowd, she noticed his eyes grew wild whenever the press of bodies around them drew too close.

Once they were inside the comforting darkness of their borrowed carriage, William dropped his head onto her shoulder. His arm slipped around her body, and he dragged her close, almost into his lap. She froze, uncertain of what William was about. He had not held her since the early days of his recovery, and then only when he had been asleep or when he was very restless. It was as if he needed someone to hold him to the earth.

He still seemed not himself, so Matilda allowed him to remain close, stroking his arm in a manner she hoped soothed him. His breathing settled during the journey, and by the time they drew up before the town house, he was still quiet but calm once more.

Once at home, she spoke for him, wished the butler good night, and requested Dawson come up to attend William in his bedchamber. His mood remained subdued, and he made no further advances toward her.

Matilda turned back his bedding and patted the mattress. "Come and sit. Mr. Dawson will be here in a moment and will help you ready for bed."

William sat on the edge of the bed in silence, appearing lost in thought, quite unlike the confident man she'd come to expect when they were alone. He was hurting, and she didn't know what to do about it.

When Dawson arrived, she wished them both a good night, then retreated to the dressing room. She struggled out of her gown unaided, then pulled her nightgown on. She left her hair unbound, which William seemed to prefer, and waited. When the valet finally left William, she hurried back in, finding her husband exactly where she'd left him but without his shirt, waistcoat, and coat. His feet were bare, though he still wore his black silk breeches.

Her pulse raced a little too fast at the state of his undress and she swallowed. She was rooted to the spot by his body and his vulnerability. "Are you going to sit there all night?"

He took a deep breath. "I considered it."

Matilda shook off her apprehension and moved toward him. "Sleep will help."

"Sleep is another nightmare."

"Nightmare?" She set her hand to his shoulder and then his brow to test him for fever. "I don't understand."

"I dream, Mattie. Even during the day." A shudder wracked him. "I'd rather be awake than remember the past."

"You dream of the war?"

His nod was brisk. "Every death I dealt, every wound I inflicted. Only it is worse than when it actually happened. I'm..."

He almost said more, but he turned away as if he couldn't face her.

Matilda's heart skipped a beat. She had no understanding of the violence of war, but clearly William could not bear it. It was months now since his participation had ended. He never spoke of his past. She had imagined he'd not cared to dwell on it.

Matilda set her hand to his shoulder, then glided her fingers softly over bare, heated skin. Touching him seemed too intimate, but he'd always responded well to her caresses during his convalescence. "I had no idea. Lie down now."

William folded to the mattress slowly. "Will you stay in my arms tonight?"

She bit her lip. Once since their marriage he had managed to wrap around her without waking her from sleep. Was that all he wanted?

He moved backward, sliding under the sheets, tucking his pillow under his head, leaving a wide space for Matilda to fill. His eyes never left her face. He held out one hand, reaching for her.

Matilda considered his request and then nodded. He was mostly dressed; Matilda was completely covered by her nightgown. She moved to blow out the candle. They were husband and wife, and he needed her.

She climbed into his bed, rather breathless at her boldness as she pressed her back against William's chest. He covered her up with the bedding, then wrapped his arms about her tightly. "Thank you."

The warmth and strength of his embrace caused her heart to flutter, as did the way he kissed her hair. "You're welcome."

After a time his breathing slowed, and his grip softened. She rolled a little away from him, but his grip firmed, preventing her leaving him. He made a sound that reminded her of his desperate pleas during his recovery when he could not speak.

Matilda wriggled to get comfortable and closed her eyes, fighting back tears. Had he suffered the nightmares even then and not been able to convey what truly troubled him?

She pressed her hands lightly over his arms, listening to him fall deeper into sleep, hoping he would not dream again.

Tomorrow would be soon enough to discover if there was any way she could help him avoid further nightmares or lessen the horror of them. He'd been so brave, stoic, hiding his troubled thoughts from her for months. The least Matilda could do was support him when he needed her most.

CHAPTER FOURTEEN

KEEPING a promise had never been harder. For weeks he'd escorted his wife around London—shopping, amusements, attending balls, dining with friends while his sisters searched for a husband, and acting utterly smitten.

Which he might very well be.

Matilda had thrown herself into the role of wife with great enthusiasm. Her retiring nature had evolved into a confidence he felt decidedly proud of. But there was one problem with his scheme. He hated every moment of the lie, especially when Matilda was the center of attention from other men.

She didn't want him, and although she did not appear to want anyone else, his palms itched every time she smiled at gentlemen, and there was to be no relief for that. He'd promised not to harm her in any way, even though she tempted him, even though she was, in all respects bar the bedroom, his loving wife.

She had grown accustomed to sleeping in his arms, at least for part of the night, and he was grateful. For the past weeks his nightmares had receded, and she respected his wish not to discuss them again. When his nightmares did return, he would cuddle up close against her until the panic faded and lie beside her until morning came.

While he listened to her even breaths at night, he considered a future that might keep her in his life. During the weeks of their marriage, he'd grown accustomed to her presence. Of taking care of her and seeing that she had everything she could need to be happy. He interrupted her conversation to pass her a glass of sherry. "For you, my dear."

"Thank you, William," she murmured with a shy smile. However, she quickly returned to her conversation with his excitable sisters, leaving him to his guests.

Polite wasn't enough for him. They did not have a true marriage.

And that lack of connection was slowly eroding his calm.

He shook his head and returned to his friends. "Where is Mr. Nelson this season?"

Cobb and James Mitchell smiled broadly. "He wrote to say he found a distraction in Wales during the winter and will stay for the summer too."

Not surprising. His friends were a lusty lot with a broad taste for amorous adventures. "Another bored married woman?"

Mitchell laughed softly. "Is there any other sort of distraction to chase after?"

"None that I know of." William smiled and then quickly expanded that remark. "However, that was before I married."

"Poor bastard," James Mitchell remarked and then toasted William's wife. "It must be such a hardship being married to that gorgeous woman."

"Oh, it is," he said, laughing as he was expected to do but secretly agreeing that marriage to Matilda was difficult for a man of his inclinations. He was a scarred war hero with a beautiful wife he couldn't touch, without means for any sort of relief in the near future. It was more frustrating than not being able to speak. Even more frustrating than knowing he couldn't kiss her again.

The fact that this sham marriage had sprung from his idea didn't mean he had to like it. As much as he tried to be satisfied with only her friendship, he couldn't control her the way he needed to. The way he wanted to bend her to his will would probably frighten her. He'd fooled himself that he could suppress his instincts when all he wanted to do was drag her off somewhere private to make her cry out in both pain and pleasure.

Cobb sidled closer when Mitchell drew away. "I thought to meet you at Fowlers last night."

William glanced around discreetly before answering Cobb. Matilda still had no idea he was a client of a discreet brothel, a place that provided willing women for patrons to scold. "I've no desire to go."

Even though he had permission to kiss other women, he couldn't do it. The idea twisted his stomach into knots of distress. What if other women were not as kind as Matilda when he kissed them? What if they laughed at him or were utterly revolted by his scar?

Mitchell returned, smirking as he pushed between William and Cobb. "She distracts you again. However did you get the lovely lady to marry you when all you can do is scowl at her?"

"There was no other choice once I got to know her." He rattled off his well-rehearsed story of falling in love with the woman who'd saved his life to his friend and waited to see if he was believed.

"I see," Mitchell said, frowning. "It's just you usually chase a certain type of woman. Is she agreeable to that?"

Damn, but even Mitchell knew which disappointments to dig his fingers into. "No."

"That must be frustrating," Cobb remarked dryly. "You should indulge at Fowlers."

"I cannot consider it." That part of his life had to be held in check until he was free of this marriage. He owed Matilda his constancy at the very least since the end of their marriage would tarnish her reputation.

He did not care to think of that future at times.

A strange smile turned up the corners of Cobb's mouth, and he leaned close. "Surely there is a way to bring her around if you possess enough rope."

He bristled. "Have a care for your remarks, Cobb. That is my wife you speak of."

"Apologies." Cobb grinned. "I forgot your tender heart prefers silk bindings on your women rather than rope."

"Stow it," William warned.

Matilda approached, and Cobb thankfully stopped needling him. "Mrs. Alderman is feeling unwell and was hoping you might escort her to her door, Mr. Mitchell."

Mitchell's eyes glittered with amusement and eagerness both. He and the lady were neighbors and had a standing weekly rendezvous. Tonight must be the night, William assumed.

"Of course." Mitchell took his leave, heading toward Mrs. Alderman and offering his arm solicitously as if she were truly unwell. The pair were well versed in their charade of congenial friendship. He would do well to learn from them and mimic their disinterest around others.

Cobb bowed. "Perhaps I will see you at the club soon, Captain."

"Unlikely," William replied tightly, frowning after his friend.

Matilda remained at his side, and after their remaining guests had departed, she faced him. "I did not know you were a member of a gentleman's club."

William raised his eyes to the heavens. "I'm not."

"Then what place was Cobb talking about?"

Damn, but he didn't want to begin lying to Matilda now. She already knew the dark path his lust took him. If he told her about Fowler's brothel, he could be guaranteed she'd never make the mistake of believing he could be changed as so many wives thought of their spouses. "A brothel. He was talking about attending a brothel I used to frequent."

She gasped out loud. "But why would you of all people need to buy a woman's affections?"

William took Matilda by the wrist and led her to the brandy and sherry table, far away from the door. He didn't want to shout out his depravity for all the staff to hear. He had to tell her himself. He wanted to be the one to explain his nature since he had a feeling Cobb wasn't going to let the matter drop.

He stared at the liquor before him rather than Matilda. "There are not many women among my acquaintances in the *ton* who wish to be disciplined. Many ladies require financial incentives to assume a subservient position. It is easier to pay for the pleasure than run the risk of a failed affair being gossiped about and me being labeled a monster for my tastes."

Matilda's hand fluttered to her neck. "Is that where you went before we married? To a brothel to spank strange women?"

Her question reflected her horror and he winced. "I went but did not. I could not because of you."

It was utterly humiliating that Matilda had his pleasure wrapped around her finger. She had always drawn his attention, but now that he was married to the woman, he was fixated. Becoming obsessed.

"Me?" she whispered in shock. "How recently did you go?"

"The night before we married," he admitted. "I hoped to calm myself."

"Captain." Her breath shuddered out. "I don't know what to say."

"The problem is mine. You've done nothing wrong." She never had, and yet he could only think of her. Want her. Matilda lived in comfort and had every luxury he could offer her, and yet she still did not want him.

Not the way he had grown to crave her.

It was utterly baffling how the idea of marriage to Matilda, of prolonging their arrangement, scared him far less than embarking on an affair with anyone else to satisfy his urges. He'd only had to lay eyes on another lady before his heart had started to race with the overwhelming urge to flee.

He'd never felt the need to marry anyone before.

He had done everything in his power to avoid the institution since he'd reached his majority. However, he'd always wished for companionship that could sate his desire to dominate. "No one else has affected me the way you do. You are extraordinary, and you don't even know it."

He was proud of her mettle and commitment to his bargain. She had managed to convince everyone they met that their marriage was satisfying, offering a shy remark on her good fortune that was entirely believable to others. He'd heard her praise with his own ears. Apparently, he was a generous and kind husband, and he was glad she said so even if it was a lie.

He shook his head. "Would you care for another sherry, my dear?"

"I'd like that very much," Matilda whispered.

William poured half a glass and handed it over. She sipped slowly, a frown between her brows. William downed a brandy and then another. There was no point dwelling on what could not be altered. "Did you enjoy your evening?"

"Not exactly," she whispered. A blush grew over Matilda's cheeks as the butler cleared his throat at the door.

"Is there anything else you require, Captain?"

"Nothing. Goodnight, Carter."

When they were alone, he leaned close. "What is wrong, Matilda? No, don't answer me here. Come to bed and tell me there."

He held his tongue until they were upstairs in the privacy of their chambers. He closed the doors on the dressing room and bedchamber. "Now tell me."

Matilda winced. "I don't understand why so many believe a newly married woman would want to share intimate details of her private life."

"You are very lovely, Matilda, but you are an unknown. They are testing your character to see what sort of marriage this is."

She wrapped her arms about her chest. "It is none of their business. None but ours."

"They likely do not agree. Even my own friends, friends who know my nature, ask impertinent questions. You are much more alluring than you can possibly understand."

"I'm nothing special."

"You are everything." He tipped his head to the side, trying to see her as others might. Glossy dark hair, simple but elegant gowns, but her eyes were without guile as they held his stare. "If we had just met at a dinner at a friend's house, I would attempt to lure you to the gardens and have my wicked way with you. Any man would, but I probably shouldn't have confessed that. You might yet throw me over for someone else."

"William," she whispered in a shocked voice.

"Are you surprised that I desire you? I am a normal man with an unfortunate fondness for punishment. I had not foreseen how much of a temptation you could be." He shrugged. Why not ask for what he wanted? Why not be direct and see if she wanted to know him better too? "I know you did not enjoy being kissed by me, but there are other intimacies that could satisfy us both."

Her hand rose to her neck to cover the necklace he'd given her on the day they began pretending to be husband and wife. Since then, he'd noticed she clung to the piece when in distress. She always chose that necklace if he did not decide on another for her to wear. "I never said I did not enjoy being kissed," she whispered.

William took a pace toward her as her eyes dropped demurely. Had he misread her? "You did not say you liked it either."

"Please. Not so loud."

Emboldened, he captured her wrist, and a soft moan escaped her. "Were you repulsed by the scar?"

She shook her head. "I could feel it at first and then I didn't notice it."

"Why did you not tell me that when I asked?" He pinned her to the nearest wall, caging her with his arms. Her gaze rose to his chest and then lifted to reveal her confusion. His pulse took flight as her pupils dilated. He eased back a little but did not retreat.

"I am not used to speaking of such things." She bit her lip. "I am often so overwhelmed by you that I don't even know what I want or how to behave."

"I only want you to be yourself." He brushed her cheek with the back of his fingers. "There is no right and wrong when it comes to pleasure between us."

Her fingers dug into his chest, holding on to him rather than pushing him away.

"Should I whisper my desires?" He pressed his body against hers. "I want to touch you, Matilda. I want to hear you cry out in pleasure tonight."

She whimpered but did not seek to leave his arms.

Encouraged, William brought his mouth to hers and kissed her gently. Her lips moved against his, hesitant at first, and then she lifted her arms and twined them about his neck.

He broke the kiss and stared down at her. "Give me tonight. Let me make love to you."

She gasped. "Our bargain?"

Of course. For a moment he'd become swept away, blinded by desire and Matilda's response. "I will keep to our bargain, and you will keep your innocence. I promise. Say you want me to touch you."

She remained silent, drawing out the moment between them until it became clear she wouldn't agree. As he straightened, intending to draw away from her and the temptation she presented, her fingers twitched on his shirt.

A chaste marriage it was to be, with the occasional discipline.

He nodded and turned away, intending to sleep elsewhere that night.

"Yes, William," she agreed suddenly. "I would like you to touch me as you did that first time."

He turned, utterly surprised he had her permission at last. A fiery blush of color consumed her face, and she seemed not to know how to stand still.

He returned to her, brought both hands up, and cupped her hot face. "Sweet Matilda," he whispered. "You don't know what you do to me."

A strange sound escaped her. "I think I might."

He stared into her eyes as her pupils grew rounder, her breath rushed. "I want to take you over my knee right now," he whispered.

Her breath caught, undeniable excitement filling her eyes.

He nodded, sensing victory, swept up in the anticipation of pleasuring his wife at last. "But perhaps a few more kisses first?"

He captured her wrist and drew her toward a sturdy chair, and when he sat, he pulled her down onto his lap. She balanced with her feet dangling an inch from the floor and a wild expression in her eyes. He caressed her face and then brought her lips to his to taste her again.

He kissed her slowly, thoroughly, until his face ached with the strain. He caressed her waist and held her trembling body still within his grip.

And then when he could wait no longer, when Matilda had begun to squirm in earnest and moan softly at the sweep of his tongue into her mouth, he gently rolled her until she lay prone across his spread thighs, her hip resting against his erection. "Hands touching the floor," he asked of her.

He took a breath to center himself, to master his desire and devote his energies into her pleasures. He had waited so long for this moment and would not ruin it with undue haste.

He placed one hand at the small of her back, the other on her ankle, and firmly caressed her leg. As he touched her, he moved her gown higher up her limbs until her stockings were exposed; he listened to her rushed breathing and felt the tension rise between them.

He teased the crease of her knee and then her inner thighs. She parted her legs a little, a nervous flinch rather than an invitation, and her head dropped to hang between her outstretched arms.

When he at last pulled her gown beyond her bottom, he was panting and aching too. In all the times he'd been with other women, he'd never felt like this—in control and utterly trusted. He adjusted himself and then slipped the buttons at the fall of his trousers undone enough to ease the pressure.

Her buttocks clenched as he caressed the firm globes of her bottom, and when she relaxed, he tapped her, a sweet and sharp strike that made his fingertips tingle. Matilda gasped as expected, a delightful sound that tested his resolve to make tonight a sweet memory for them both.

He brushed his hand over the reddened globe that filled his hand and then squeezed. His wife. She wanted him to punish her and had unwittingly given him a reason earlier. "Three more for not using my name."

He struck her, smoothed her skin, and then struck again but harder.

A dark moan left Matilda's mouth.

"You like that."

She shook as she nodded. "Yes, William."

William struck her again, hard enough to rock her forward, which was why he'd asked for her hands to be outstretched. He exhaled loudly, his urge to punish satisfied for now, but Matilda required more than pain. And he wanted to please her so badly.

Even though the punishment was over, Matilda remained still, ready for more across his legs. William admired her body, resting one hand possessively on her tender rump. "Sweet Matilda," he whispered.

He slid his fingers between her legs. She was damp with arousal and sensitive enough that she squirmed against his fingers. He stroked her clitoris lightly. "Does that feel nice?"

"Oh," Matilda cried out and lifted her head. "Yes."

He leaned over her. "What more can I do for you? Tell me."

"More of the same," she said, her voice tremulous.

"Ask for what you want." He slapped her left cheek. "More punishment?"

"Yes," she choked out.

She bowed her head as he swirled his fingers over her clitoris again.

"More pleasure?"

"Yes." She gasped as he slapped her right cheek. "Please."

"Pleasure and pain require two hands," he whispered.

"Yes, William." She was silent a moment, then added, "Please touch me the way you did before."

Success.

He employed his left to spank in an inconstant rhythm and his right to toy with her sex. Matilda relished the attention and soon was puffing and gasping out loud. She dangled over his lap but moved restlessly against his fingers in a way that had nothing to do with the beat of his hand against her skin and everything to do with heightened desire. He brought her to her peak swiftly and rejoiced in her strangled cries of ecstasy. When she quieted, he leaned back in his chair and buttoned his fall, wincing at the renewed confinement but satisfied as never before.

He brought her up to hold her in his arms on his lap. She hissed a little as her bottom pressed against his thigh, but the sound was music to his ears.

He set one hand lightly over her bottom and held her close against his chest with his other arm. "Thank you."

"For what?"

He turned his lips to her brow, noting the high heat of her skin. In his previous encounters with other women, he'd never encountered such an honest response to his lovemaking. There had been no affection after, or so little he'd not remembered feeling so possessive. "For letting me take care of you like that."

She turned her face into his shoulder and gripped his shirt tightly. Embarrassed, he thought, by the simple act of giving in to desire.

He should have held her after the first time he'd spanked her, and he cuddled her closer against him now so she would feel safe. He should have shown her how much the moment had meant to him instead of allowing her to run away to hide from what he'd started.

While she caught her breath, he unbuttoned her garments, let down her hair so he could run his fingers through the soft strands. When his erection had subsided enough to pass unnoticed, he stood, placed her gently to her feet, and let her outer garments fall to the floor. The strength of her body, the beauty of her curves, never failed to move him. Her body was his to touch now, to caress, to bring pleasure and pain to.

He was wealthy beyond words.

And happy.

He undressed her, then put her in a prim nightgown and lifted her up into his arms. He carried her to their bed and tucked her in. "Sweet dreams, Matilda."

He took a pace back.

"Where are you going?"

To bring himself off with his own hand so he wouldn't embarrass her with an intimacy she wasn't ready for. "I have something to take care of in my study. Go to sleep, and we'll talk in the morning."

CHAPTER FIFTEEN

DAWSON HELD up two waistcoats—one bright and the other dark. "Captain?"

"The bright one," William decided. It suited his optimistic mood.

He cast a glance at the closed door to his bedchamber. He'd given Matilda time alone that morning to recover from their interlude last night. Her bottom was sure to be tender. "Is my wife awake?"

"She rang the bell for breakfast an hour ago," Dawson announced in a tone that hinted disapproval. Dawson had been odd since William's marriage. "She asked what I knew of Lloyd's demise before your dinner guests arrived last night."

He moved close to the valet, studying him. "What did you tell her?"

"Nothing, as you insisted." Dawson scowled. "But do not forget she is clever. She will figure it out or..."

"Lloyd might seek her out." He frowned at that idea. "His return will place her happiness at risk."

"Perhaps she should know what kind of man he was and what

happened to the last woman he planned to marry." Dawson flushed a dull red. "Lying to protect her isn't much better than the reason you married her."

"How did you...?" He squinted at the man hard. "You had your ear to the door."

Dawson shook his head. "I thought she was going to resign. Imagine my shock at your dishonorable suggestion that she pretend to be your lover. Can you blame me for worrying for her state of mind and what happens to her when it's over?"

"No." William grimaced. "That's why I married her."

Dawson scoffed. "You only married because the duke made you do it."

William scowled at his valet, a man who'd been at his side through thick and thin, who acted as his conscience occasionally. He was annoyed with him until he registered what the man had said to justify his eavesdropping. "Why did you think Matilda was going to resign?"

"Someone had salted her tea that morning. It's not the only problem she's had with the other female staff I've since learned. They were making her situation unbearable. She was waiting for Harry Lloyd to marry her. To save her. She got dragged into your scheme instead."

William swore.

"She doesn't deserve to have her reputation dragged through the mud."

"Trust me. This arrangement benefits her, and I will make sure she is never troubled again." He had no doubt about that, but he wished he'd known the extent of her problems here. He had already set aside the funds she required and had inspected a resi-dence, a neat and vacant town house a few blocks away, that should suit her very well. It was in a good part of town, close to the park and with decent neighbors. She would be very comfortable there, and he could also keep a discreet eye on her future affairs.

"How could divorcing or having the marriage annulled be desirable? You know that she will be labeled by society. That sort of scandal will never go away."

William hated being questioned. He pinched the bridge of his nose to rein in his temper. "You will trust me on this. I know what I'm doing."

"You had better hope so." Dawson's expression grew mulish. "After all she did to save you, it had better have been worth her while."

"It will be." William turned away. Dawson obviously felt protective of Matilda, and he approved of that to a degree. He had once suspected that Dawson had romantic feelings for Matilda. That he hadn't acted upon them, not even to kiss her, spoke of a very platonic friendship.

His Matilda was never free with her affections. She might have considered marriage to Harry Lloyd, but she was as pure as the driven snow if his was the first kiss she'd ever received.

He did not overlook the importance of that discovery.

He was willing to overlook Dawson's impertinence because he was feeling so optimistic about life with Matilda.

Their tryst last night had given him hope that one day she might think of him warmly. However, he could not depend on that continuing. It was not often a lover of his enjoyed being spanked as frequently as he might wish to discipline them. He and Matilda had made a bargain that had suited them both then. Now, though, he was not certain he wanted to be rid of his wife.

He had never expected that complication.

There were many advantages to being married. Pleasure could be found at home if she remained willing, conversation was available when he liked and for as long as he liked just for a start. And even with the restrictions of their arrangement, the lack of physical release on his part, Matilda had made the experience of marriage not too painful.

And then there was Matilda herself. He no longer needed to make a mess for her to clean up as an excuse to see her whenever he wanted to. She was right there, beyond that door.

When he finished dressing, he sent Dawson away. Sex with Matilda was obviously out of the question, though he dreamed of being inside her one day. He shook his head. Best not to think too far beyond the present moment. Discipline and control were what he craved most and what Matilda allowed. More? He would be patient and let her behavior guide him.

He took a breath, caught the cold brass handle of the bedroom door, and then let himself inside. Matilda was sitting on the side of the bed, a faraway look in her eyes.

"Good morning, wife."

"Husband," she said, but her expression remained troubled.

"I trust you slept well."

She nodded slowly enough that he was concerned. He crossed the room, cupped her face, and pressed a gentle kiss to her lips. "I couldn't sleep and got up very early today. I watched the sun rise over London for the first time since my recovery. I hope I did not wake you when I left our bed."

"You didn't." Her shoulders sagged a little. "I had wondered where you had gone. I don't remember your coming to bed. I thought perhaps you had gone out to that place."

"Never," he assured her before he brushed his fingers across her warm cheeks. He didn't want anyone else while he had Matilda. She must not realize how fixed his attentions had become. "Whenever I have gone there, it is to discipline, and you had already allowed me that. I had everything I needed last night with you."

Her frown lifted and a hesitant smile turned up the corners of her beautiful lips. "I was not sure if I should dress myself or wait."

"I'm here now to do that." He caressed her neck and enjoyed the view down her nightgown. Her breasts jiggled as she moved, and her nipples hardened to points as he caressed her. He began to silently count backward from one hundred in an effort to curb his arousal. "I am on my way out shortly, and I hoped you might wish to accompany me."

Her frown returned. "Where are you going?"

"I have a meeting with my man of business at ten in his offices, and then I have a second meeting in Mayfair to look at a house at one o'clock. In between, I thought you might like to do some shopping or perhaps visit my sisters for luncheon."

She groaned. "More shopping? Captain, you have already spent too much on me."

"That's one." He drew closer to her, warming to the idea of spanking her again and then spoiling her afterward. Something light in a pale shade of pink to accent her blushes would be just the thing. "If you believe that, then you will be surprised to learn I have not spent a tenth on you yet that is not already spent on my youngest sister for her come-out next year."

Her eyes widened. "Surely not."

He nodded. "I have seen the bills of sale for Evelyn, and it is far larger than your upkeep. Besides, is it not my privilege to pay your expenses for the next two years as part of our arrangement?"

"I suppose. But I already have more gowns than I can possibly wear."

"Nonsense." He glanced around. "We shall see what else I think you need today."

Matilda leaned back from him, resting one hand on the bed so that her nightgown slid down, exposing her shoulder. "You are disturbingly opinionated about my wardrobe."

"I am." He liked knowing she wore what he chose, but that bold pose was causing him to thicken in his trousers beyond his ability to stop it. He would be counting all day at this rate. "That will not change. Matilda, you should understand your husband. I do have strong opinions about how a lady should look. I don't agree that her assets"—he glanced down at her bustline—"should be on show for just anyone to admire. I prefer modesty in a woman's attire in public. We may not be married for life, but I intend to protect you from any unwanted attention. Even my own."

She smiled a little and gave a halfhearted laugh. Her gaze flickered downward, and then her eyes widened. She swallowed as she stared at his hips, or rather the bulge of his erection growing beyond his control between them. Her lips parted a little, and there wasn't chance he could restrain his arousal when she stared at him like that.

"Matilda, look at my face."

She glanced up quickly, though her eyes were wide. She licked her lips, swallowed, and then darted another look at his arousal. She sat up, and his breath caught as she drew near. What would she do? Ignore his condition or explore him?

He hoped the former since they had appointments to keep.

"So you sent those three gowns back to the modiste because they were immodest?" She clenched her hands in her lap and looked up into his eyes. "Evelyn was very enthusiastic about the design and colors."

"Far too revealing. You must remember that a gentleman of greater height than you could have been granted a most extraordinary view of your cleavage that he would not have deserved." He took in that same view but kept his hands back. Now was not the moment for indulgence, but he had always enjoyed the anticipation of touching the things he craved.

Matilda's gaze flickered from his face and back to his arousal. "I liked how I looked in those gowns."

His cock twitched. "So did I, which is why they went back." He stroked his fingers over the exposed skin of her leg. "Far too tempting, like you appear now."

Matilda glanced up at him, eyes wide, and then glanced down at her bare legs where he touched her. For a change she did not seek to cover herself. Her legs were slightly parted, revealing the softness of her inner thighs.

"I should get dressed," she whispered.

"Indeed, but first a kiss to start the day, just to make sure I have this right." He cupped her face and kissed her softly, moving his lips over hers in a gentle possession.

Matilda kissed him back after a moment. She was shy, very hesitant to touch him, so he ended the kiss with no regrets. But he was painfully aroused, as he had been last night by the time he'd left her in bed. Kissing Matilda made him long for more. For permanence, passion, and punishment as a regular part of his life. But he wanted a willing partner who knew all his vices. Someone who would enjoy those private moments, anticipate the next ones as much as he would.

Someone willing to be tied up, masked, and disciplined properly with an array of implements before being pleasured all night long.

He drew Matilda to her feet and without further discussion dressed her in a modest gown of sky blue even though he ached to run his hands along her arms and bind her with silk strips. He clenched his hands, forcing them to his sides. "Reticule, hat, gloves."

Matilda spun around at his tone. "William, what have I done wrong?"

"Nothing at all. The fault is mine." He went too fast, as usual.

He took a deep breath and forced a smile. "I'll be below in the little parlor. Do not make me wait long."

He turned away quickly and hurried from her presence. He wanted Matilda to want him as he did her. He though he wanted her to stay beyond the time of their bargain. But was it possible to convince her that their marriage was the best thing that could have happened to either of them? Could he persuade her to explore every dark sin and vice he craved forever?

CHAPTER SIXTEEN

"WHAT IS THIS PLACE?" Matilda asked for the third time as William unlocked the front door and gestured her inside. The cold hit her first and then the emptiness of an abandoned country house. "Does anyone live here?"

She shivered when the front door groaned closed again as William shut them inside. His footfalls rang loudly as he led the way. "This could very well be home if my man of affairs is correct about the suitability of the space."

"My home?"

"I suppose you could say that."

She glanced up at the cobwebs drifting on the currents created by the opening of the door. It could take a long time to bring this place up to scratch. She almost rubbed her hands together at the challenge of so much work to occupy her time. "This might be a bit large just for me. I wanted to stay closer to the city."

"It occurred to me that it would be a good time to invest in property. I have no faith that my involvement with the navy will suddenly increase, even if I were to pester the admiralty daily for a new command and ship. I have time to spare and am in need of a diversion. I have lived in my grandfather's homes for ten years, but I will eventually need additional income to support a family. This will be my first investment."

"You'll move here?" The idea of William living so far from London seemed impossible. He had friends in London. Family. It had taken an hour by carriage just to reach this place.

"For now, and there will be others to manage." He nodded and set his hand to the doorframe, smiling down at her, his expression unreadable. "After the separation, you will remain mistress here if the house pleases you. If not, you can choose another closer to town."

She blushed and glanced away. He had said they would discuss the separation, but she had not expected the conversation today. Not after last night's spanking, which she was ashamed to say she had thoroughly enjoyed, or after this morning's flirting, which had appeared to arouse them both.

William had left her breathless and strangely happy both times. Especially the part after the spanking where he'd held her close to his chest. The tenderness after the punishment had been a revelation about him. She had not thought he wanted her affection, but he had proved otherwise. Matilda had been the first to pull away. She wished she'd not done so soon after. She would have liked to spend the night in his arms, but he had taken himself off and she'd fallen asleep alone.

She had missed him. She had missed his occasional snores and odd twitches.

Matilda took stock of the features of the property even as she was astounded by her own revelation. She did miss William when he was elsewhere. However, she was merely a temporary part of his life, just like this property would be the first of many conquests. Her life with him would come to a close very soon, and he would eventually have a real family.

His beautiful sisters had three firm contenders for their hand in marriage so far that she could tell. Victoria had charmed an aged duke, Audrey a gentleman of modest means, and Evelyn, even though she was not out in society yet, had charmed an entire horde of gentlemen as they called on her sisters. Her bargain with William could be over before long. "When we made our bargain, I hadn't considered moving so far."

"And you don't have to if you don't wish to. I have already enquired about a house in London that might suit you. It is one extra block farther away from my family than where we currently live. Close enough that you will not be removed from the friends you make in society in the coming months. Remember, you're my wife until my sisters marry, and no matter how long that takes it is my intention that we stay friends."

"I would like that too," she whispered. The discussion of endings made her sad though. She glanced around, studying the raw space with fresh eyes. It needed a great deal of attention to make it a home, and making it suitable for William could be a good distraction from thinking about the future.

"For as long as we decide to remain married, I would have you comfortable, and I am also thinking beyond that too for my own life," William said.

He moved away, drawing her attention to his body. A body she had seen very little of but had imagined when she was alone.

"This room should do for a drawing room," he said, "and those rooms for a study and dining room."

She moved slowly through the house in his wake, imagining it how William described. Soft reds and muted greens would make the house very pleasant. Not that she expected to have a say in the decoration if William moved into the space before their parting.

He moved on, opened two sets of doors, and stepped into a

glass-walled room. "This space should be sufficient for your butterfly house."

Her jaw dropped. "How did you know I like butterflies?"

"I've made it my business to discover everything I can about you since the day we met. Butterflies fascinate you." He smiled slowly, and the effort transformed his face. Her heart did a little leap and he leaned close. "You used to chase after them whenever you came on our picnics. Hands in the air, you'd leave us behind in an attempt to lure them to kiss your skin."

She stared at him in surprise. "You always became angry with me for that."

"For wandering away into the woods alone with only butter-flies for company. You could have been left behind a few times if I'd not missed your being underfoot." He brushed her cheek with his fingertips. "I spoke to Lord Deacon about his country butterfly house, and he assures me it is possible to have them here. If I go through with the purchase, he will arrange to have a man come and fill the space with what is needed for their survival. It will be up to you to see that they thrive."

Her eyes stung at his words. She had not expected him to have noticed or remembered what she had done in her first year of service. In her first year she'd occasionally forgotten that she was not meant to enjoy herself on their outings. But she had always loved chasing after the small, winged creatures to study their design and colors. Giving her a part of his house to keep as her own was the kindest thing William had ever done for her and completely unexpected. Yet he turned away the next moment as if to make light of how great a gift he'd just delivered.

Matilda flew after him, wrapped her arms about his body, pinning his arms at his sides. He stiffened in her awkward embrace, but Matilda didn't care. She squeezed him tightly, uncaring if she'd be in trouble or not later. "Thank you," she whispered against his back. "A thousand times thank you for remembering."

He turned in her arms and drew her against his chest. "I am glad you like the idea. This is the only property I have seen with an existing enclosure, so I hope it will suit. Deacon's man will let me know if I must continue the search or not. They are few and far between."

He'd turned down other places simply because they hadn't met her needs? But why? In a year they might not be married. "It will be beautiful. I promise."

"Not as lovely as you, but I look forward to seeing you dance with them again." His lips pressed together hard. Was he ashamed he'd watched her in the woods before calling out? She'd known he was there, hiding in the shadows of tall trees. She had smiled and kept dancing, completely forgetting her place until he'd ordered her back.

She expected him to retreat into gruffness immediately now, but he caught a curl of hair hanging down her neck and played with it. A slow smile spread over his face, and laughter filled his eyes. "Perhaps one day if I am very lucky you might invite me to dance in the woods with you too. There is a copse of trees to the west of here."

"I would like that," she said. Imagining him twirling with her under the trees brought a blush to her cheeks, and she patted his chest. He was always uncomfortable when it came to expressing his feelings, as if he expected to be rebuffed, but then so was she when it came to him. Matilda forgave William his earlier gruffness because she could now understand his hesitation to reveal his softer feelings. Hers were growing for William in a way that threatened to spread well beyond their arrangement.

She had grown to *like* her husband.

Matilda rose up on her toes, and before she considered

whether he'd like it or not caught the back of his head and dragged him down so she could kiss him full on the lips.

He appeared startled at first but soon took charge, moving her toward a wall and pressing her into it with the strength of his body. His kiss was hungry and thorough, demanding her response in his usual dominant fashion, a manner that Matilda had grown to crave. She did not want him turning to other women to scold them. She wanted him to reserve his punishments and attention for her.

She broke the kiss, turned her lips to his scarred cheek, and kissed him there. "I would dance with you anywhere, Billy."

He shuddered at the name, and as she trailed her lips along the full length of his injury, she grew aware that his hands were tightening around her waist. His skin was rough against her lips, coarse but warm. He was becoming very familiar, and she wanted more, to explore him if he was willing to indulge her curiosity.

She slipped her arms about his waist beneath his coat and pulled him close, overwhelmed by the need to feel him firm against her skin. Last night, pinned by his strength and passions, had been wonderful—arousing and painful—and yet her heart had never felt lighter as she'd reclined in his arms afterward.

She nibbled his earlobe and he groaned.

He jerked up her skirts and squeezed her thigh roughly, grinding his hips against hers. She felt, for the first time, the part of him he kept hidden beneath his clothes. She aroused him, and he tried so hard to keep her ignorant of all his desires.

His hand moved along her sides restlessly, sending her pulse flying. "Don't tempt me, woman."

"Billy Boy," she said again as his hand slid over her rear.

He squeezed, his breathing rough and unsteady against her throat. Matilda gasped and pressed her head against the wall as William nibbled at her throat.

She marveled at the power of his lips and body to overwhelm

her senses, but his reluctance to take his own satisfaction with her was troubling. At first, she had been embarrassed to notice his erection. Proper women were not supposed to consider such things or mention them. However, she did not imagine that many married men would be capable of holding back for so long.

She ached for his touch already even though her urges had been satisfied last night.

William kissed her neck up to her hairline and tormented her senses with a flick of his tongue behind her ear. He drew back. "Say it again. Once more."

One more impertinence would see her punished. He'd warned her of his limits. Three remarks he didn't care for would provoke him beyond reason. And he hated being called Billy.

The idea of deliberately goading him simply to be spanked held a definite appeal. He liked to spank her. Matilda loved to see him reveal his hidden nature when he turned her over his knee.

"Billy," she whispered into his ear.

William shuddered against her, cock rubbing directly against her sex in a way that made her ache intensify. He lifted her into his arms and carried her toward the front hall. He stopped there, placed her on her feet, and turned her to face the locked front door.

"Are we leaving already?"

"Hands on the brass knobs and no further questions."

Matilda trembled at his angry tone but complied because she wanted this.

William rearranged her stance until her bottom stuck out toward him, then lifted her skirts high. "You know how I feel about that name."

"Yes, William. You'll punish me for using it."

"I must. Are you ready?"

The first time he'd given her no warning, the second she'd

been already overwhelmed by their conversation. This time Matilda knew exactly what it would feel like to have his hand beat against her skin. And she wanted it. She wanted to feel William.

"Yes, Billy Boy."

"Count silently until the pain becomes too much to bear, then tell me the number." The first strike was immediate and hard. It shook her from head to toe and stung like the very devil. The next and following strikes alternated from one cheek to the other, without pause or any hesitation. She'd unlocked the devil in William, and there was no stopping him now. She didn't even want to.

She counted until her bottom began to hurt in earnest, and when it became too much she peeked back over her shoulder. William's attention was fixed on her rear, and he was smiling like she'd never seen him before.

His eyes lifted to hers, and his hand froze in midair. "How many?"

"Thirty-three," she managed to get out even as she was on the verge of tears. Her body ached. Trembled from his touch and desire for more.

"Stay like that," he whispered before dropping to his knees.

He kissed around her hurts gently and then burrowed his face between her legs to kiss her throbbing quim. She gasped at the shock of his actions, but as his tongue lapped at her wetness, she arched her back even more as he teased her clitoris.

"Oh, stars." She wanted more this time. She wanted him to feel good too. Matilda widened her legs.

He lapped at her hungrily, brought his hand up between her legs to rub her with his fingers when he moved back to kiss her bottom. She moaned brokenly as the pleasure mounted until she was crying out, almost crawling out of her skin with the need for release.

And then he stopped, rose to his knees, and pulled her skirts over her tingling bottom. He stumbled away, gasping.

Matilda slowly straightened, cringing a little as her bottom stung. She kept her hands on the door handles as he'd instructed, using them to hold herself upright. She leaned against the doorframe as her legs trembled. She had been so close. "William?"

"Tonight, after dinner, we will continue," he promised, still gasping heavily.

Matilda closed her eyes as her quim twitched in anticipation. Tears spilled down her cheeks. Did he not desire her innocence at all? "Why did you stop?"

"Anticipation is a heady feeling," he whispered. "For both of us. This abandoned country house is not meant to hear your cries of passion yet."

She glanced his way, noticing his clenched hands and tense shoulders, the fullness of his trousers around his erection. "I would not have minded."

"I would." He unclenched his hands and stared at the right one. He brushed his fingers over the hand that had punished her so thoroughly. "Harder than I thought to stop when I'm with you," he admitted.

She smiled and then started to laugh at how their situations had reversed. Matilda hadn't wanted him to stop touching her, but he had. She'd never expected that.

He straightened and held out his hand. "Come, let us go home to an early dinner."

Matilda took a step toward him and cried out. "The pain is going to make sitting down to dinner a problem," she warned him.

"I'll find you a very soft pillow for your chair." William grinned, clearly unrepentant for her suffering, and moved to support her by putting one arm behind her back. He held her against his side a long moment, and she appreciated the comfort of his attention.

"You'll manage beautifully," he whispered. "Though I should warn you my sisters are coming to stay for a few days. They promised to be no trouble and keep to the house."

Matilda turned her face into his shoulders and hid her blush. His sisters could never know what she and William did together. They would never understand what was truly going on. Evelyn, Audrey, and Victoria were still convinced William must love her and hoped Matilda might feel the same about him one day. She hoped they kept quiet on the subject. Marriages like this, if there ever was another like it, had nothing to do with love. She was lucky William was so considerate, even if he did force her into gowns of his choosing rather than her preference.

"I hope they can amuse themselves. I don't think I have the presence of mind, or body, to chase them after that interlude."

William held her close, fingers cupping her face. "You asked for it. You enjoyed being disciplined."

"I did," she admitted. "A year ago I would never have imagined I would want to provoke you ever again."

"A year ago I hoped I would have a second chance to make things right with you," he murmured before straightening.

Pleased with his remark, she accepted his aid to step out onto the drive. Their carriage had been moved away to the river where the grooms were lounging in the sun. After William had locked the house, Matilda hobbled the first steps, then straightened so the servants would never suspect anything was amiss. Nothing was actually wrong, but her bottom was going to pain her for some time.

William put his arm behind her back, and they strolled along as gracefully as she could manage until they reached the dim interior of the loaned Newberry Park carriage.

There were many advantages of being married to William Ford, but there was one side of their life she'd not anticipated. For the entire journey she had to sit awkwardly to the side, leaning into William to keep the pressure off her tender rear. William allowed it, grinning the entire way home. There was no predicting how two people would get along, but she'd never once imagined she'd have the power to make the bossy William as happy as he appeared to be now.

CHAPTER SEVENTEEN

WITH THE DRESSING door closed and locked behind William, Matilda could breathe freely. Dinner had been a long and torturous affair with his innocent sisters chattering company. The discreetly placed pillow had not muted the awareness of what William had done to her bottom. It had constantly reminded her that their interlude was not over yet.

William took her hand and led her deep into his bedchamber, stopping when they reached the side of his wide bed. Her heart beat very fast as he turned her around.

His expression had been very serious all night. His manner direct, almost cold. If she did not know his nature so well, she might think he'd forgotten what had happened between them earlier in the day. If she did not know where to look for signs of his arousal, she would think him unaffected.

But he *was* affected. His restrained bearing was a sign that he was in control of his body and emotions, whereas Matilda was far from it.

She trembled every time he held her gaze, and she'd fought a blush all night long.

He unhooked her gown at the back and had her step out of it, all without saying a word to soothe her or seduce her. He brushed his fingers over the chain about her neck but left it hanging there as he took her hair down, tossing away the pins carelessly.

She had never been undressed in this room, so close to the bed they shared at night. She shifted her weight from foot to foot, anticipating William's touch eagerly. He gathered and straightened her hair, plaited some of it into a rope, then swept it forward to lie over one shoulder.

A small smile twisted his lips as she faced him again. "Lovely."

He drew back holding one of her hands and took a good look at her body. She was still wearing her corset and chemise but felt as bare as she was when he dressed her each day. The more she came to know him, touch him, the more she craved to see where his passions would lead her next.

He pulled her close suddenly, slamming her against his hard body. A gasp escaped her at the contact, and she instinctively put her arms about his neck as he embraced her. She held on to him, which she soon concluded had been his plan all along judging by his devilish grin.

He brushed his good cheek against hers, and she shuddered as his evening whiskers abraded her skin. He turned his lips against her cheek and kissed from her jaw to her ear and then proceeded down her throat, only stopping when he reached her pulse. He dragged his tongue slowly across her skin.

She tightened her grip around his shoulders and brushed her fingers up into his hair. A low growl left William, his hands squeezing tighter around her waist.

When he lifted his head, his eyes were two black orbs of unguarded emotion, the same look he'd regarded her with when she'd been holding him down on his sickbed. Desire for her and determination not to lose control.

She grinned at the realization. At last she understood what he wanted—her absolute trust.

She knew him. She was growing to appreciate him. She most definitely trusted him not to hurt her body more than she needed it done.

With that understanding, Matilda accepted him and closed her eyes before she leaned into him.

William kissed her—deep, drugging kisses that made her pant and moan. His hands roamed her back, squeezing and sliding over her skin as if he couldn't get enough. He avoided touching her bottom, deliberately tracing around the tender flesh, which she appreciated for now.

But she was learning that what would not please others aroused her. Matilda tightened her grip on his hair and kissed him back, flicking her tongue across his until he growled against her mouth. He lifted her and staggered the few steps toward the bed.

He tossed her high, and she landed on her knees on the thick mattress. William followed, crawled across the counterpane, and sat on his haunches. He pulled her close enough that her legs straddled his thigh. And in that upright position, he kissed her witless once more, guiding her ever closer to his lap and his hidden erection.

When his thigh brushed high between her legs, touching that secret place that clenched when he stroked her during a spanking, she let out a soft moan and blushed scarlet.

He set his hand to her hips, nudging her closer until she was pressed tight against his hot body. Matilda braced her hands on his wide shoulders as he lifted her chemise at the back and tucked it beneath the material of her corset. She glanced over her shoulder as his hands covered each globe of her tender bottom.

She felt a twinge of apprehension and met his gaze. "You're going to punish me like this?"

"Most definitely, but you'll also feel pleasure too. I promise."

His hand landed hard on her right cheek, and she jerked forward with a gasp into the hard mass of William's silk-covered thigh. Matilda clutched his shirt as he struck her again, and once more she rubbed against his unyielding flesh.

The twin sensations were a thrilling combination that stirred her arousal to life beyond what she thought she could feel.

William's fingers dug into her bottom, and then he ground her against his leg. Matilda gasped as her senses rioted and he continued to spank and brush her sex against his thigh in a steady rhythm. She was burning up with embarrassment and equal parts lust. How could she like pain so much that she found it pleasurable?

How could William have known what to do with her so well?

He stopped suddenly, panting hard against her throat.

The pause gave Matilda time to think about William. Should she touch him, or was the experience of spanking her all he wished for himself?

Risking rejection or further punishment, Matilda slipped her hands across his shoulders and down. He was tense beneath his shirt, hot enough to sweat. She teased her fingers over the skin of his chest, across the part exposed by the open neckline of his soft white shirt. William drew back, ripped his shirt off over his head, and placed her hands directly over his skin.

"Oh my," she whispered. His skin was so pale, so pliant beneath her touch.

"Beautiful, sweet Mattie," he said and then brushed his lips over her temple. "I think that might be the nicest thing you've ever said about me."

He caught her wrist and shifted her hand slowly down his body. She skimmed over his hard muscled chest, past his taut belly, and lower. There was a long, hard shape beneath his tight breeches, and touching him did strange things to her own body. He was aroused, and Matilda caught her breath, uncertain what to do next.

"Touch me. Please," he whispered.

He struck her bottom, and her hand bumped against his length. A strangled growl left his throat. "Again."

He spanked her once more as she traced the shape of him beneath his garment. He was very different from her beneath his clothes, something she'd known but never fully comprehended. He flexed his hips as she traveled the length of him, and when she reached the top, she could see the tip wedged between his belly and the tight waistband of his breeches.

William spanked her and grasped her breast while she stared, fascinated by a mere peek at his manhood. Her body quivered at another strike of his hand and hard rub against his thigh. Pleasure was new to her, but not to William. Emboldened by his patience with her fumbling, Matilda ran her knuckle up his length, and when she reached the top, she brushed her fingertips over the head.

While William cursed out loud and struck her bottom sharply, she reveled in the softness of his skin. She skimmed the tip of him, finding moisture had beaded at the tip, but after a moment regretted her limited view. She wanted to please him. She wanted to see and know his desires.

William paused, breathing hard against her shoulder. Impulsively Matilda unbuttoned the fall of his breeches, exposing him. His long length jutted proudly from a thatch of dark hair and curved all the way to his belly. His skin appeared so pale beside her hand that she was fascinated. She wrapped her fingers over his length without considering if he'd like it.

A rough moan left his lips before he claimed her mouth in a

deep kiss that left her in no doubt that he desired more of such caresses.

She brushed her fingers up and down his length until he covered her hand and had her squeeze him harder. It was not unlike the way he held her wrist sometimes, and she gripped him tightly in her hand, lost in the wonder of the moment. He shifted his hips and thrust between her curled fingers.

Matilda glanced at his face as he began to move the two of them against each other. His eyes were hot on hers, focused but wild. The pressure on her sex was exquisite and arousing, her hand pleasuring him even more so. They were completely tangled together, each exciting the other. His teeth nipped at her throat. "Is this what you want from me, Mattie?"

She squeezed his length tightly and moved her hand in opposition to the thrust of his hips. A dark moan left his lips.

"Is this what you need, Billy?"

He struck her so hard she cried out.

"Yes." He took her mouth again and sped their movements.

Matilda held on to him with one arm and with the other squeezed and stroked him firmly.

He pushed her down on his thigh and rocked her against him. Matilda closed her eyes as her breath caught. She was beyond excited and lost, with no idea how to continue without his help.

William pinched her nipple suddenly, twisting it until it hurt. The sensation surprised her, the pleasure increasing. Her body tightened and she shuddered, crying out the next moment as wave after wave of sensation swamped her. She clung to William.

William groaned darkly as hot moisture coated her hand where it was wrapped tightly around his length. They shuddered together, climaxing in unison, and then Matilda collapsed into William's strong arms, utterly spent.

She complained when he parted their limbs. The loss of his thigh against her sex proved her very sensitive.

He eased her to her side, keeping her throbbing bottom off the sheets, her sensitive quim pinched between her thighs. He returned quickly with a washcloth. "Just lie there. Let me take care of you."

"I am capable of nothing else."

"Good. That is very good for me."

William fussed and then moved off the bed, occasionally brushing against her tingling bum with his fingertips as he moved around, removing their clothes from the room.

She pushed her hand under her cheek after he'd removed her corset and chemise, lying in a contented daze. "Do you like to view your handiwork?"

"Yes." His lips grazed the back of her neck in a soft kiss. "All of you too, but especially after touching you intimately."

And yet he covered her with a nightgown, then the bedsheet, even tucking the counterpane tightly around her so she would be warm and cocooned.

If he hadn't just spanked her silly, she'd think him the most doting and gentle man in the world. She was growing to appreciate the differences in him. He acted in keeping with their situation.

He doused the light, climbed into bed, and when he was lying down, he took her hand in his. "Good night, wife."

Matilda smiled in the dark. William wasn't so complicated. He thrived on routine and orders. Pleasure. Pain and a firm set of rules to guide them on their journey was all they needed. "Sleep well, husband."

He kissed the back of her hand like the most ardent of suitors. "Until tomorrow, my Matilda."

"I hope you know my bottom will hurt like the very devil every time I sit down tomorrow." She sighed. "That will make you content, I suppose."

"Indeed it will," he whispered with an amusement to his voice that she thought very sincere. "Until the next time you call me by that name again. The next time I might not be so lenient."

Matilda groaned as her body quaked with anticipation for their next painful interlude. "It won't be soon. I need time to recover from that spanking."

"I'll wait."

CHAPTER EIGHTEEN

"I TELL you he is out there."

William carefully folded the newspaper he had been reading and moved to stand at the window beside Dawson. It was a gloomy day outside, but he could make out a solitary shape leaning against a wrought iron fence across the street. "The height is about right, but I cannot make out his features."

"It's him," Dawson insisted. "What are you going to do?"

"Nothing."

"She'll find out you lied to her."

"That was always in the cards." He stared at his valet. "Dawson, you continue to worry about my wife unnecessarily."

"Begging your pardon, my lord, but your lady is worth worrying about. I have always thought she was far too trusting. The other servants did not treat her very well while we were away." Dawson's expression grew grim. "Speaking of the servants, when will you do something about how the house is run?"

He moved away from the window. "Those responsibilities belong to my wife."

Dawson's expression grew troubled. "She's not changed anything so far."

William considered her inaction. They had not spoken much about their expectations, but their marriage was based on an arrangement—wed for a while, then separate. A separation that was growing less and less appealing every day.

He was still elated by last night's tryst. Making love to Matilda had been worth the wait. He wanted nothing to upset the ease growing between them. Last night had felt like a first great step forward. The first of many, he hoped.

But had his desire to dominate Matilda convinced her she could not impose her will on anything else around them? He hadn't meant for that to happen. It was not even what he wanted. He would have to discuss what he really wanted from marriage and hope she might understand the difference. "She will soon."

"Good. The younger servants are suffering, being bullied into doing more chores than they should whenever my back is turned. The boot boy fell asleep at table this morning and was slapped severely for it afterward. I intervened, but I cannot always be belowstairs. I don't have the authority if the butler turns a blind eye."

William cursed. His discussion with Matilda had to be handled carefully.

Dawson bowed. "I'll do my best to keep him out of the house, but I'm not the one answering the doors. You'll need to alert Carter not to admit him."

"Thank you."

Harry Lloyd's reappearance was as ill-timed as any bad omen. He did not want Matilda upset. Not when their marriage had finally begun to progress in a promising direction. She had opened herself to him at last, accepting that passion and pain were one and the same for them, confided in him, but he did not know what she would do when faced with her former betrothed. Since she'd never experienced intimacy before their marriage, he felt strangely confident the lie would not completely shatter her trust in him. He took care of her, he asked for her opinions, and after last night... Well, she might be growing more and more fond of his brand of affection.

He felt no compulsion to bring their arrangement to a close. Separation would be a very messy affair, and Matilda's reputation would be harmed, even more so than his own. And she was still very much an innocent. The thought of how other men might consider her, assume her much more experienced in pleasure than she was, set his teeth on edge.

He folded the paper briskly and collected the day's letters. The more time he spent with her, the more uneasy he was about a separation that would leave her without his protection.

He would have to confess his deception. With luck, he wouldn't be sleeping on the chaise come nightfall.

Victoria plopped down at Matilda's side in the drawing room and took her hand. "Is everything all right between you and William?"

"Perfect, why?" Her bottom still ached from William's spanking, but she couldn't share that with his sister.

"I heard a commotion coming from your rooms last night, and I am concerned."

Matilda frowned. "There was no commotion."

"I thought I heard someone being slapped." Victoria winced. "Quite a number of times, in fact."

Dear God, the sound of William's spanking had carried outside their bedchamber.

Matilda had been so wrapped up in William that she'd never

dreamed their activities would come to anyone else's attention. She glanced away, thinking of how to explain the situation in terms Victoria could accept. Their interlude had taken a while, and William had been most thorough in warming her bottom with his hand. She couldn't tell his sister that, however. She had to find another explanation. "A spider. There was a spider in our room, and William was hunting for it."

Victoria's brows rose. "Did he kill it?"

"What?"

"Did he kill the spider?"

"Oh yes, I think he must have. He was quite dedicated to chasing it around."

Victoria's eyes narrowed. "Are you sure that's all it was? My brother can be a little hard at times."

"Absolutely."

"Matilda, what are you agreeing to?" William's voice was the best sound in the world.

She jumped to her feet and hurried to stand before him. "I was just telling Victoria that you saved me from a very large spider last night." She widened her eyes, hoping he'd catch on quickly. "But it took a while before you managed to flatten it. The sound disturbed her a little bit."

William took the lie in stride but shuffled the unopened letters in his hand. "You know, I'm not completely sure I did get it after all, but I don't want you to be alarmed, my dear. I will take another closer look tonight and make sure you're not frightened again. Just ignore any further nighttime ruckus from our rooms, Victoria. I fully intend to look after Matilda. I promise."

Matilda's toes curled in her slippers as desire for his touch reared its head. She was not used to feeling that way about him, and it was highly distracting.

Apparently appeased, Victoria let the matter drop and stole a glance at his correspondence. "Ooh, the Malvey masquerade."

"To which you girls will not be going," William announced sternly. "Where is Evelyn today?"

"She needed to speak to Aunt Pen, and stop changing the subject every time I want to discuss the most popular entertainment of the year." Victoria set her hands to her hips. "Malvey's masquerade is not even considered that shocking or scandalous anymore. Why can we not go?"

His gaze landed on Matilda, and he studied her. "Because I would like a night out with Matilda on my arm without having to watch over three girls who can get into enough trouble when I simply blink."

Victoria huffed but then tossed her head from side to side. "Oh well, fair enough. But only because you'll take Matilda. I'll help her choose a costume."

"That will not be necessary." William passed Victoria a letter absently. He passed another to Matilda. "Hold on to that, my dear."

Matilda bit her lip at his endearment and quickly dropped her eyes to the invitation. The flowing script invited Captain and Mrs. Ford to an evening of lively entertainment that was to end at dawn. She smiled to see their names side by side.

"But really, William," Victoria exclaimed. "She simply must have something divine to wear for her first masque."

William pursed his lips. "So I thought too. Which is why I ordered a costume for her and a mask when I remembered the event was coming up. It was meant to be a secret gift, but there you have it—a surprise ruined by your curiosity yet again."

"My very own mask?"

William winked. "You should never wear anyone else's. Not while I live and breathe."

Matilda pressed her lips together, excited by William's thoughtful and generous purchase. He planned everything so carefully, often making decisions for her many days, weeks, in advance. She had glimpsed his appointment book and seen her name written several times. It gave her a warm glow to see their names written side by side so often.

Victoria closed her eyes briefly. "Well, she does deserve something nice for putting up with you."

He grinned widely and retrieved the invitation. "Nice and painfully expensive, I promise."

"Excellent." Victoria clapped her hands and embraced him suddenly. "You really are a good husband. Who would have thought you'd be so considerate?"

William's gaze flitted to Matilda. "I must have married the right woman."

Matilda could feel heat creeping up her cheeks. She moved away as embarrassment made her throat tight. They were not going to be married for long, only pretending to be man and wife for a time, and then they would go their separate ways. Even if, at times, she couldn't imagine not being with William. He was very considerate and generous, except when punishing her. And even that seemed to please her now.

It would be very strange to go on without him.

Victoria hurried away with her letter clutched in her hand. When she could no longer be heard, Matilda sank into a chair, wincing a little as her bottom throbbed.

William moved close, squeezing into the space at her side and kissing her neck. "What are you thinking about?"

"You."

A delighted smile burst over his face. "And I was thinking about you. Especially about last night and what we did together. Chasing spiders was thrilling."

Matilda grew hot. "I thought you would have done more."

"Taken your innocence?" His breath beat hot against her throat. "I considered it."

"Why didn't you?"

"I don't know." He sighed and then nibbled her neck again. "Perhaps my conscience got the better of me."

"Because we're not truly husband and wife."

"We had an arrangement, and I don't mean to dishonor it." He nodded. "Once you give your innocence to me, there is no going back. Last night was wonderful, and I loved arousing you. But I think if I were to slide inside you and make you mine, I would prefer to keep you in my bed forever."

Matilda panted. "You should probably be more worried that I'd become your slave. You can be very persuasive when you try."

William slid his hand across her belly. "Are you not that already? You have an obedient disposition made for me, and I crave that and more."

"I suppose I am very malleable."

"But only with me." His fingers slid up her side, coming to rest beside her breast. "I won't lie. Last night I ached to be inside you."

Hearing the confession of his lust made Matilda smile. "That pleases me," she said, aiming at mimicking his confessions of wanting to spank her.

"I will, but only if you truly understand what that means for you." He met her gaze, serious once more. "I can't change who I am. I will always want to correct your behavior, take you over my knee and spank you. I will always tell you how to dress, order your days and nights. It is who I am, but I can understand if that makes you uncomfortable."

"It does make me uncomfortable. I have always been a woman who worked. I'm not easy being so idle, but you will likely punish me for attempting to fill the hours."

He was silent, and then he kissed her neck once more. The fast quality of his breathing gave her gooseflesh. "Let us compromise," he whispered.

Matilda struggled to concentrate. His lips were traveling along her collarbone, and she began to shiver. He might have had doubts about the appeal of his kisses, but Matilda was putty in his hands, near reduced to ash by his scorching passions. "What kind of compromise?"

"I will always give you three warnings before a correction is delivered."

"You'll tell me what I'm doing that displeases you?"

"Yes." He cupped her breast, the one he'd pinched the previous night, and then slid his fingers to the tip. "It will be up to you whether or not you continue the activity and provoke me."

Matilda shivered. He held her nipple lightly between his fingers as her breathing hitched. "Billy."

"That one will always bring punishment."

She met his gaze and smiled. The things he did and said to her had produced an ache between her legs she couldn't control. "Make love to me."

"That's another matter that must be addressed." He moved his hand away, leaving her bereft. "I decide when and where we meet for intimacy."

"Do I have no say at all?"

"Some, but only when preceded by a punishment. I get so damned excited when I lay my hands on you, but you can stop me. You can always stop me."

Matilda nodded, already believing that to be true.

A wicked smile played over his lips. "You might even come to enjoy my delays. Anticipation can be a powerful aphrodisiac. I will tease you, tempt you, but hold back your fulfillment until I am certain that you enjoy every moment to the fullest extent."

"That is what you do now. Hold yourself apart until you have to act."

"Yes, but it is not without risk of disastrous results."

She studied him. "The first time you spanked me, you said after that you had made a mistake."

He winced. "I was too overcome with emotion to prepare you properly for my actions. That will not happen again."

Matilda glanced at him shyly. "I am very prepared today."

He stood and caught her hand. "We are going out."

She stood quickly. "To where?"

"That is going to be a surprise. There is something we need to talk about, but not here. I want to be alone with you."

He wrapped her hand around his arm and held her to his side. It was a possessive gesture—did William ever behave another way?—that sent a burst of happiness through her whole body.

"I'm growing to like your surprises." She glanced down at his groin where the outline of an erection showed. "In fact, I could get very used to more."

"Captain Ford, a word," Mr. Carter said suddenly.

The butler's interruption brought a blush to Matilda's cheeks.

William shook his head. "Carter, we were just about to go out."

"A messenger has come, sent by Miss Evelyn. You are needed at Newberry House urgently, Captain. Something to do with an accident and your aunt. She does not know what to do."

William glanced at her swiftly.

"You had better go," Matilda urged. "We can talk another time."

He seemed indecisive. "The thought of what Evelyn might do to aid my aunt sends a chill down my spine," he confessed.

"Mine too." She pushed him away. "You had better hurry or

else she might water the woman's feet with sherry. She wanted me to do that with you."

William sprinted for the front door. "Dear God, I hope I'm in time to prevent such a travesty. "

CHAPTER NINETEEN

MATILDA COULDN'T HELP but laugh at William's words about his sister. Surely Lady Penelope Ford couldn't be in too much danger by having her feet sprinkled with the best sherry. She glanced at Carter and saw his frown aimed at her. Her merriment subsided. "Was there something else, Mr. Carter?"

He turned away rudely without answering.

Matilda's happiness dimmed only a little. If not for William and the acceptance of his sisters, Matilda might have taken the butler's rebuff to heart.

She did not today. She was the lady of the house, and Carter had to do her bidding. "I should like tea at three o'clock, Carter," she called out.

"Very good," Carter intoned. But she heard the remark that followed, "The second-best cups will do for the likes of you."

"Thank you," Matilda called after him, little caring if the man liked her or not. Once she would have. There had been a time when she'd been afraid to upset the applecart.

Not now.

Being William's wife was turning out to be much more enjoyable than she'd imagined. There were so many things she could do. She could be busy or sit idly, make plans, and discuss them with William when they lay together in bed at night. She was making friends slowly in society and enjoying having a family. She was happy with her life. Content in a way she had never expected. She turned around, filled with excitement and a wish to surprise William later, but stopped dead when she saw she was not alone.

Standing in the doorway was a man she'd never expected to see again. She cried out in shock and then covered her mouth to whisper his name. "Harry Lloyd?"

"In the flesh." He grinned widely and held out his arms. "Did you miss me, sweetheart?"

Matilda stumbled. "They said you were dead."

"That's troubling." He pressed a hand over his heart and tapped his fingers in a regular rhythm. "No. Still beating."

Matilda hurried across the room and took his hand in hers to be sure she was not dreaming. His hand was solid beneath hers. Warm. She dropped his hand quickly. "You're not dead?"

"No. I'm flesh and blood and come back to claim my girl," he said, grinning broadly. "It's time for me to settle down."

Matilda's heart stopped beating altogether. "I am settled."

He glanced around the room. "I see you're still keeping to the same schedule. Polishing his nibs' brass and smoothing his sheets right when I knew you would be at this time of day."

She shook her head slowly, her head full of horror for what she'd done. How could this be happening? He was dead. William had told her so. She'd married William. She had made her decisions and had trusted him to keep his promises. How could William be so wrong? Unless he had meant to mislead her just to get his way. She swallowed the hard lump in her throat. "I don't dust anymore," she whispered.

"Moving up in the world?" He nodded approvingly, and then

he flopped down on the chaise, resting his feet on a pillow. "I thought I saw Mrs. Young below, but are you running the place now?"

She winced. "You could say that."

"That's the ticket. Bet you've saved us a pretty penny over the past year. So did I. We'll pool our funds and make like fish in a new pond far away from here."

Matilda twisted her hands together at her waist. A chill swept over her skin. Harry had kept his promise and come back to marry her with no idea her faith in him hadn't been as firm. She had allowed Captain Ford to drag her into his life and let him punish her whenever he liked. "Where have you been? Why didn't you write me and tell me where you were?"

"I've been everywhere in England, luv. Why all these questions?" He scowled. "I came here to collect you as soon as I had money enough in my pocket to spare for the mail carriage and our future. I thought you'd at least show a little bit of appreciation at seeing me."

Matilda flinched. She'd cut herself off from Harry the moment she'd said yes to William. "You should have written to me with your directions."

He shrugged. "And let Cranky Young snatch my letters from you and read them aloud to everyone? Lord, I haven't missed that old biddy one bit. I convinced the skinny boot boy to help me slip upstairs to avoid meeting her. Can't wait to see the old trout's face when we walk out of here arm in arm today."

He picked up a book that had been left on the chaise by William and leafed through the pages. A scrap of paper dropped out and fell to the floor, unnoticed by Harry. He snapped the book shut without marking the place again. William would not like that.

"Don't touch anything else." Matilda snatched the book and scrap of paper and tried to find William's place. He'd been reading some of it to her at night, and she flipped the pages until a familiar expression jumped out at her. She put the scrap of paper there, hoping she recalled correctly where he had read to last night.

"Still following Captain Bloody High and Mighty's rules, I see. That man is a tyrant. There'll be no need to worry about what he might say once we're married."

There was every need to worry. "This is his home. He does not like anyone touching his possessions. He will become very angry that you just lost his place." Matilda lifted her chin.

Harry appeared unimpressed. "What he wants doesn't matter anymore. There's a whole world waiting for us outside these walls. You'll see. You'll love the adventure of never knowing what will happen next as much as I do."

Matilda couldn't continue without confessing the very big change that had occurred in the past weeks. She twisted her wedding band around her finger. "I can't leave with you."

Harry patted his pockets and searched until he held a dull metal band out to her in triumph. "Cost me a penny we couldn't afford to lose, but here's the ring you said you needed. Now come and give the man you love the kiss he's been waiting for."

Her heart lurched, but she somehow found her voice. "Captain Ford has been ashore for over three months, recovering from an injury."

"So? He'll be gone again soon." Harry shrugged, pausing to admire the ring in his fingers. A ring that looked a great deal less valuable than the gold band gracing her left hand. "What difference does it make? I have it all planned out. A night at the theatre and then the stage for Southampton and beyond."

The past months had made all the difference in the world to Matilda's heart. She took a step back. "I cannot go anywhere with you."

Harry continued without listening. "I've gone into partnership with a fellow who runs a tavern down there. Very classy, mind. None of that watered-down ale in our establishment, I promise you that."

"I am pleased for you." She heard footsteps behind her, echoing up the main staircase, and froze. Someone was coming. She trembled that it might be William. "You have to leave. Now," she whispered.

Instead of leaving, Harry merely slipped behind the door and held a finger to his lips.

Matilda faced the doorway. Thankfully it was Dawson.

"Is everything all right, madam?"

She ignored Harry's widened eyes at the way the valet addressed her. "Everything is fine, Mr. Dawson."

Dawson appeared unconvinced as he shuffled his feet. He frowned and glanced around. "I thought I heard another voice with you."

"No," she promised him.

Dawson had paused just at the doorway. If he took three steps more into the room, he would discover Harry's hiding place behind the door. He could not be allowed to find Harry. "The servants are all downstairs, I believe, if you are looking for one of them."

"Thank you." He bit his lip a moment. "Is Captain Ford returning soon?"

"I hope so." William had quite a bit of explaining to do. "Thank you, Dawson."

Dawson retreated, and Harry stretched out his hand to the door and pushed it slowly shut. "Madam?"

"Yes, I am married now."

Harry's brows shot up. "To whom?"

"To Captain Ford."

"To that stuck-up piece of board?" He started to laugh. "That's a fine jest."

"It is no jest. I am married to him."

Harry's face shifted into anger. "Well, well, well. I guess mine wasn't ever going to be the right ring on your finger. Did you make him promise to marry you before you'd allow him a kiss, too?"

"It didn't happen like that."

"What was it then?" he ground out. "He felt compelled to make an honest woman of you on a whim? There had to have been something between you."

She blushed. William had married her for his own reasons. "I will not explain my marriage."

Harry's expression turned to disgust. "You don't have to. I can see your plan plain as day. You were always too interested in him, making sure you followed his orders to the letter, all with a plan to force him to marry you. Clever girl."

That stung. It was what everyone assumed had happened. "You don't know what you're talking about. I never set out to become his wife."

"I thought you were different, but you're just the same as all the others. You'd suffer that man's company in bed, produce a brat every other year, and play the part of an adoring wife just so you can have at his money." He grabbed her hand and glanced at the plain gold band on her ring finger. "You should have demanded better than that, sweetheart," he said, sarcasm dripping from his lips. "Next time make sure it sparkles with sapphires or rubies."

Matilda hid her ring in the folds of her skirt. Whatever William had given her had always been enough. "I didn't marry him for his money."

"Well, you didn't marry him for his charm," Harry hissed. "Everyone knows he's got a temper and a half. Good God, the way he bossed you about made me furious."

"He's very pleasant with me," Matilda insisted.

"Pleasant?" Harry spat. "Damning him with faint praise."

"How I feel about my husband is no one's business but mine."

"Spoken like a true woman in love." Harry peered at her hard, and then his anger drained away. "A man with his connections could have anyone he wanted. Did you have any choice in marrying him?"

"No."

Harry turned away before she could continue. "I'll make him suffer if it's the last thing I do."

"You will not harm him," Matilda shouted. "I won't let you touch him. I chose to marry him. I wanted to."

His jaw worked, and then he spun around. "So this is all yours?"

"No. Everything you see belongs to my husband, as always."

He snatched an empty snuffbox from the mantel and stared hard at her even as he pocketed the trinket. "Even you."

"Give it back." Harry had often palmed small items from the house, but he'd once claimed it accidental. Matilda held out her hand for it when he did not put it back of his own accord. "You should leave."

Harry shook his head, eyeing their surroundings with keen interest. "Not until I've been compensated."

He came close, invading her personal space. He eyed her body boldly. "I'm owed, madam. How would you like to soothe my disappointment?"

He grasped her about the waist and planted a kiss on her lips. It was wet, disgusting, and she fought to get away from him. He released her with an oath when she bit his lip. "Still a prude."

Matilda raised her fists, prepared, however feebly, to fend him off. She'd never hurt anyone before, but she would defend herself. "I am married."

"Like that ever stopped any woman from taking a bit of pleasure on the side. Even your precious husband has dipped his wick in one or two maids. Don't get all hoity-toity with me, *Mrs. Ford.* I deserve some satisfaction after the fool you made of me."

She lifted her chin. She had always believed a woman should wait until marriage before being intimate, even if she was marrying the man. Harry had said he understood her wishes and grudgingly agreed to wait. Apparently, he placed little faith in a woman's fidelity after marriage.

There was such a vast difference between William and Harry's attitude toward women that it defied description. William would never try to take what she hadn't willingly given him permission for. He was adamant Matilda should keep her virtue intact even if she had not been so sure it was necessary anymore.

Matilda would not allow herself to be used in such a way. She was no man's plaything. She made her own decisions. She calmly walked to the door and opened it. "Dawson?"

William's valet appeared immediately, his expression tense as he peered into the room and spotted Harry Lloyd. His stare turned furious. "Yes, Mrs. Ford?"

"If you'd be so kind as to see this gentleman out immediately." She gestured to Harry with considerable embarrassment. "He has no business being under this roof ever again."

"It will be my pleasure." He rolled his shoulders, hands bunching into fists. "Immediately."

"Dawson, check his pockets first," Matilda said. "Mr. Lloyd seems too fond of the captain's possessions."

Matilda took a chair in the drawing room as a scuffle broke out between the men. Harry fought off Dawson, eventually throwing the empty snuffbox away.

But finally he was gone.

Matilda sat alone in the quite drawing room and began to

shake. She put her fingers to her lips and attempted to scrub away Harry Lloyd's kiss.

William had lied to her about Harry's demise.

She had married William believing she had no chance to marry for love. Harry could not love her now. She had accepted William's offer of a temporary marriage that would leave her with funds but ruined socially, seeing that as her only chance for a comfortable life.

Now that lie was revealed, had she any incentive to remain as William's wife and keep to their bargain?

CHAPTER TWENTY

WILLIAM RUSHED up the front steps of his home. Coming home to Matilda felt so right, and he couldn't hide his anticipation of seeing her. He was sorry he'd gone out on a fool's errand and left her behind when they'd had plans to go out together. There had been no summons from Newberry House, indeed his aunt and Evelyn had been away from home and couldn't have sent any message.

Dawson's unhappy face greeted him in the entrance hall. "He came."

William passed off his hat and gloves to the butler. When Carter did not leave immediately, William sent him away. He drew Dawson into his library. "What happened?"

"Your wife met Mr. Lloyd. Somehow, he managed to get into the house, past every servant, and arrived upstairs. He was in the drawing room. I warned you the servants needed to be dismissed for their lack of propriety and respect to you both. He must have had someone's help, because I made it very clear that he was never to come here again the last time I saw him."

William curled his hands into fists. "So she's gone off with him."

"No, she is in the drawing room. But she is weeping again." Dawson drew closer. "She's had a shock. The man revealed a little bit more of his nature than she was prepared for."

"What do you mean?"

"Nothing happened, but I think he might have forced her had I not intervened."

"I'll kill him." William considered his options. Chasing after Harry Lloyd appealed, but Matilda was upset. He'd see to her first. "Thank you, Dawson. I had better go and meet with my wife."

He trudged upstairs, more than a little worried about what sort of reception he'd receive today. Sometimes she smiled, sometimes she seemed wary, but after discovering he'd lied to her about Harry Lloyd's death so there was no impediment to their marriage, he expected any number of greetings. None of them could be good or in his favor.

He stepped into the drawing room, spotting Matilda far down the large chamber, and closed the door behind him to ensure their privacy. Her gaze was pensive as she stared out the nearby window. He drew closer, tense with both anger and apprehension.

She didn't acknowledge him, so he sat at her side and waited for her to speak.

Her head turned a little toward him. "Dawson told you I had a visitor."

"He did. I will go after him directly and make Lloyd regret ever coming to see you."

"You will do nothing." Her jaw clenched. "Do you understand me? You will never raise your hand against Harry Lloyd."

"But he has upset you."

"No, Captain. You have upset me." She played with the ring on her finger. "Why did you say he was dead?"

"I didn't." He winced. "It was you who twisted my words to take on a more permanent meaning."

"You could have corrected me." She blinked rapidly, dislodging a tear. "You always correct me."

"I know he meant something to you, but you deserved better than that scoundrel. He would not have treated you well. He would have used you."

Her breath caught. "You used me to avoid marrying Miss Chudleigh."

"You knew I was going to do that." William stared hard at her face, trying desperately to read her mood. "You agreed, and I've never imposed on you. I thought this, we, were becoming more than a business arrangement."

"Our bargain is based on a lie."

"Our marriage is not. Have I not kept my promise that I would protect you and never ask for more than you are comfortable with?"

She laughed bitterly as she studied the plain band gracing her left hand. "I accepted you because I could see no other way to escape servitude. I could not see the truth of your character, only the lie that you were a gentleman with somewhat honorable intentions."

"Lloyd did not have honorable intentions toward you. He fooled at least one other maid into sharing his bed."

"I never did."

"I never suspected you had. When you told me he offered to marry you, I was livid," he said. "I can recall the misery of another maid who'd been charmed by Lloyd's smooth tongue perfectly well. I wanted to spare you the unpleasantness."

"He had a ring." Her brows drew together. "He came to marry me."

William swore. "I don't believe it."

"Well I do, and that is all that matters," she whispered, turning away from him. "So you decided to save poor, gullible Matilda. To keep me in this gilded cage until you are bored with me."

"You are not gullible, and I would never tire of you." He nudged her arm. "What we have is not easy to describe, but I am happy with it. I thought you were becoming so too."

She hugged herself. "How can I trust you now?"

"Because you know me, better than anyone else ever could or will. I have done everything I can to protect you. I accept your limitations. I will never ask for more than you want to give." He frowned, trying, and failing to define how he felt about Matilda. It was more than need or want. He couldn't bear to lose her over this. "Lloyd was dismissed from service for lifting the skirts of another maid. He filled her belly and denied any responsibility."

Her skin paled. "Why did I not hear of it?"

"Luck and quick action." He sighed. "The girl had been Dawson's particular friend—not an intimate acquaintance, he assured me—but they confided in each other. She only told him, and he appealed to me. When confronted, Lloyd fled. I never imagined he would return. I never imagined you had formed an attachment to him until the moments before you accepted my proposal."

Her brow furrowed. "He said he was going to make his fortune, and he has."

"That surprises me. Lloyd barely worked a day here as it was. Dawson has revealed tidbits of how the servants' hall is run, and I have to say I'm not pleased with what I have learned has been going on behind my back. I am sorry if you were imposed upon when you were a maid here."

"I was not imposed upon," she whispered. "But I was worked very hard. I used to go to sleep at night so exhausted that my whole body ached. Morning always came too soon."

He clenched his hands into fists, furious. "I'd no idea. I'm so sorry, Matilda."

"Why should you have troubled yourself over me? I was just a servant."

"My dear woman, right or wrong, you were never just a servant to me." He considered whether to touch her, take her hand or wrist, but decided against it. He was patient enough to wait. He would let Matilda make further overtures if there were to be any at all before their arrangement came to an end. "It has always been up to you what our marriage entails. I have tried to give you time to adjust to your new role. I care about you. From the moment we met I wanted to protect you. I hired you without references because I couldn't bear the thought of you leaving my house."

"Thank you, Captain." A half smile curved her lips, but her tone dripped sarcasm, something he'd never heard from her lips before. "It is pleasant not to be exhausted anymore. To sleep uninterrupted in a soft bed until after the sun has risen."

He clenched his jaw. Was she so upset that she never noticed her slip into formality? He'd grown so accustomed to her using his given name that his rank on her lips was insulting. "I like to wake you solely to have the pleasure of your company."

She smiled sadly at that. "So you can move me around like a puppet on a string."

William sighed as his patience was tested with that remark. She might see herself that way, but he did not. Matilda had grown to enjoy his fussing until this moment. "The household needs firmer guidance from you if it is to function properly from now on."

"Mrs. Young is very set in her ways." She shrugged. "She won't listen to me. Why would anyone?"

"Because you are my wife. You must stand up to her. If she wishes to remain in our employ, she must adapt." He clenched his hands between his knees. Dear God, he'd never heard Matilda so defeated before. It made him afraid he had lost her good opinion forever. Did she even want what he offered her? He had to know today if he'd ruined their marriage. "If you wish to separate now because of what I led you to believe about Lloyd, then that is your decision, and I will make the necessary arrangements so you can follow him and hope he will offer for you again. He'd be a fool not to."

As she closed her eyes and her lips pressed together tightly, William's heart gave a horrified lurch. Did she wish to go?

He pressed on, knowing he must. "If, however, you want to remain as my wife for the season and beyond, I will be pleased and support any changes you wish to make within the staff and how the household is run. I want you to be happy here. I want our staff to be happy here too, but there is a thickening layer of dust on all the furniture. They must do some work for their wages. I can only assume the dust has formed because you are not working yourself to an early death to clean our house."

She did not react to his words, but tears began to slide down her cheeks.

He took a calming breath to better voice a third option. "But if spending the rest of your life with me is something you would consider, I would be the happiest of men. We are, despite your misgivings, a very good match. I have trusted you with my life, Matilda, and I have no doubts about that decision. Yet I know it cannot be easy to accept my rules and restrictions. Trust me with your happiness and allow me the privilege of making this a marriage for forever."

He stood when she remained silent. "I'll be downstairs if you should wish to talk again tonight. And unless you say otherwise, we will go on as we have been—sleeping beside each other at night, dressing together in the morning."

On a sudden impulse, he kissed the top of her head. "Think about it, Matilda. I can give you everything you need and more. A home, wealth, security, passion, and friendship. I don't want to crush your spirit. I want to nurture it. Reveal it until others can see your worth too."

William looked for signs of agreement, but her eyes remained closed, her face stained with tears. Should he tell her his secret wish? A truth he'd never been sure how to voice? But this moment was the worst time to confess that he loved her. She might think he was trying to manipulate her again. Better to say nothing and wait until the time was right if she stayed.

He strode out with a heavy heart. The truth was always a discomfort, and loving Matilda had always been a secret he'd kept close to his heart. He made his way to the library and stopped before the window.

Outside, Harry Lloyd waited on the street, eyes fixed on the upper drawing room window where William had left Matilda to decide the fate of their marriage. Miss Chudleigh's carriage rolled past, and the woman's face turned to him. She waved.

William glared at them both until they went on their way, and hoped they would never darken his door again.

CHAPTER TWENTY-ONE

MATILDA WIPED at her eyes as tears continued to fall. Indecision gripped her. She was furious, confused, bound up in lies and desire, and hope, with no certainty of what lay ahead.

Seeing Harry again had been such a revelation. He'd forced her to see a truth that had been staring her in the face all along. She preferred to keep the easy life she was living now. Despite the lie, she wanted to remain with William.

If Harry Lloyd did actually go into a partnership at a tavern and married her after her marriage to William ended, Matilda as his wife would have to work, and work very hard, for the rest of her life.

Every form of the life William offered was very easy in comparison.

She stared at her hands. Once red and chafed from hard work, they were soft and paler than she'd ever seen them since her father's death. William hated it when she even tidied a room.

She was also appalled at the idea of running out of her marriage, even if William had lied to her to obtain her agreement.

She drew her knees up to her chest and placed her chin upon

them. Harry was right too, after a fashion—she was always in this part of the house for the latter part of the day. Even when William had been at sea, she had gravitated to this pretty room—seeking a moment or two of peace from the other servants. For a short while she had pretended to be the lady of the house rather than the lowly maid who cleaned it.

And now, thanks to William's new and startling wishes, she might live with him forever.

All she had to do was believe in him. To trust him without reservations.

She liked this house, and she'd grown accustomed to her easy life here. His family was kind, and she was slowly growing accustomed to them being around.

She had even grown accustomed to William's scolding's and rules. He was very steady in temperament once she had figured out his quirks and made allowances for his desires.

She'd learned to understand her own.

Matilda looked forward to the next punishment so much that the very memory of the last made her body quiver with anticipation. But despite the pleasure of her situation with William, she had never believed she belonged in his world. She'd always known she could never stay with him.

And yet the thought of leaving, of never seeing him and his scowl again, brought unbearable pain.

There was a tap at the open door, and she quickly placed her feet on the floor so she would appear a proper lady. "Come in."

As it swung open, her disappointment was acute that William had not come back to her. "Yes, Dawson?"

"Captain Ford begs me to ask if you would be joining him for dinner."

She frowned, unable to decide. She didn't want to leave the comfort of this room yet because the moment she did she would have to decide what to do with her life and their marriage. "Tell me about your friend, the one Harry Lloyd stole from you."

Dawson shut the door quickly and took a few paces into the room. "Not stole. She was never really mine. Marta worked as a kitchen maid. She was young, pretty, and very shy, just like you in some respects. A little flattery, and before I knew it Lloyd had a claim on her heart."

"Marta? I think I remember meeting her when I began working here. I was sorry when she left. She was nice to me. I thought we might have become friends one day."

Dawson winced. "I think she would have liked you too. I didn't understand until it was too late that Lloyd had promised her marriage in return for her favors. Marriage was never his goal. She came to me in tears as soon as her condition became apparent and told me how he'd disappointed her. I had some money saved, and I gave it all to her, and after appealing to the captain he gave me leave to escort her into the country myself. My sister had married well to a carpenter with his own shop, and was willing to harbor Marta until she found her feet. By the time I returned, the captain had dismissed Lloyd from his duties. I had thought Lloyd might have done the right thing and married Marta, but in the end, she lost the babe and remained with my sister in the country as her housekeeper."

Her throat tightened at the similarities between her and Marta's past. She had almost succumbed to Lloyd's seduction once, made a little too merry from punch she'd later learned had been embellished with alcohol. It was probably pure luck that she'd not been ruined, but Matilda had never been comfortable in her own skin, or bold enough to risk behaving in a manner that might lose her a position. Not until William's strict instruction and seduction had educated her a little about the truth of her nature. "Do you still see her? Marta?"

"Not for over a year now. My sister writes that she is well and asks for news of me on occasion. I will most likely ask her to marry me next Christmas, if she's not found someone else."

"I hope she hasn't for your sake." Matilda was filled with sadness and wiped at her eyes. "You are a good man, Dawson."

"I wish I had known he'd promised to marry you. I could have saved you so much trouble by revealing his flaws." Dawson came closer and perched on a chair nearby. "He was desperate for coin, but then you knew he had light fingers, didn't you?"

"He always swore it was accidental." Matilda grimaced. "And then would talk about how wonderful our life would be far away from here."

"You can't leave with Lloyd."

The idea of a liar and seducer of innocents in her life was decidedly uncomfortable.

Dawson continued. "I am sure it seems unforgivable that Captain Ford lied to you. I am equally sure he did it because he cares about you so much more than he reveals. He never meant any harm, and he is a much better match for you in my opinion. Please give him another chance, or at least don't be fooled by Lloyd's claims that Captain Ford chased after all the maids."

"I know William wouldn't do that." Matilda drew in a sharp breath. He'd focused his attention on her from the moment they'd met though. She'd sensed his interest, been flattered by it a little. He'd claimed he'd tried to fight his attraction. "I am quite done with Mr. Lloyd, I assure you."

But was she done with William too?

She did not know the answer to that, but she would have to decide and soon. Despite William's claim, their marriage could not stay the same. "I'd like to be alone now."

"Very good, madam." Dawson released a heavy sigh, as if he'd been truly afraid she'd throw over her husband so quickly. "Shall I bring up your supper tray?"

"Yes, please." The sun was setting, her favorite time of day. "I will remain here for the evening."

"And the captain, ma'am?"

She glanced at the ring on her finger. The only thing she had that made her a respectable woman. "I have no message for my husband."

Dawson added more fuel to the fire and then fled. By the time he'd returned with her supper tray, Matilda had decided what to do. Everyone believed her properly wed and bedded. It was only a matter of time before the inevitable fall happened. Why deny that her own nature required William's firm hand to bring her peace?

If pleasure and pain were all she could have, she'd take it. Her hope of being loved would have to go begging.

CHAPTER TWENTY-TWO

SINCE MATILDA HAD NOT COME down to speak with him or left the house to meet with Harry Lloyd, William kept to his regular schedule as best he could. He ate, read, and at the time he felt right, he climbed the stairs and strolled to the dressing room. Thank God his sisters had returned to Newberry House earlier. He could not have borne their questions or disappointment in him.

He'd made a bloody mess of his marriage. The question though was could their friendship be saved?

He went into the dressing room first, but the space was empty of Matilda. Her nightclothes were still laid out upon the chaise next to the gown she had worn that day. He stared at her stockings, corset, and chemise and glanced around. What was she wearing?

He picked up her chemise and held it a moment, pulse racing as he breathed in her scent. Rosemary and lemon. Familiar scents that always decided his moods. She stirred his passions and his temper.

Matilda never slept without clothing.

To do so was immodest and sure to tempt him to break their bargain.

He hoped she knew by now that her bare skin excited him beyond reason.

Although he should not read anything into her nightgown being in the dressing room still, the sight of it made him tremble with hope. Matilda hadn't chased after Harry Lloyd and had two options before her—keep to their terms, which ended with separation, or become his wife in every way that counted.

He had expected to talk about her choice and move forward in the manner they agreed. He needed to know her limits so he could do his best to always meet them and never stray beyond.

He undressed slowly, stripped down to his breeches, and then approached their dark bedchamber, his candle held aloft. Inside, sheets rustled as she moved in their bed restlessly.

When he stepped through the doorway his heart raced. Matilda lay in the exact center, her dark hair spilled over his pillow, but the sheets were pulled up to her chin modestly. He couldn't tell if she was naked under the sheet, but after a moment of silent scrutiny he assumed so. She seemed more than a little nervous.

He put the candle aside on a chest of drawers, moved to the bed, and pulled back the sheet only a little so he could climb in next to her. "Matilda."

"William," she whispered.

He rested on one elbow, watching her carefully, and then slowly peeled back the sheet an inch or two. Her shoulder was bare. He fought jubilation and traced a circle on her skin with his fingertip, unwilling to rush to any assumption that might lead to embarrassment for either one of them. "Does this mean what I hope it means?"

"Our bargain wasn't fair. Not to either of us." She met his gaze. "I want to be your wife, William. I want to be the wife you want me to be."

"You already are." He smiled and flung the bedding away.

Matilda jumped, startled by his actions. "William!"

He loved his name on her lips. He kissed her shoulder, her neck, overcome with hope for their future. "So very beautiful, and all mine."

"And you'll be mine too." She captured his face and pulled him in for a kiss. Her behavior was a little startling since she usually waited for him to act. He couldn't say he didn't like her wanting him, but there was an order to his amours.

He leaned over her a little farther and sank into their kiss. Her fingers wormed between them, and she unbuttoned the fall of his breeches. She eased them down over his hips until they bunched at his thighs, and he was too shocked to utter a word of protest. Too excited to slow things down. William rid himself of the garment and returned to Matilda, expecting to talk honestly about her change of heart.

Except she caught him in her hand and stroked his length until he was unbearably aroused and very nearly incapable of coherent thought.

The very thing he'd been secretly longing for since they'd met, acceptance of his nature and affection from his wife, had become his most gratifying experience. His Matilda was the strongest, most forgiving, bravest person he'd ever met. By God, he loved her.

He drew back a little, staring at her lips. "I don't deserve you," he whispered, "but I will treasure every moment we have together."

"Make me your wife," she asked, eyes huge and trusting. "Make me feel you want me for myself and not just as a means to keep others from having you."

"I do want you, Mattie. I always have." He eased into position between her thighs, fighting his instincts to claim her immediately. But she was so untouched, so truly pure, that he feared no matter his hesitance that he would cause her pain. To keep her as his wife, and William wanted nothing else but that, he would have to be very careful not to disappoint her again. "This might hurt."

"No more than I expect."

She was warm against him, and he held her close as he made love to her mouth and body, trying to prepare her. She was restless beneath him, but he would not be rushed.

He slipped his hand between her legs, discovering warmth and moisture between her lower lips. He teased her, sliding over her clitoris and the entrance to her quim. He'd never had a virgin. He'd heard all manner of things could go wrong though. Nothing could ever go wrong between them again. Matilda had to enjoy this too. He wanted her to love everything they did together. He wanted her to love him.

He carefully inserted his fingertip into her tight sheath and pushed in.

Matilda gasped.

"I'll go slow," he promised, easing his finger back out immediately.

He moved back to her clitoris and swirled his fingers around. She was used to his touch there, and her body relaxed again. He returned to her opening, teased, and toyed with her until she grew accustomed to his invasion. When he had two fingers gliding in and out of her body, when Matilda's breath was coming in short little pants, she tightened her arms about his neck and rubbed her nipples against his chest with a happy little moan.

He eased down the bed and lightly suckled her breast, flicking his tongue over the hard point as Matilda twisted and moaned on his fingers. "Oh, William. That feels so strange."

He raised his head enough to ask, "Good, strange?"

"Yes."

He shifted downward, lapping her belly, and bestowing firm

kisses over the flat surface. He moved lower to the nest of curls that protected her core and buried his face there, flicking out his tongue to tease her clitoris too. He loved her taste.

Matilda held his head, tugging at his hair in her distress and arousal. "Don't make me wait."

He withdrew his fingers, rose up to stare down at her. "I choose the manner we come together, or have you forgotten?"

"No, but... I'm afraid you might stop before I'm truly a wife."

He turned her hips a little and slapped her bottom. "Impatience will only lead to pain."

"I like your pain. I want it. I need it, William. Please."

William flipped her over to her back and joined with her before she could issue any more demands or doubt him again. They belonged together.

Her shocked cry and tight confines brought out every fear and secret longing as he pressed deep. She hadn't been ready. He should have taken more time.

He should have gagged her so she couldn't goad him on.

He held still as the idea made him quake. He had only ever gone so far with women, but there were more opportunities for dominance with a wife than his imagination could conjure up. Binding Matilda would be so wonderful. Exciting for both of them too.

He kissed her lips before he thought too much about that, thrusting his tongue into her mouth the way he wished to take her sweet body. Her fingers moved on his chest delicately, and he drew back. Tears slid from the corner of each eye and disappeared into her hairline. She offered a tremulous smile.

"Oh, Mattie mine." He hugged her tight, lost in the wonder of her unflinching spirit. "I hurt you."

"Am I complaining?"

"No, but then again you never do." He began to move, slowly

at first, giving her time to grow used to him being inside her. After a time he pulled back, resting his weight on his hands so he could see her face as he quickened his rhythm. Her eyes fluttered closed, and she took her bottom lip between her teeth.

Fearing he was hurting her, he froze.

Her hands clamped down on his hips and her legs brushed his. She lifted her gaze to his and he saw desire, pure raw hunger in her expression. "Don't stop," she begged. "Oh, please stay with me. I never expected this. I'm so close."

He moved again, watching her face now. She frowned, grimaced, and twisted against him, clearly enthralled by their tryst and desperate for the inevitable conclusion. He cupped her breast with one hand then pinched her nipple hard. Matilda gasped softly, a sound he'd grown to love hearing as he spanked her, and he twisted his fingers to give her more pain.

She came around him, a soft shriek filling the room, and he released her breast to watch her face relax. She lay beneath him afterward gasping, a wondrous smile spreading over her face. Her body quaked around him for a long time, and when she was spent, her hands slipped off his skin slowly. "I'm glad it was you."

William shifted over her fully, cock hard and eager to pump into her body every feeling he possessed. No one ever but him would have this honor. He would never give her up now. He braced his forearms around her head and flexed his hips, driving into her tense sheath, relieved that she appeared not to be in any great pain.

A dreamy smile lingered on her lips. "Do that again."

"I have wanted this for so long," he confessed as he thrust again and withdrew with a little more vigor before claiming her again. "I never expected for one moment to have my heart's desire in my bed."

"And I have mine. I belong to you now, Billy Boy."

He raised a brow while he loved her as gently as he could despite the provocation. "Careful, darling. I'm on edge already. I don't want to hurt you more than necessary tonight. Corrections can wait for another time."

"For the first time in my life, I know what I want. I am happy that I am with you like this. I want you to be this happy too." She stretched her arms over her head, pressed her palms against the wooden headboard, smiling, and then chanted, "Billy, Billy, Billy."

"No," he gasped, fighting an arousal that threatened to overtake his control.

"Yes, Billy."

Her defiance was like lightning stroking down his spine. The taunt snapped his control and he shuddered at her provocation. He shoved into her hard and then withdrew, pumping his hips while lust filled his mind with desire and passion and unstoppable love. Matilda braced herself against the headboard as his thighs slapped into hers. He rose above her, desperate and wild not to miss a moment of pure bliss. He hooked her leg around his hip, and she curled the other around him too. With her hips raised from the bed, he could take her the way he needed to. The way she seemed to want him to, as well. He twisted her a little to the side, exposing her rear even as he thrust. He slapped her bottom—once, twice. And then fucked her long and hard until he could wait no more.

He slapped her bottom again and then held her steady as he pumped his seed deep into her body with a hoarse shout that should have been heard all the way to the attics of the house. His spasms lasted forever, but he struggled to focus on her face. She smiled at him; her face flushed a deep red but no tears. "Thank God," he whispered.

All the pain and uncertainty had been worth the wait. Matilda offered a shy smile, the kind that never failed to affect him. He collapsed in a tangle of her arms and legs and held her to him. Her softness was a balm for his soul, her trust the most precious gift.

He'd known, that first day when Mrs. Young had introduced Matilda as a prospective employee, that he'd sacrifice his honor to be with her just once. She had been forbidden to him then, and he'd carried his desire for her in secret. Now he could treasure every moment, shape every interlude to bring them both happiness.

She stroked his hair from his face, and he recalled a memory from his time as her unwilling charge. He shifted down the bed, lying between her spread legs, and rested his chin gently on her chest, watching her face closely. "You did that when I was first brought home. I remember thinking it would be the last caress of my life, the best thing that ever happened to me. I did not deserve your kindness then."

She did it again and raised one brow. "I surprised myself that day too. I didn't want you to die. It seemed unthinkable."

"How fortunate for me. How lucky that we didn't miss this opportunity to know each other."

Her face clouded but then she smiled. "Was it luck? How did you know I could like what you would do to me?"

"I didn't know. How could I suspect that beneath such beauty lay a woman after my own heart? I'm glad you agreed to marry me. I'm grateful for this time with you." He brushed his lips across her skin, overcome by emotions that threatened to unman him. He was truly in love. He'd never felt this way before about any woman.

"Me too."

He jostled to glimpse her face. "Sleep in my arms tonight. If you can bear it, I'd like to make love to you in the morning before we start our day."

She pushed him off and then settled in his arms, one arm slung across his chest, her bare leg pinning his down in a way she had not embraced him before. It was possessive and made his heart skip a beat.

Matilda took a long breath and then kissed his skin. "I would not deny you."

"Thank heavens." He kissed her brow and then cuddled her close. Marriage was what he needed. Marriage to Matilda and all the tenderness she could spare him.

CHAPTER TWENTY-THREE

MATILDA TAPPED the papers in front of her on the drawing room table. "You will dismiss Jenny and Jane today."

Mrs. Young gasped. "On what grounds?"

"On the grounds they're not working for their wages and never have." Matilda kept her expression neutral, but inside she was anxious. Giving orders to Mrs. Young was within her rights and expected by her husband, but she did not anticipate that the woman would give way without a fight.

"They are excellent maids, the best I've ever trained," Mrs. Young protested. "You may not have ever liked them, but that does not mean they do not do their job."

"Oh, I liked them the first month I was here until they kept pressuring me into doing their work for them." Matilda grimaced. "The longer I worked here, the more they did not do, and you turned a blind eye. They put salt in my tea, dirt in my shoes and worse, and you never looked out for me. I would not be surprised if you had not encouraged them too by talking about the pranks played in other grand homes."

Mrs. Young spluttered. "You've always possessed an active

imagination, seeing faults in others before your own. It was not I that trapped the master into marriage."

Matilda had been trapped too, by William and by her own nature. She'd accepted that a woman had few options in life, some of them brought pleasure, others brought pain. She could be happy as William's wife, enduring both, if she dared trust in herself and in him. She turned her attention back to the matter at hand. "You believed their claims that I was dragging my feet while I worked their chores on top of my own. I was not lazy, I was exhausted."

"You were dangling after the captain from the first day you arrived."

Matilda shook her head. She had known Mrs. Young would resist change but had hoped the woman would see she had two choices—either follow Matilda's orders or accept the consequences of not doing so. Matilda still hoped for agreement. What had been done to her was in the past, and it was the future she cared about most. She had made a promise to William; she would straighten out his home. She found the sheet of paper she'd prepared earlier in the day and glanced over it to mask her dislike of confrontation. "This lists the chores Nora completed on the last day of my employment as a servant."

Mrs. Young attached her spectacles to her face and studied the note. "Seems in order."

"According to Captain Ford's own instructions for the house-keeper, half of those chores belong to Jenny. So, after the chores I was doing for Jenny and all Alice has done too, Jenny was left with dusting the entrance hall and dining room. Hardly taxing enough for a woman of her age and stamina, and yet both rooms remain undusted this week."

Mrs. Young made a noise. "She had other duties this week."

"Yes, but those other chores are the responsibility of the housekeeper. I do not wish her that much responsibility. Nor does the captain." Matilda scowled. "Tell me, Mrs. Young, what exactly have you done this morning except slap Alice's face for yawning at the table and imbibe half a bottle of red wine with your breakfast? Don't deny it. I can smell the drink on you from here."

Mrs. Young's face colored. "How dare you!"

"Be careful, Mrs. Young. Do not forget who I am now and what I can do." Matilda said, remembering William speaking to her in such a manner. "I am the lady of this house, and you will do as I wish or leave."

"I won't stay here and listen to this slander. The Duke of Rutherford hired me, and only he can dismiss me. Which I am positive he will not do." Mrs. Young pushed to her feet, most certainly in an attempt to intimidate Matilda.

If Matilda had not already been intimidated by a master of manipulation, William, the housekeeper might have had some hope of winning the day. As it was, the housekeeper's behavior only made Matilda weary. She smiled, having already anticipated this tactic from the woman. In truth, most of the servants here had been originally employed by the Duke of Rutherford. "By all means, speak to my husband's grandfather and call me a liar. I am sure the great man will immediately side with you."

"He's a fair man, unlike some who think themselves better than others simply because of marriage."

Matilda had expected that too. Her elevation had likely upset the old woman, but until now she'd held back her spite. Matilda had no right to think very highly of herself. She had married for money and security, after all.

"Should you change your mind about speaking with him and accept the termination of your employment graciously from me, I have written an adequate letter of reference for a housekeeper of your years of experience and set aside appropriate severance money. I do not know that Rutherford will offer you so much in its stead."

"He will certainly hear of this outrage. So will the captain." The housekeeper stormed off in the direction of the main stairs. Since William was currently reading in the library, she felt a twinge of pity. She was certain the two would meet directly. She experienced unease for the unnecessary disturbance of his day. Matilda usually tried to avoid any interruption to his routine.

What could she do if others refused to follow the captain's rules?

Matilda tapped the letter of reference on the table, then slid it away into the desk. She would not offer Mrs. Young the letter or severance money again. Her pride had already been stretched enough to offer that much after the woman's years of neglect and gluttony.

She glanced up at a tap at the door. "Come in."

Nora and Paul Franks filed in, scullery maid and boot boy siblings, their faces mirroring confusion and worry. Guilt ate at her that she had not seen to an improvement in their circumstances sooner. She had been so wrapped up in her changed situation that she had overlooked their needs. But she would take steps today to ensure they were never overworked again under this roof.

"Good morning, ma'am," the two said.

"Good morning." They stood nervously near the open door, and with a start Matilda realized it might be the first time the pair had ventured into these rooms. She smiled at them warmly, hoping to put them at ease. "And I hope it will be a better morning for you soon."

Dawson arrived, carrying a heavy tray. Milk, bread, ham, and cheese. Everything a pair of growing youngsters could want to ease the ache of an empty stomach. He set it on the table before the fire. "Is there anything else?"

"No, but please see that we are not disturbed by anyone."

When he was gone with a polite nod, Matilda gestured to the food. "That tray is for the pair of you. Please eat. I am sure you are very hungry."

They looked at her a long moment and then scampered to the tray. While they ate their fill, Matilda collected the letter for their mother, and the coins from their wages she meant to send home with them and waited patiently.

The boy finished first, wiping his mouth with the back of his hand. The girl used the napkin and then stood stiffly. "Thank you, ma'am."

Matilda smiled. "Now. I want you to do something for me. I want you to take this letter and these coins and go straight home to your mother."

The pair cried out. "Don't turn us out."

"Oh, no. Never." She hurried to them and caught the girl's hand. As the elder, she was the one who needed to understand they were not being punished by being sent away. "The letter explains everything for your mother, but I want you to have a little holiday from your duties. I know how hard you have worked here and how little freedom you've been allowed. The other servants have not treated you very well, and I'm sorry I have not done more before today."

"You were always kind to us, and we don't want to go."

She was glad they thought well of her, but it was best they be removed for now. She was about to set the house into an uproar, and she didn't want these mere children caught up in the chaos. She passed the note and money to the girl. "You are to go directly to your mother, no stopping to buy treats along the way since your tummies are full already. Help your mother if you can with your siblings, sleep, rest, and do as she says. Then next Tuesday you are to return to your duties here. By eleven if you can, or earlier if you want."

They appeared confused. "Are you sure, ma'am?"

"I am very sure," she promised them.

"You're not mad at me because I let Mr. Lloyd in," the boy whispered.

"No. Not at all." Matilda smiled at the boy. He appeared very worried. "I had something to tell him anyway, so you did me a very great favor."

Brother and sister glanced at each other quickly. "Thank you."

She walked them to the door, fretting over them finding their way alone. Mrs. Young had not given them leave in the past year. Would they get lost? "On second thought. Dawson!"

He appeared within seconds. "Yes, my lady."

"Would you be kind enough to hail a hack for this pair? I am sending Nora and Paul home for a short holiday. It is a very long walk to their mother's home, and I would not like them to become lost."

The boy's eyes widened considerably. "A carriage ride? Truly?"

Dawson beamed, ruffling the boy's hair. "Only too happy to arrange it. If I may, I'd like to accompany them. The hack will take them the whole way and not half the distance for twice the fare."

Matilda nodded, removed sufficient coin from her pocket, and handed enough to him for the round trip. "A wise precaution. Hurry back. There are still a great many changes to make today."

Belowstairs, the sound of Mrs. Young's complaining could be clearly heard. She shrieked and the younger servants ran to the rail and glanced down while Dawson and Matilda listened from a safe distance. He smiled suddenly as Mrs. Young's protests about her dismissal became clearer.

He nodded to Matilda approvingly. "Looking forward to it actually."

"I thought you might." She grinned. "We are going to need a new housekeeper."

"Do you have someone in mind?"

"Indeed I do, and that can be discussed later. But first let's get Nora and Paul away on their holiday." She put her hand on the boy's shoulder. "I will see you both next Tuesday, and by then I hope to have everything improved belowstairs."

The girl, who had always been more reserved than her brother, dipped a curtsy and led her brother away. Matilda held Dawson back. "Make sure no one interferes with them on the way out of the servants' hall. I have no proof of this, but I want to be sure their wages reach their mother without subtractions."

"Agreed." Dawson rushed after the children, speaking in low tones as he ushered them into the servants' staircase.

So far, all was proceeding as Matilda had hoped. Next was dismissing Jenny and Jane herself if Mrs. Young refused. She didn't anticipate too much trouble from that pair of imbeciles. She'd pay them enough final wages to send them off smiling with their passable letter of reference. After that, she had enough time to place a notice in the paper for new staff and to draft a new outline of duties. The days where a young or harder-working servant bore the brunt of chores was over. She would personally oversee the staff until a suitable replacement was employed as housekeeper and judged sufficient for her needs.

She was hard at work on a revised and far simpler menu for Cook when William strolled in.

"That was not pleasant," William remarked as he tossed a book onto a chair and stopped inches away. "You might have warned me you planned to upset the applecart today."

Matilda stood and faced him. "You told me action was overdue."

Her heart skipped a beat. They'd made love last night. She'd finally given herself completely to their marriage and had no regrets. The loss of her virtue had been her decision. William had seemed surprised, and he'd been so considerate afterward.

"Indeed it was." He kissed her cheek and then glanced over her writing table while she blushed. His mouth had been between her legs. A part of him had been inside her body, and she'd enjoyed every moment. "I had no idea Mrs. Young thought so meanly of you. I dismissed her too, by the way, without a letter of reference, simply for her unfounded spite. She's planning an appeal to my grandfather, but I doubt he'll see her."

Matilda shrugged and placed her hand on William's arm and squeezed. "She has always resented that I was capable and could work without her instruction."

William's arm crept around her back, and he held her a moment. "That she thought to warn me to keep an eye on the silver because of you was beyond insulting."

Matilda winced and drew back. "She must resent my heritage."

"Heritage?"

"Hmm, I suppose you deserve to know the truth about my family. You asked about my mother." Matilda clasped her hands at her waist. "Romani." Although she whispered it, the confession seemed to boom through the room.

"She's one of the Rom?" William tilted his head to the side as he studied her. "Oh."

"Thankfully, aside from her coloring, I inherited nothing of her nature."

"When you would not talk of her, I assumed your mother was

French or Italian or such. That you were ashamed of the connection because we had been at war with her people."

Matilda shook her head quickly. "My mother's family is in England somewhere." She studied William's face, watching for signs of disapproval. Her heart might break if he turned away because of her mother. "I do get restless at times but not, as my father often remarked, as much as she once did."

William captured her face in his palm, turning her into the light. "I have always been fascinated by your features."

She grew uncomfortable as he continued to study her. "Unconventional."

"Unique. So calm and yet so subtly wild beneath the surface. Like the way you dance in the woods and watch the sunset from this room every day. You are drawn to nature as much as I'm drawn to you. From the moment I laid eyes on you, I have tried to capture your attention and never once managed the feat to my satisfaction. There is something so elusive about your face and eyes. You bewitched me, and at last I know why."

Matilda glanced away at his remarks, unsettled by them. "My father said as much of my mother. Marrying a Rom did not turn out so well for him in the end."

"He lost her too soon." William brushed his thumb across her lips. "I can understand the wish to keep you safe from harm at all costs. I am only surprised you allow me so much latitude."

"It feels right between us, William." She blushed though. She had not the strength to fight her own nature. She liked being disciplined. "My mother didn't die, William. She went home to live with her people because she could not abide society or my father's rules and restrictions."

His eyes widened in shock. "Your mother is alive?"

"I imagine so." Matilda shrugged. "They fought before she left. My mother wanted to take me with her, but my father refused to part with me. He would not deny his daughter a place in the world, he said. He promised to educate me, something my mother wished for but could not provide if she resumed her life with her people. She gave me up. She never came back."

William caught her wrist and held her firmly. "Do you want to search for her? I will help you find out what has become of her."

"That is very kind of you, but it is not necessary. My father and I lived in the same house until his death. In all that time, she never sought us out again." Matilda shrugged, unable to recall much about the woman who'd given birth to her or stir up the longing to seek her out. "If she had wanted to see me, to be my mother again, she would have come long before now."

"Her loss. She should have been proud of the woman you've become. Here now, lift your chin." He raised her face with his knuckle, his brow creasing severely. "You have nothing to be ashamed of, Matilda Ford."

Matilda studied his earnest expression, astonished by his remark. "I married for money, William. For that I have every right to be disappointed in myself."

"How can you think that? If not for you, I would have died. You had no idea how lost I was until you came."

Matilda traced the scar on his cheek. "Our lives prepared us for each other, but it is up to us how we live those lives."

"Indeed it is." He grinned and studied her notes. "You'll need to advertise for a full complement of servants for the new house. I completed the purchase this morning. We can move next week."

Matilda bit her lip. "We have the perfect butler already. He simply needs a promotion and a kind word from you."

"Dawson?"

Matilda nodded. "He will be perfect in the position and can help Miss Marta if she accepts my offer to come back and work for us as housekeeper."

William raised a brow. "Are you offering the woman the position so you may play matchmaker?"

"I am offering her the housekeeper position because I feel she and I will get along. If Dawson and Marta rekindle their romance, then two needs are served at once." She shuffled her papers. "I assume you have no objection to fraternization between people who intend marriage."

"No." He chuckled softly and caught her up into his arms. "What did I do before you came along?"

"I don't know, but I prefer not to speculate."

His hand smacked against her bottom. "Dearest Matilda, my wife, my darling, my savior. You are the only woman who has ever spoken to me with so much honesty. I don't know how I survived without you, and I couldn't live without you now."

She blushed at his promises. Accepting his rules and punishments was easy. Keeping her place in his world took all her strength, but she was willing to be instructed. She wrapped her arms about his neck, smiling up into his face. "I can be all you need, Billy."

He kissed her hard. "Darling, say that again."

"Billy," she whispered into his ear.

William hoisted her off the floor and moved toward their dressing room.

"I want you over my knee right now, Matilda," William said before drawing up her skirts. A cold draft tickled her bottom, and his fingers teased the back of her thighs in a distracting dance. She loved him when he was bossy.

But there was one thing more she needed to say before he would continue. Something vitally important. She whispered his name. "Billy."

CHAPTER TWENTY-FOUR

WILLIAM LET himself inside their new home and smiled at the change Matilda had already brought to the place after just a few short days. Mirrors were hung, hall tables placed exactly where he'd expected them to be and topped with flowers gathered from their own garden. He pushed the door closed on the outside world and placed the heavy wicker basket on the floor gently.

He'd been away, attending to the final packing of their possessions, which should arrive in the next day to conclude their move from London to the country.

The move had gone smoothly and was completed so quickly that he was impressed. Matilda had handled everything beautifully. He'd allowed her to stay here without him for two nights, but only because Dawson and the new housekeeper had already assumed their new roles.

He was standing in his first-ever home, and quite proudly too. He imagined many happy moments in this place with Matilda. He imagined raising their family here together one day too.

He made his way to the butterfly house but stopped dead in his tracks when he saw what was going on. The room was filled with plants now, a cozy pair of chairs and a side table had been placed in one corner. But it was his Matilda that stilled him. His beloved was kneeling on the floor, her beguiling bottom swaying back and forth as she scrubbed at something she shouldn't be touching. "What is this?"

She spun around, eyes wide. "William, you're back!"

She scrambled to her feet and removed the soil-stained gloves that protected her fingers before she hurried to greet him with a peck on the cheek.

William put his hands on his hips. "I've come for my Mattie, but who is this urchin scrubbing at the tiles?"

"It was just a small spot," Matilda promised, appearing not the least bit guilty. "It was stubborn, and I could not stand it there a moment longer."

He grunted. Stopping Matilda cleaning their new home had become something of a battle between them. The minute he went out of a room she moved things, dusted, or started polishing windows. The number of times he'd spanked her for infractions, and she'd not complained, was a little alarming. "Very well. I will let this go just once."

She fell into his arms. "You were gone a very long time."

"Three days and two very long nights." He cupped her face with both hands and lifted her gaze to his. "An eternity."

"It was." She took her lower lip between her teeth but then smiled brightly. "I trust you left your family in good health."

William kissed her. Hard. Pleasantries could wait a few minutes. Gods, he'd almost run mad with missing her. "Victoria had a marriage proposal just as I left Newberry House. She's going to consider it on the journey back to Newberry Park and write to let us know what she decides."

Matilda's face grew serious. "She did? Who?"

"Lord Thornton. He's a kind man. I'd be very happy with the match if she accepts him."

Matilda turned away. "Does she love him?"

"Hard to say. Victoria keeps her feelings to herself much more than the other pair. Do you know how they met? My sister almost skewered him with an arrow of all things. He's a brave man to offer. He must wonder if he can survive the marriage." William laughed heartily, recalling how Victoria had blushed and stammered when she'd recounted the story. "Do you remember our wedding day?"

Matilda nodded.

He tweaked her chin. "You were so scared of what our marriage might entail. I hope you see now that your fears were unfounded, and you belong with me."

"Yes, William." She turned away. "I know what you want from me."

A shiver raced over William's skin at the flat quality of her response. He tried to catch her eye, but she kept fiddling with other things. "Maria Chudleigh showed her face again. She asked after you particularly."

Matilda turned away. "Oh, what did you tell her?"

Something subtle had changed since they'd become intimate, but couldn't work out why. He had wondered perhaps if his nature was driving a wedge between them. He'd given her everything he was. His name. His time. His attention. His wealth.

"I told her that when I returned to our home, I expected the nursery to be ready. She almost fainted at that suggestion. You would have laughed about it later with me." He placed one hand on Matilda's shoulder, and she jumped. "Are you all right?"

"I am not increasing," Matilda whispered as she resumed her work, tidying pots and shovels away into the workbench he'd had made especially for her use.

"Good. I confess to being entirely selfish. I want you all to myself for now."

She said nothing to that. "Did you see your friends too?"

"Yes, Mitchell and Cobb. We had dinner and drinks at the club the first night I was away. Both send their regards."

She nodded, but then her face fell. "You went to the club?"

"Yes. Grandfather pulled some strings and arranged a membership at White's."

Her breath whooshed out of her lungs suddenly. She rubbed her temple. "Are you happy with what I've done with the house so far? Do you approve?"

"What I have seen of it, yes." He pursed his lips, wondering what he'd done. "Now you must come with me. You have a visitor waiting to meet you."

She glanced down at her gown. "I'm not dressed for guests."

"You are perfect, as always, for this. Vicar will approve of my urgency and will not care what gown you are wearing."

She stared at him for a very long time. "I did not know you'd had time to attend services here too."

"Not that kind of vicar." He kissed her cheek. "Come and meet him."

William took her hand and brought her toward the front door. Before they had reached their destination, however, he heard whimpering. "Ah, Vicar has awakened."

The basket wobbled wildly.

"What is that?"

"Our dog. He was old enough to come home to you."

Matilda knelt on the ground and unlatched the heavy wicker basket. The dog, who'd thankfully slept most of the journey, burst out and proceeded to jump all over Matilda as if he remembered meeting her before.

All of a sudden, Matilda burst out crying and tried to hide her emotions from him. She hugged the squirming animal tightly to her chest. "He's just as I remember him, but why call him Vicar?"

"You said his little white spot at his throat reminded you of a catholic priest's robes. If you don't care for the name, it can be changed." William knelt at her side and patted the dog too. "He's had some training, but a little more would be a good idea."

"I will. I'll look after him and you'll never know he's here, I promise."

Her promise startled him. "Why would I not want to know he's here? That was the point of having a dog again. We'll both have company."

"But you like your peace."

"But not utter silence, Matilda. Dogs bark, our children will cry, and my wife has the most beautiful voice. I missed hearing you while I was away." He lifted her face to his as she sniffed back tears. "Darling, what is wrong? Don't ever hide your feelings from me."

"I'm sorry."

He took in her distress and pressed his head to hers. "Matilda, do you have any idea how much I love you? I would do anything to make you happy."

Her eyes darted to his, wide and full of surprise. "You love me?"

"Of course I do." Her lips parted and drew back in shock. "How can you not know that you've claimed my heart completely?"

Her eyes widened further, as if she did not trust his claim. "I have?"

He nodded quickly. "I spent the entire time I was in London gushing about my incredible wife to anyone who would listen. Cobb left dinner at Whites Club in a sulk, and Mitchell is probably still laughing at my impatience to return to you. I told Miss

Chudleigh that you might be setting up our nursery because one day, eventually, I hope we are blessed with children."

"Oh," she whispered.

"I've loved you for so long and never could put my feelings into words." He peered deep into her eyes, trying to show the depths of his devotion. "I wanted you, a servant in my home, when I should have known better. I exposed you to my desires without warning you that I'm not like other men. I wanted you so badly at times that I was jealous whenever you smiled at others."

"I wanted you too."

"No, you didn't. Not in the beginning." He held her face, brushing his thumb across her cheek. "I wanted so much to stay away from you once and I made that ridiculous bargain, intending to keep you safe. I tried to convince myself I could keep you at a distance and let you go later. But leaving you alone is impossible for me. I want you to be my wife, Matilda."

Her lashes fluttered, and then she smiled so warmly she lit up the room with her happiness. "I am already your wife, William."

"You are my best friend. The one person I can share my hopes and dreams with. You drive away my nightmares with your touch; you share my enjoyment of passion without ever making me feel I am wrong."

"What we do could never be wrong."

He kissed her cheek, pushed the dog aside, and held her there on the floor. "You got under my skin from the moment we met. But because I had blundered so badly, I had to start all over again." He brought her hand to his mouth and caressed her knuckles with his lips. "I am not an easy man to live with, but you found it in your heart to bear with me."

"I cannot imagine ever being afraid of you again."

At a sound behind them, he caught her elbow and helped her

stand. "Dawson, come and take the dog outside for a short walk. Teach him how to fetch a stick or something."

"Yes, Captain." Dawson rushed in, snatched up the dog, and hurried away.

"That will teach him for listening into our private conversations again. We need to get him a woman of his own to worry over."

Matilda laughed. "It is too early to be sure, but that matter might be solved soon if all goes well. I have detected a flicker of mutual interest between our new housekeeper and butler."

"Good." He steered her toward the steps that led upstairs to their bedroom. "Forgive my haste. It's been a very lonely week."

"I missed you too." She leaned against him with a deep sigh. "But when will you tell me all your secrets?"

"Soon." He brought his hand down on her rear hard. Muted by her gown, it wasn't at all a satisfying slap for either of them. Once on the upper level, he caught her hips and directed her toward their bedchamber at speed. He'd show her the depths of his desire one day, but not when he was desperate to be inside her.

She glanced at him shyly. "You love me?"

"Now and forever."

EPILOGUE

Christmas, 1815
Newberry Park

MATILDA WAS OVERWHELMED. Too much food. Too much laughter. Too much acceptance.

A thing she'd never expected when she'd agreed to marry William.

She leaned a little to the side, resting against the well-padded arm of a chaise in the white drawing room of Newberry Park while she petted her sleepy dog's head. She was glad Vicar was finally still. He'd spent the whole of the day either chasing or running from the horde of angry cats that populated the Duke of Newberry's country estate.

It was a miracle, in her opinion, that she'd not been scolded for the young pup's antics. Everyone, though, seemed to find the great chases hysterically funny. Everyone seemed to accept her presence. Even Lord George Ford had wished her a merry Christmas.

A pair of silver eyes regarded them belligerently from under a nearby chaise. "He is asleep," Matilda promised the hissing black cat.

"Oh, don't worry about Horace," Lady Sally Hastings, William's cousin, assured her. "He's just annoyed he's missed out on all of tonight's table scraps."

"I can't believe how much Vicar has been eating."

"The dog and his master too." Sally's eyes slipped to William where he stood in talks with his aunt. An amused smile turned her lips up. "It is good to see my cousin has not lost his competitive nature."

Matilda winced. William had both surprised and worried her this past week. He was quite different around his family. He laughed more. He talked more and dragged her into everything eventually. "He's happy."

"No one can miss that he is," Sally assured her. "Happy Christmas, Matilda. I'm glad you could be with us this year."

"To you too."

She sauntered away as William dropped into the space at her side. "Are you warm enough, darling?"

"Yes, Will," she promised. On her lap, a thick woolen blanket covered her legs to ward off the chill of any draft. All the Ford women had their own, which meant she must have one too. She had been supplied with a nip of warm rum and a plate of shortbread to nibble on. Matilda had never experienced a Christmas like this, not even when her father had lived.

She'd never imagined being as included as she'd been this past week.

"I think I ate too much," William complained, pressing his hand to his belly and groaning.

She glanced at him but smiled. "Well, what do you expect when you keep sneaking extra helpings of the plum pudding?"

"To win." He burped into his hand and then apologized profusely. "I had to keep up with Hastings."

She glanced across the room. Mr. Hastings and Sally were currently kissing beneath mistletoe. The pair had married months ago and still appeared inseparable and very happy together too. "He was trying to impress his wife and seems to have succeeded."

"I can understand that desire." William winked. "But I beat him, I'm sure."

"Yes, William. I'm sure you taught him a lesson he'll soon not forget." She smiled fondly at her husband. William's playful streak was a rare commodity, and she cherished each and every glimpse into his lighter soul. "What happens next?"

The family Christmas gathering was quite a bit more involved than she'd first imagined. After a communal breakfast, they had taken to sleighs and delivered gifts to all the tenants of Newberry Park. William, despite his naval career, was well known at Newberry, and he'd greeted many of the farmers with such joy in his eyes he was breathtaking. He'd introduced her to everyone and remained with his arm around her back, supporting her during the lengthy conversations.

"Next we all troop outside carrying torches, light the bonfire, and watch it burn."

"All of us?"

"Perhaps not Aunt Pen this year. She was just complaining of the cold and plans to retire shortly."

Matilda fingered her blanket. "I should give her my blanket before we go out."

"That would be very kind of you, but I was hoping you would take it with us. It is very cold outside tonight, and I had plans to wrap us both in it."

"It's not a very large blanket, William."

"Large enough for me to wrap my arms about you and huddle

together under it while we watch the fire burn. And after a while I had hoped to slip away with you. Somewhere private where we might be ourselves."

A blush heated her cheeks and she squirmed. She had plans for the night that required them to remain indoors. Matilda just hadn't told him yet. She had finally figured out her husband's secret, the one thing he dared not reveal about his desires. She'd known he was holding back but was rather astonished it had taken her so long to figure him out. "I'd like that, but can we stay indoors if I promise to be very quiet?"

"You're hardly ever quiet these days," he complained without real disapproval in his tone. It had been a week since he'd laid a hand to her bottom, and she missed the warmth and comfort such touches inspired. He glanced at her quickly, considering her request with the gravity it deserved. They would have some explaining to do if they were overheard. "Perhaps the bonfire can wait."

"Thank you."

"Let me take Vicar to Dawson for the night, and then we can make an escape."

It didn't take William long to dispatch Vicar to a secure room for the night. When everyone began talking loudly about going out, they slipped from the room hand in hand. The cold of the hall almost took Matilda's breath away. Although she was bundled up in her blanket, the chill in the air made her nose burn and she hugged the fabric closer to her skin. William led her firmly away from the white drawing room, and Matilda pulled him up the stairs. "I have a Christmas gift for you in our rooms."

"You do?"

Matilda nodded. It had taken all her cunning to hide his presents in her luggage and not have them discovered. "It is warm there. Come and let me show you."

They hurried toward their guest bedchamber as voices burst out laughing below and doors clattered shut. Matilda was breathless with anticipation for the surprise she was about to reveal and quickly slipped into the bedchamber assigned to them on their arrival.

"Darling." His kiss was fierce and consuming as he pressed her against the door. Matilda flicked the lock when they drew apart a few moments later. "Billy."

"That's my Mattie, always seeking the fastest way to please us both." He kissed her some more, but they both were aware that time was short and privacy paramount. He turned her around and placed his hand at the back of her neck. "You are a terrible tease, my love."

She shivered as he steered her toward the huge four-poster bed. "Then punish me, Billy."

She had already laid out his present. A mask, red silk strips of cloth, riding crop, and an unworn snowy white cravat cloth of his waited.

His fingers tightened on her neck. "Matilda?"

"Surprise." Matilda took two bold steps forward, halted at the foot of the bed, and dropped her arms to her sides. "Merry Christmas, Billy Boy."

William came up behind her, glancing at the items she'd spread out over the bed. "They were in a locked chest in the attic at home. What are they doing here?"

"They belong in our bedchamber." Teasing William was always pleasurable for her. Matilda wiggled her bottom, bumping against his groin deliberately. His sharp intake of breath made her smile. She glanced up, making sure he noticed the hook dangling from a length of rope tied to the high rail.

William reached for the hook and tested it. "This will not be quiet," he told her. "You might cry out a little more than normal."

"Then tie me up and gag me," she said as she cast an innocent glance over her shoulder and then gestured to the cravat and the other things. His eyes widened farther. "That is what they are for."

He nodded slowly.

It had taken Matilda some time to figure out what each length of red cloth was used for. She had studied the creases on each until she'd figured out William must enjoy binding women during sex. Since he'd not done so yet but often held her wrists, pinning her against the bed or walls, she decided he would probably like to do it with her one night.

This evening was the perfect moment to experiment, but time was short. "You do want to restrain me, don't you, William?"

"Hell, woman." He raked his hand through his hair and then shook his head. "I love you, Matilda. Even more than I thought possible."

Her gown disappeared, corset and chemise too, until she was standing naked before him. His hand struck her bottom, and a pleasant burn warmed her cheeks.

He secured the first long silk tie around her body, so it crossed between her breasts, and tied it firmly at her back. "I told you not to touch that chest."

"Thank you for this perfect Christmas," she whispered, smiling at the tension in his voice.

"My pleasure," he said, winding another around her right thigh firmly. He reached for a third strip and tied it around her left leg. "Or it will be very soon."

Matilda widened her stance, bent over the bed, prepared and eager for more punishment.

He hooked his fingers in the silk band tied about her chest at the back and held her firmly in place. Then he spanked her with his hand until her legs trembled. Moisture coated her thighs, and her sex quivered with need by the time he stopped. She did not feel the cold, only the heat of her husband's regard.

He drew her upright using the silk bonds, bound her wrists in front of her briskly, and then reached for the long white length of cloth. He twisted it between his hands and then pressed it to her lips. Matilda opened her mouth, accepting the gag, and breathed deeply through her nose as he secured it at the back of her head. Her mask slipped over her face next. She loved to wear her mask. It made her feel mysterious and safe all at once.

A rough growl left William's throat as his skin pressed against her from behind. He was naked, aroused, and ready to punish her. His arms wrapped around her body instead. "Darling."

Matilda couldn't respond with the gag in her mouth, but lifted her arms up toward the hook. With his help, she dangled from the mooring point, her toes barely touching the ground.

"When the punishment becomes too much," he whispered, "bring one knee up onto the bed. I will stop immediately."

She nodded her understanding, excitement filling her with restlessness. She swayed from the hook, but the first light smack of the crop against her nipple caused her to groan. He brushed her body all over with the crop, sliding the leather between her legs too, and tapped lightly over her clitoris. Matilda moaned around the gag as her body began to throb.

William stopped touching her and silence lengthened.

Although she expected punishment, the first strike of the crop was a shock, and she could not contain her cry. Although muffled by the gag, she could have been heard by anyone passing their room. The second strike burned, and her eyes filled with tears as she fought her instincts to moan loudly. The third and fourth strikes had her tears falling. She sobbed at the fifth and sixth.

"That's enough for the first night," he promised after the

seventh strike, despite her not signaling for him to stop. He set his warm hand to the back of her neck. "I love you."

He threw the crop away onto the bed before her. William removed her gag and released her from the hook. He kept her hands bound, the silk ties wrapped around her body, and laid her gently over the bed.

A smooth, hot caress stroked over her flaming cheeks, and then William hooked his fingers beneath the ties on her legs to part her thighs and entered her from behind.

She arched her back. He always felt so very good when he was impatient to be inside her body. His use of the ties to control her was no detriment to her pleasure.

Her arousal only increased the more he used them.

Matilda held on to the ends of the ribbons of silk bound around her wrist as he began to move. Her bottom stung every time he pressed hard against her skin, but the slide of his cock brought bliss. She would find that perfect moment again where everything ceased to be and there was only her and William. Billy.

His grip on her hips eased and then he touched her between her legs. Matilda closed her eyes, and desire surged through her body as he made love to her roughly and thoroughly, leaving her in no doubt that her gift of complete trust and submission had released his hidden passions. She enjoyed their time together the most when he was on the verge of losing control, as he seemed to be now, until she was sobbing his name and ready to scream.

His hand slid up and covered her throat and then her mouth, muffling her cries of passion as they drove each other crazy.

He turned her head a little so they could see each other. "When are you going to tell me?"

She frowned and his grip on her mouth eased. "Tell you?"

"When are you going to tell me you love me?"

His hands moved to cover her breasts and then down to cover her stomach. He patted her stomach lightly. "And that we're having a child."

"There's no babe."

"I think there is." He hovered over her, barely moving against her, but still full and hard inside her trembling body. She wriggled but he caught the ties at her back and held her still. "And about time too."

It was always hard to think when he was inside her. Harder now that she was restrained as she was. She frowned, concentrating on his lips rather than how her position made her vulnerable and even more aroused by that. "You really do want a child so soon?"

William kissed her cheek. "Getting you big with our child is all I think about lately. Have you not noticed a lessening of your punishments and an increase of ease in your schedule?"

"Yes, but I had thought it simply your growing accustomed to me. I thought, perhaps, you had grown tired of punishing me so often."

He drew back and thrust deep. "Heaven forbid I ever grow that accustomed to our marriage. I have never been so aware of another person as I am of you, and you test my limits every day. Your breasts have been tender to my touch of late. Your waist has thickened too. All things I love, I hasten to add."

Matilda's cheeks blazed with embarrassment. She had given the chances of conception absolutely no thought. She had been too wrapped up in her new life, in William's astonishing love, to think any further than her next punishment. Provoking William in unexpected ways could take hours of planning and effort on her part. But could he be correct about a babe?

If so, they would have to take greater care in bed. William

cradled her hips between his hands. "A daughter for you, a son for me. A dozen or one, but I will never get enough of you."

She blushed. "Or I of you. Of moments like this with you."

"So what is your answer?"

Matilda struggled to bring her thoughts in order. She had never dreamed of this life, but she thrived on it. She thrived with William. He had become the center of her world, and she had accepted she was the center of his. They made a good pair. They made magic together. "I do love you," she confessed.

"Thank God," he whispered and drew back to slap her bottom. "I have needed to hear since I met you."

He slammed back into her, and his thrusts quickened until they both cried out soon after.

Wedged beneath William, Matilda fought for breath. She hadn't thought he was waiting for her to say it. She'd thought he already knew she loved him.

"Don't call me Billy again tonight," William said as he wrapped his arms about her waist and drew her tight against him. He was breathing hard and rough against her ear. "Dear God, that name on your lips drives me insane."

"I had noticed that," she whispered. Warmth filled her soul. Happiness. Contentment. She liked what they did together. She liked that she could drive him wild so often. She loved being bound and punished too.

As her breathing slowed, William shifted off her and then eased her into bed, wrapping her warmly against the cold. He moved to the windows and peeked out. "A large group is coming back."

Matilda smiled. She had love, she had desire and discipline, and exquisite pain from the one man she'd never expected to care about her. She curled her bound hands under her cheek and admired the man she'd married. When William had demanded she pretend to love him she had never intended to. She had thought a few turns about a society ball would be all that was required of her. But a fake marriage to William had become all too real. Too tangible. He had invaded every moment of her life and shown her how to live in his world.

She had once resented the Fords' easy, undemanding, pampered life, but there was nothing easy about loving William and nothing she would do to change him. "Will I be punished for unlocking that chest?"

"Undoubtedly, but not too soon," William said, coming close to fiddle with the knots to release her wrists. His eyes glowed as they held hers, warm with love, and desire betraying his heightened emotions. "There is a lovely spot not far from here where I can take you over my knee again before we go home if the weather is agreeable. The spot is on the edge of the woods, protected from casual notice. No one goes there in winter, not even the hunters. You'd like to be spanked in the outdoors, wouldn't you?"

"Yes, William." Truthfully, Matilda didn't care where they were as long as William was with her. There was darkness in his soul, but she wasn't afraid of him—his darkness excited her beyond reason. She craved more adventure with him like tonight—his hand burning her skin, his body thrusting into hers, passion exploding from every nerve as he made love to her with wild abandon.

Matilda bit her lip as her body responded to her thoughts. "I'd like that above anything, Billy."

"Matilda," he growled as his eyes darkened with lust. "I already asked you not to provoke me again tonight."

"But it is Christmas. A time for giving." She smiled and fluttered her lashes at him. "I think I would enjoy making love in the outdoors as much as I enjoyed being tied up, Billy."

She laughed heartily as William drew close and pressed the

gag lightly to her lips again. She really did love to provoke him. "I really do love you, Billy," she mumbled around the cloth before he stopped her talking by making love to her until the sun rose the next morning.

The End

PREVIEW: THE CHRISTMAS AFFAIR

A lonely shopkeeper offers shelter to a not so innocent miss to overcome the bitter memories of Christmases past, but could such a wicked connection ever lead to a happily-ever-after?

Amy Mellish might never be warm. She would freeze and no one would ever know her name. She would be just another homeless, unknown body they found during the spring thaw if she did not keep putting one foot ahead of the other.

She blew on her hands, encased in her late mother's best-but-worn gloves, and surveyed the bustling street ahead. Bond Street less than a week before Christmas was a busy time, though so cold this year. Few looked at her directly. No one moved out of her way.

It certainly was not the best time to lure a man to take their pleasure with her so she might afford a corner of a room in a drafty boardinghouse.

"A pox on the happily married," she muttered bitterly as a laughing couple almost barreled over her.

Amy had been overlooked all her life. As a child she had not had friends or family aside from her mother, and as an adult of two and twenty years, that was not likely to change. She was utterly alone, and as a result of her lack of proper protection in the form of chaperones, she was not innocent.

She was one of the impure, a fallen woman who relied on the wickedness of her customers to survive the harsh world of London's streets. It was not the life her mother had wanted for her, but it was the life she must live no matter how hard it seemed.

Unfortunately, she was not that successful in attracting interest in the middle of winter and had taken to the streets of London's busiest district in desperation for coin and customers.

She pushed on through the happy crowd, fretting over her desperate situation. She could do what one of the light-skirts on the last street corner had just done—made a show of unbuttoning her threadbare coat and flashed her breasts to a passing gentleman. The portly fellow had ogled her but had not flicked out a coin. He had smiled and then moved on with his own business. The woman had taken the loss of custom with good spirits and hurried to cover herself again. Amy considered her very brave. Undressing, even partially, while the snow fell, and the winds howled, was not pleasant. While she silently applauded the woman's tenacity and fortitude under trying circumstances, Amy was not willing to surrender any more of her body heat to the uncertainty of fickle male whim.

She had to be practical and thrifty with her favors.

"Watch where you're going!"

Amy jerked up her chin and met the hard stare of a well-heeled heavy-set gent of middle years. On his arm was an expensively dressed woman who positively sneered at Amy's presence on their path. Amy shuffled aside, feet sinking into a deep patch of snow that reached above the top of her ankle-high boots. The couple took their time passing, and Amy was shivering in earnest once more when she could proceed.

She stamped her feet after they were gone and shook the snow from the hem of her heavy garments.

"People are always in too much of a hurry," a contemptuous male voice remarked nearby.

She turned around for the source of the voice and found a fellow standing just inside an alley in the shadows, smoking from a weathered pipe. He seemed of middle age or perhaps older, but it was hard to tell with his cap pulled low over his eyes.

Amy smothered her disappointment. She preferred a younger customer. They were a little more giving of their coin and often cleaner, but she would make do with whatever she got. "Some are indeed."

He moved to the edge of the shadows but did not step out into the street to meet her. His eyes beneath the cap were fierce and his expression sour. "Most don't see the beauty they cast aside. Not me though. I've got my eyes wide open. I see you."

"How kind," Amy said calmly enough, but her skin prickled with a warning.

From time to time, Amy had met men whose interest in her brought unpleasant sensations. She did not feel at all safe near this fellow. Despite his neat outward appearance, there was something about his demeanor that warned her to keep a distance. He could be dangerous.

His clothes were good quality, but it was what lay beneath that made a difference. Even the best-dressed men could hurt a whore. She had heard enough, witnessed enough firsthand, to heed her own instincts. She nodded to him, intending to move along.

He jerked his head toward the alley behind him. "Why don't you come over here and we can warm each other for a bit?"

She pretended to be shocked. "Sir!"

His expression grew menacing in an instant. "Think you're too good for the likes of me? I know what you are."

Amy needed coin desperately, but not so desperately as to risk misadventure with someone as changeable as him. "I am a lady, sir, and what you suggest is indecent. Leave me be or I shall call the watch."

She spun around, but not before she heard the sound of a soft moan come from the dark alley behind the fellow. Amy hurried on, crossing the street to the bakery side, and slipping in behind a chattering group. She took a moment to catch her breath, stealing the warmth from the ovens deep into her lungs for as long as she dared. And then when an older woman swept past carrying a heaped basket, she followed her out onto the street again.

A quick glance around confirmed the dangerous fellow had not followed her to the bakery.

The woman with the basket turned to her. "Can I help you, dearie?" She had the face of kindness, but her eyes were shrewd as she took in Amy's threadbare coat.

"No, but thank you."

The older woman hesitated. "You're very pale."

"The cold," Amy murmured, but then that moan she had overheard from the alley came to mind. "A conversation with a stranger a short time ago has overset my nerves. It's nothing, I'm sure."

"Oh, what did he say?" The woman adjusted her basket, waiting for a juicy bit of gossip.

"Nothing untoward, thankfully, but as I was walking away, I swear I heard a moan come from the alley behind him."

The woman's eyes widened. "Not again."

The woman spun back for the bakery, shouting a man's name, and disappeared with her basket of baked goods.

Amy sighed, lamenting the fact that the memory of the smell

of freshly baked bread was going to torture her all day and likely all night.

Unfortunately, Amy had no choice but to push on in search of a customer. A shy smile, a flutter of lashes, were all she had to bring a gentleman into her arms in the right circumstances. In the biting cold of the afternoon, however, she was not having much luck, and she needed funds to escape the aching cold of winter that was sure to envelop the city tonight.

Another couple passed her, laughing as they went. "A pox on all happy couples," she said aloud and then prayed she had not been overheard.

She had best keep her thoughts to herself, or she would never appeal to anyone. Aside from the dangerous fellow, she usually had good luck in the shopping district, though her usual haunts had attracted a rougher crowd of late. Amy had no wish to be passed around a group of men for the fee of a single client. As long as she was not overly brazen about what she was there for, she had found she was left largely to her own devices in the proper neighborhoods.

And it was usually so much cleaner, safer, nicer all round in this part of town. She lifted her thoughts to the path ahead and arranged her face into a pleasing expression.

There were certain shops, however, that she did not like to linger near for long, and they were just ahead. The pastry shop always made her empty stomach complain, and the fine merchandise displayed in the Cabot's Haberdashery windows made her yearn for the past and the coin she did not possess.

The dream of one day having funds to buy whatever she liked gave her something to hope for though. If her circumstances changed and she had funds at the ready to spoil herself with, she might yet be a regular customer at either establishment.

However, she would not be able to frequent either if one of the proprietors—both very proper gents and handsome—discovered how she earned her living.

Purchase your copy to keep reading.

ABOUT HEATHER

USA Today Bestselling Author Heather Boyd believes every character she creates deserves their own happily-ever-after—no matter how much trouble she puts them through. With that goal in mind, she writes steamy romances that skirt the boundaries of propriety to keep readers enthralled until the wee hours of the morning. Heather has published over fifty regency romance novels and shorter works full of daring seductions and distinguished rogues. She lives north of Sydney, Australia, with her trio of rogues and pair of four-legged overlords.

Find out more about Heather at:
Heather-Boyd.com

facebook.com/HeatherBoydRomanceAuthor

instagram.com/heatherboydbooks

bookbub.com/authors/heather-boyd

goodreads.com/Heather_Boyd